UNTOUCHABLE

AVA MARSH

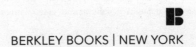

BERKLEY BOOKS | NEW YORK

BERKLEY

An imprint of Penguin Random House LLC
375 Hudson Street, New York, New York 10014

Library of Congress Cataloging-in-Publication Data

Marsh, Ava.
Untouchable / Ava Marsh.—Berkley trade paperback edition.
pages cm
ISBN 978-0-425-28113-0 (paperback)
1. Escort services—England—London—Fiction.   2. Prostitutes—Crimes
against—Fiction.   3. Suspense fiction.   I. Title.
PS3613.A76979U58 2015
813'.6—dc23
2015018185

PUBLISHING HISTORY
Transworld Publishers paperback edition / August 2015
Berkley trade paperback edition / October 2015

PRINTED IN THE UNITED STATES OF AMERICA

10 9 8 7 6 5 4 3 2

Cover art: *Woman* by Serg Zastavkin, *Man* by
Paul Gooney/Arcangel Images, and *Background* by Olavs.
Cover design by Lesley Worrell.
Interior text design by Kelly Lipovich.

Penguin
Random
House

For JR. And everyone else I've neglected while writing this.

ACKNOWLEDGMENTS

Gonna keep this short and sweet. Big thanks to everyone who helped launch Grace into the world, particularly my agent, Stan, for his boundless enthusiasm, patience, and sage advice. Also my lovely team at Berkley Books: my editor, Jackie Cantor; production editor, Stacy Edwards; copyeditor, Randie Lipkin; and art director, Lesley Worrell. Thanks also to the rest of the Berkley crew, who've worked so hard behind the scenes to make sure you're reading this now.

PROLOGUE

S o, *Grace*," he says. "Here we are."

The temperature in the room drops several degrees. The breath catches in my throat and I swallow hard.

He knows my name.

He knows my fucking name.

"Why are you here?" I ask, struggling to keep any trace of fear from my voice. "What do you want?"

He smiles, finally, but it has no warmth in it. "I came to deliver something, Grace." His tongue sliding over my name, caressing it.

"What?"

He raises his hand, and I flinch, but he strokes my cheek.

"A message from Michael."

The hand drifts lower to my neck. He stares deep into my eyes, his features giving nothing away as his grip around me tightens, his fingers digging into my skin while his thumb traces the line of my throat. At the base, in the hollow where it joins my chest, he presses down. Not enough to stop my breathing. Just hard enough to make me very afraid indeed.

My pulse starts to sing in my head, and all I can feel is the constriction in my throat, this man's breath on my cheek as he leans in and whispers three words in my ear. Three words like punches, like a kick to the guts.

"Michael says hello."

ONE

You expect more the first time you turn a trick. You hear about women who throw up the moment the client walks out the door. Some resort to hysterics, or the bottle. Others are overcome with remorse, resolving never to do it again.

In my case, nothing. He came. He came—eventually. And then he left.

Sliding the lock behind him, I felt no more than a vague sensation of having lost my virginity all over again. I walked into the bathroom and examined my face in the mirror above the sink. Searching, as after fumbled, hasty, anticlimactic sex at fifteen, for clues to what had changed.

Not much, it seemed. Same sleek dark hair, though underneath eyes more weary two decades on. The hint of a wrinkle I allowed to elude my focus, this not being the time for self-doubt.

So that's that, I told my reflection. *You've sold yourself for money. You're a whore, Grace Thomas, a prostitute, a hooker, a harlot, a working girl.*

I released myself from my own gaze, feeling slightly numb and slightly elated. I'd crossed the line and there was no going back.

Once a tart, always a tart. Another thing I'd never live down.

TWO

Forget violent clients or venereal disease, the true scourge of working girls is tax returns—at least for those of us who bother to file one. How to describe your business, for instance? The get-out clause on every independent escort's website—being paid purely for "time and companionship"—won't wash with the Inland Revenue.

I opt for my standard evasion: personal therapist—vague enough to obscure the real source of my earnings, truthful enough to pass muster should anyone dig deeper. Grabbing my calculator and diary, I tot up my appointments. Three hundred and thirty-six hours at an average of £250 per hour gives me an income last year of . . . *blimey* . . . a gratifying £84K.

That's before expenses, of course. I tap my pen against my teeth, trying to remember what I can claim for. Condoms and lube, certainly. Cost of website and updating photographs, yes. Taxi fares—probably.

But stockings? Clothing? Makeup? Brazilians? Vibrators? Batteries?

And how much for working from home? Assess how many rooms you use for business, suggests one website, and for what proportion of the day. Hmm. I see around half my clients as in-calls, here at my flat. So if I spend around seven hours a night sleeping in my bedroom and, say, an average of three or four a week fucking in it, what proportion does that make for business use?

And what about the lounge? If I screw someone on the sofa, does that count as using the room for work purposes?

The trill of my mobile cuts through my ruminations. I check the screen—a London landline. I answer on the fourth ring.

"Stella?" He sounds American. Or possibly Canadian—I can never tell the difference.

"Yes?"

"My name is Gerald. I wonder if you might be free this afternoon. For an hour?"

I think for a moment. I should really get this done—the deadline's in a few days. "Where?" I ask.

"The Randolph Excelsior. Knightsbridge."

I check the clock on my phone. It's nearly one. "What time?"

"I was hoping two o'clock. Does that suit?"

Another set of calculations. An hour to finish this—or at least wrestle it into submission. Five minutes to eat. Ten to shower and run a razor over all the bits that count. Add ten to dress and slap on some makeup, fifteen to dash to Boots for more condoms, and at least twenty to get to the hotel.

"Three would be better," I say.

He hesitates. "Three o'clock is too late. A quarter after two?"

I inhale, make up my mind. Tax dodging it is.

At exactly 2:15 P.M. I'm standing outside Room 759, savoring my last few seconds off the clock. And the anticipation. You never quite get over it, having no idea who's about to appear at the door, knowing in just a matter of minutes you'll be as intimate as two people can be. Suspense has proved an enduring aphrodisiac.

The door swings open to reveal a tall, slim man with an unexceptional face. Probably in his early fifties, judging by the lines around his eyes and the recession in his hairline. Though his teeth as he greets me are improbably white—I'm guessing he's had them bleached.

Gerald Archer stands aside to let me in. I give the place a quick once-over. The room is larger than a standard suite, the bed flanked by two dark, solid bedside tables. The curtains and walls are all muted beige; even the art print on the wall confines itself to tasteful neutrals.

Meanwhile Gerald conducts his own evaluation, his face expressionless as he takes me in. I smile, but he barely responds, and I wonder with a slight lift in my stomach if this is going to be one of those occasions when a client gets cold feet. It happens sometimes. A crisis of conscience, perhaps, or simply a case of not particularly liking what he sees.

I hover in the middle of the room, waiting for some kind of reaction. Gerald's lips lengthen into a tight smile. "Would you like a drink?"

I shake my head. "No thanks."

He nods. Pours himself a Scotch from a bottle on the desk. Takes a sip and sets the glass back down.

"You warm enough?" He gestures toward the thermostat on the far wall.

"Thanks, I'm fine." To prove the point I remove my jacket, folding it over the back of one of the armchairs.

Gerald eyes me again as the TV chatters away in the background. He makes no move to switch it off, but then I've lost count of the number of North American clients who think it's perfectly normal to screw to a sound track of CNN.

"I apologize for it being rather last-minute," he says finally.

"No problem." I'm wondering now if I'm here because another girl canceled.

"I wasn't sure of my schedule, you see. Not till this morning." His lips barely move as he speaks, giving his face a shifty look. I glance at his feet. He's wearing red socks, a blaze of color in a room full of understatement.

"You look nice," he says, taking in my gray Whistles sheath dress and black executive-height stiletto boots. "Very chic."

I relax a little. Perhaps I was actually his first choice.

Gerald picks up the whisky glass and downs the remainder, then steps toward me and plants his mouth on mine. *Cut to the chase, why not?* I taste the Scotch on his breath, and beneath it something more pungent. Garlic, maybe. I repress the urge to draw away. This, after all, is what I'm paid for—the willing suspension of disgust.

"I've been looking forward to fucking you," he murmurs, drawing back, eyes locking with mine. His are the kind of blue that fades with age, surrounded by heavy lids that echo the hint of jowls along his jawline. Otherwise, he's not too bad. Handsome, even—or at least was once.

"Do you mind?" I nod toward the TV. He reaches for the remote and switches it off, then slips an arm around my waist, dropping his head to kiss my neck.

No awkward small talk. No inane attempts to make this feel like anything other than what it is.

He releases me and I bend to unzip my boots, then take his hand and lead him to the bed. We undress each other quickly. He pushes me onto the pristine white sheets, burying his head in my crotch, his tongue drumming against my clitoris with an insistence that makes me flinch.

He doesn't take the hint. I endure it for a minute or so, then fake an orgasm. Nothing showy. You don't have to go all *When*

Harry Met Sally. A hitch in your breath, a couple of urgent gasps, a final undulating moan—that usually does the trick.

Gerald lifts his head, chin glistening, eyes glinting with satisfaction. Nothing flatters a client more than thinking they've got you off; it's the challenge, perhaps, or the reassurance. They may pay for every minute of your time, but most want to believe you're enjoying it as much as they are.

And sometimes I am. Just not today.

"One second." I slip off the bed and grab a condom from my bag, tossing it on the bedside table. It's then I notice the book—an Anne Tyler novel, the one about the couple who marry during the war. Next to it a pair of reading glasses, lilac with small diamanté chips on the outside of the frames. The type only a woman would wear.

Why not hide them? I wonder. A simple omission, possibly, or is he trying to make me uncomfortable? I consider asking, then remind myself I'm not his therapist; I'm here to deal with his cock, not his cognitive style.

I turn back to Gerald, who's stretched out on his back, arms folded behind his head, watching me. I avoid his gaze. Look instead at the dark nest of his pubic hair. There's no sign of an erection, so I bend down and take him in my mouth, changing the rhythm as he enlarges, trying to keep my thoughts on the job at hand. Done with full concentration, fellatio can be almost meditative: just my mouth and a prick, a little dance of mutual satisfaction. But my mind keeps wandering to the glasses on the table.

No wonder he was so antsy about the time. I feel a wave of revulsion, and drag my focus back to his erection. Cocks, in themselves, are rarely repellent. It's easier to hide your antipathy if you concentrate on this—the business end—rather than the dick it's attached to.

"Stop." A slight gasp in Gerald's voice tells me I'm in danger of going too far.

I sit upright, offering him a languid smile. "Too much?"

"Nice," he says, his eyes not quite meeting mine, "but maybe a bit too nice."

"Let's take a breather." I glance at the travel clock on his bedside table. Still half an hour to go.

Three years in the business and I've learned that pace is everything. It's not rocket science. You're working on roughly one ejaculation an hour for most guys over thirty—any more is too much effort, and puts you at risk of going overtime; any less and, well, you can forget that repeat business.

But Gerald clearly has other ideas. "Come here." He beckons me back up the bed. I fold myself into his outstretched arm. He reaches over and caresses my breast as I trace a line down his belly with my forefinger and curl my hand around his balls, giving them a gentle squeeze of encouragement. I don't want him wilting on me.

Premature ejaculation and a flaccid penis—Scylla and Charybdis, the rock and the hard place. The two hazards every working girl has to navigate.

Twisting round, I grab the condom from beside the clock. Rip the foil with my teeth, checking it over briefly before unfurling it over him. It's tight, the rubber extending only two-thirds of the way up his shaft and pinching a bit at the top. It'll have to do—Boots was all out of large.

I sit up and straddle him, lowering myself onto his erection. Gerald closes his eyes as he eases into me, slowly, firmly, lifting his hips to meet my downward thrust. I toss out a few responsive noises, until Gerald stops moving. He pulls out and removes the condom, then pushes me on my back and thrusts his cock in my mouth. A few jerks and he shudders into stillness. I swallow fast, but the hot, saline tang of his semen scalds my taste buds and I fight the urge to grimace.

"Well . . ." Gerald says as I wipe my lips with my fingers. "That was fun."

"Mmmm." I try to sound appreciative.

Gerald sinks back into the pillow. His face is impassive, his mouth a half smile.

"So tell me, Stella." His tone deeper now, more relaxed. His gaze cool. Assessing. "Does your boyfriend mind?"

"Mind what?"

He raises an eyebrow. "You doing this."

I eye him steadily. "Does your wife?"

Gerald's left eyelid twitches. Slowly, stiffly, his lips contract, then he looks away. He's up and off the bed before I can even think how to excuse myself. Wrapping himself in a dressing gown, he retrieves his jacket and, with a tight expression, hands me the envelope.

"Thanks," I say, taking this as a dismissal. I dress quickly, silently. Gerald stands with his back to me, pretending to examine something outside the window. Turns only as I head for the door. His cheeks are flushed and I can't tell if it's from the sex or my verbal indiscretion.

"A word of advice, Stella." His voice has a hint of quaver; there's a tension in his expression as he speaks. "When you manage thirty years of marriage, you get to judge. Okay?"

I nod, genuinely abashed. Let myself out the door.

Neither of us bothers with good-bye.

Pressing the button for the lift, I dig in my bag for my inhaler. Release a blast of albuterol deep into my throat. My chest feels hot and tight. I want to get out of here, into the fresh air, find the nearest bar or café. Get something to chase away the taste of Gerald, of this whole inglorious episode.

What the hell happened back there? I ask myself as I will the lift to arrive. I never used to be so touchy. I'd let the crap clients said wash right over me, just deleted it in my head, like so much junk mail.

Another minute passes. I press the button again. Wonder if I should take the stairs. At that moment the lift doors slide open. I dart in, too fast to see the woman exiting. We collide awkwardly, and I drop my bag.

Half a dozen little foil packets spill onto the floor.

"I'm so sorry," she gasps, though it was conspicuously my fault.

"No, no. It was me." I stoop down to grab the condoms. Praying she hadn't time to register what they are.

"These elevators you have over here," she says, in a distinctly American accent. "They're so small. It does take some getting used to."

I stand to see a middle-aged woman, a Hobbs shopping bag in one hand, a man's suit fresh from the dry cleaner's in the other. My cheeks start to burn. My hand trembles as I fumble with the clasp on my handbag. I force myself to look at her face: worn, plump, but amiable. Kind.

Giving me the benefit of the doubt.

"I'm so sorry." I jab the button for the ground floor. "All of it. Entirely my fault."

Her smile is warm. "Don't worry, dear. These things happen." The lift door closes between us, sparing me the sight of her walking away.

But not the sinking, certain feeling that I know exactly where she's heading.

THREE

'm halfway through my Murakami novel when the phone rings, its shrill sound filling the tiny room. I answer the call, giving the name of the center.

No response.

I repeat the name. This time it's followed by a muffled sob.

"I'm listening," I say. "I won't hang up. I'll wait until you're ready."

No reply. I let a minute pass. I can't make out much, only the occasional sniff, and start to wonder if it's another prank call. You wouldn't believe how many people think it's funny to ring up a rape crisis center and jerk us around. And not only bored kids—plenty of so-called adult males.

"Do you want to talk?" I ask. "I don't mind. I'm happy to stay here if you just need somebody on the end of the line."

A voice clears its throat. I'm fairly sure it's female.

"I don't know what to say." She's barely audible, but I can hear she's young. Probably a fair bit younger than me.

"How about you start by telling me what happened?"

A wet, sniveling noise followed by a long, low howl. "He . . . he . . . oh God, I can't."

A click, then the dial tone.

I put down the phone and rest my elbows on the desk. Glance up at the clock. Forty minutes to go before Stacy arrives to take over. It's a Friday night—generally our busiest time—and we try to keep the lines open till midnight. We'd keep them open longer if we could get the funding.

Through the glass in the door I see Mel, one of the outreach workers, mime drinking a cup of tea. I give her a thumbs-up just as the phone rings again.

"Sorry," a voice says on the other end of the line. Hers.

"No need to be."

"I just . . . I feel so . . ." She goes silent.

"Embarrassed? It's hard to talk about something so personal, isn't it?"

She clears her throat again. "Yes."

"Do you want to tell me your name? Your first name. It's good to know what I should call you."

"Andrea."

"Thank you, Andrea. And my name is Grace. How about I ask you some questions. You don't have to answer them if you don't want to. You don't have to tell me anything you're not comfortable with."

"Okay," she says uncertainly.

"Did this happen recently?"

"Yes."

"May I ask how long ago?"

She coughs. "I'm not sure exactly. A few hours."

"And you're alone now?"

"Yes. They've gone."

They. I swallow. "So you're safe, then. No one can get back in?"

"Only my flatmate, but she's on holiday. She's not home till Sunday."

"I see. Andrea, can I ask you if you've got any injuries?"

"How do you mean?"

"Cuts, bruises. Perhaps a bump on the head. If so, you should get it checked out straightaway. If you think you need to, I can call an ambulance."

She coughs. "No, I'm all right."

"You're not bleeding anywhere?"

"No . . . I don't think so." She starts crying again. A whimpering sound like an animal in pain.

I let her continue for a moment, then ask: "Andrea, do you feel strong enough to tell me what's gone on?"

"Okay," she gurgles, and coughs again.

"In your own time. No pressure."

A sigh, like her breath collapsing. "There were two of them."

"Do you know who they are?"

"Yes. Well, no, not really. One of them is called Michael. I don't remember the other one's name."

Michael. Something ignites inside me, a curl of dread and dismay. The desire for a cigarette blooms and I have to crush it before I can speak. "How do you know him?"

From the café, she tells me, across from the travel agency where she works. He asked her out when she called in for her morning coffee, suggesting a drink in a local pub. It went all right, she says. His mate joined them briefly, then disappeared.

"I made my excuses after an hour or so, and he asked if we could do it again. I said maybe and left it at that. I could tell he was disappointed, but to be honest, I just wasn't that into him. I didn't think . . ."

She stops. I hear her inhale, then release it slowly. Imagine her heart racing as she remembers. One of the first things you learn as a psychologist is that processing memories and feelings is the primary treatment for any trauma.

But that doesn't make it easy.

"He must have followed me home," Andrea continues. "About five minutes after I got back the doorbell rang and it was him. He wanted to come in, but I said no. He asked, why not? Was anyone else there? But he knew there wasn't. He knew my flatmate Dana was on holiday because I'd told him . . ."

She sniffs, followed by the sound of her blowing her nose. She's crying again. Mel lets herself in silently and places a mug of tea on my desk, along with a chipped china plate topped with a couple of chocolate biscuits.

"How could I have been so stupid?" Andrea's voice is full of self-reproach. "I'd said I'd got Dana this really cheap deal to Crete and he'd asked when she was getting back and I told him. I didn't think anything about it."

Forethought, I realize, making a note. Premeditation. *Michael, you cunning little fuck*.

"Then he pushed his way through the door and he . . . the other one . . . was suddenly there behind him. And . . . and . . ." Her voice breaks off. That wounded noise again.

"And they raped you," I say. "Forced you to have sex."

It isn't a question. More a statement of fact.

"Yes," she sobs. "Michael first, then him. Twice."

Michael. Even hearing that name makes me want to vomit. The coincidence of it. And despite myself I'm picturing *his* face. *Him* attacking this girl. Though I know it can't be. That Michael is still inside.

I take a deep breath, place the pen down on the pad, and pull myself together. "Andrea?"

"Yes."

"Listen, honey. I'd like to suggest a couple of options, but you don't have to do either if you don't want to. I recommend you go to one of the sexual assault referral centers. I don't know where you live and you don't have to tell me, but I can give you some addresses or a link to their websites. They can check you're not hurt and can do a forensic assessment, if you're undecided about going to the police."

I pause, but she doesn't speak.

"Or you can go straight to your local police station. Is there anybody who could go with you?"

A long sigh at the end of the line. "What's the point?" says her voice. "We both know what will happen."

"The police are obliged to . . ."

"They'll say I invited them, that I consented. There'll be witnesses to us all drinking together in the pub."

"Andrea, we can't be sure that—"

"Yes, we can," she cuts in. "I'm not stupid. I've read how hard it is to get a conviction. I wouldn't stand a chance. They'd make me look like a slut, like I asked for it."

I open my mouth to object, then change my mind. Because the fact is she's right—and I know better than anybody how right she is.

"I only wanted to talk," she says. "I don't want to take this any further. I just needed someone to know the truth."

Andrea starts crying again, heavy, resigned sobs. And I think of those two men and wonder where they are right now. If they have any real sense of what they've done.

Then I wonder whether they've done it before—or will again.

A rush of heat. Of anger. I have to clear my throat before I can speak.

"Okay, Andrea, I understand. But think it over, will you? You could go and get the forensics done and then decide." I try to keep my tone calm and measured.

"It's too late," she says miserably. "I've washed myself, my hair, down there . . . everything. And put all the sheets in the washing machine." A pause. "I'd throw them away, but they're not mine. They took me into Dana's room."

I suppress a groan. Wonder if she'll tell her flatmate when she gets back from Greece, or remake the bed so it looks like nothing ever happened. I get a picture of Andrea, sitting alone in her flat, the phone in her hand, and my heart aches for her.

I lift my gaze from the desk to stare at the bare walls of Consultation Room Two. We never use this place for face-to-face work, so there's little to alleviate the starkness, save a cork notice board studded with aging council notices and a list of referral numbers.

"Is there anybody you could ask over, Andrea? A friend? Family?"

Another pause. "I think I'd rather be on my own."

Then I'm certain. She won't tell anyone. For the rest of her life and mine, I'll be the only other person who knows what happened in that flat this evening. She'll bury it inside and let it fester, until her whole world is poisoned by what seeps out.

I squeeze my forehead with my left hand, pinching the skin above my nose until it hurts. I have no more advice. And no more questions.

Just a prayer she'll somehow be spared.

"Grace," she says suddenly. "That's a lovely name."

"Thank you."

"Like in the hymn." She sniffs. "I always loved that one."

"Me too."

"Grace, I have to go now." A sigh. Resigned and heavy. "Thank you for listening. I'm sorry to take up so much of your time."

"It's what I'm here—"

A click on the end of the line.

FOUR

Cruising past a line of black limousines, the black cab deposits me at the entrance of the Mayfair hotel with a good twenty minutes to spare. The po-faced concierge barely gives me a glance as I stride through the lobby. Not surprising, since I'm dressed more demurely than half his female guests.

I check my makeup in the ground-floor loos, then install myself in one of the leather seats with a panoramic view of the lobby, its giant chandeliers and high-polish art deco glory. The eyes of the concierge settle on me briefly before sliding off toward the main door. I cross my legs and smooth down my skirt. Hard to tell whether he's sussed me out or not.

Not that it matters. There's an unwritten rule in the best hotels: don't make us have to notice you. It's in no one's interest to interfere with visiting escorts—we're here to entertain their guests, after all. An unofficial room service.

I check the time again. Fifteen minutes to kill, but there's no shortage of distractions. A minor celebrity strides across the lobby to the bar. Over at the check-in desk, conferring with one of the receptionists, a group of übersmart French women, sleek and chic in their tailored couture. An older lady, dressed defiantly in neck-to-knee fur, waddles toward the lift with the side-to-side pendulum movement of the very stout.

So far, so normal.

Less typical are the four men in dark suits stationed around the various doorways, their demeanor alert and attentive. I'm just wondering who might merit the heavies when several Arabs emerge from the nearest conference room, all wearing formal gowns and white headdresses crowned with black bands. They're flanked on each side by more henchmen, eyes scanning the hallways like predators on the prowl.

I pick up a copy of the *Wall Street Journal* to mask my curiosity, but my gaze drifts back to the entourage. Three Western men are bringing up the rear, faces bowed as they step forward to shake hands with each of the Arabs. A double handshake, palms layered one over another.

As the foreign dignitaries sweep out to the waiting limousines, the Westerners confer. Serious expressions. Nodding heads. More handshakes, smiles, a slap on the shoulder. Then they leave.

All but one. Medium height and build, his hair heavily silvered, though he doesn't seem particularly old. Late forties, maybe fifty. He pauses, looks down at the floor for a moment, then heads toward the lift.

He's almost level with me when his head turns and his eyes meet mine. His lips stiffen, his expression darkening into something like irritation as he holds my gaze before finally walking away.

I stare dumbly at his receding back. What the hell was that about?

Paul Franklin's room is on the ninth floor, at the end of the corridor in the smaller eastern wing. I find it quickly, used by now to the arcane numbering systems in places like this. I straighten my jacket, run my fingers through my hair, then knock quietly. I may blend in well downstairs, but a woman calling on a man in his room will always raise eyebrows.

No response. I knock again, a little louder this time. I'm just wondering if he's a no-show when the door swings open.

"Stella," says my client. "You're nothing if not punctual."

I gaze at the man who eyeballed me down in the lobby. Take in his faintly sardonic expression. He's changed out of the suit he was wearing ten minutes ago, I notice, into a navy polo shirt and well-cut beige chinos.

"Sorry," I say. Though really I've no idea what I'm apologizing for.

Paul Franklin gives me a derisory smile. "Come in."

I pass through a wide entrance hall into a large sitting room decorated in creams and pale yellows, one of those haut monde designer affairs the hotel is famous for. Sharp-lined leather sofas and armchairs in complementary shades of duck-egg blue and beige. Splashy art prints on the wall, a bold geometric rug covering almost the entire floor.

Christ knows what this place must cost. A grand a night?

More, probably.

"Drink?" asks Paul.

I hesitate—I don't normally indulge on the job. But today I feel edgy, strangely off-kilter. How did he know who I was?

Sod it, I think, sitting on one of the blue leather couches. "What have you got?"

Paul Franklin opens an elegant marquetry cabinet to reveal an array of spirits and liqueurs. A small inset fridge. "Whatever you like."

"You choose." I watch him remove several bottles. Pour liquid into a couple of glasses. A minute later he hands me a martini, complete with an olive.

"Impressive." I take a sip.

Paul sits on the sofa opposite. He's left the top buttons on his polo shirt undone, revealing an inch or so of lightly tanned skin and a suggestion of hair. He's lean, muscular. Attractive without being overtly handsome. He mirrors my scrutiny, no expression on his face beyond the faintest hint of a smile. I wait for him to speak, but he just inspects me, not attempting to disguise it.

"So, you're here on business?" I ask eventually, giving him the chance to acknowledge our brief encounter downstairs. I'm hoping for an explanation. He clearly recognized me, but I can't imagine how. I don't reveal my face on my website, though I'll e-mail over pictures if a client asks.

He never did.

Paul's mouth widens into something approaching a sneer. It's unnerving. As I suppose he intends it to be.

"Come on, Stella. You can do better than that."

Okay. No small talk, then. I take another sip of martini, wait for him to break the silence. Paul leans back, one arm resting across the back of the sofa.

"So, Stella," he says finally. "Tell me more about yourself."

"Such as?"

He shrugs. "Anything you like."

A shift in my stomach. A discomfort born of annoyance. "There's really nothing much to say."

He laughs. A short, sharp bark of a laugh. "You've led such a dull life, have you?"

"Nothing exceptional."

"Nothing exceptional," he echoes, looking as if he knows better.

I bite my lip. "Nothing that would interest you."

Paul Franklin crosses his legs, cradling his martini, his eyes never leaving mine. Christ, the man doesn't even blink.

"On the contrary. I'm very interested."

I feel the martini start to hit, the gin and vermouth flooding my empty stomach, making me a little woozy. He's playing with me, I realize. I stay silent, forcing him to make the next move.

"Indulge me, Stella. Tell me how a girl like you ends up in a hotel room with a man like me."

It's not an unusual question from a client, and one I usually deflect with a quip about job satisfaction. But this man doesn't strike me as the type to be fobbed off with a double entendre.

"I lost my job," I say. "I had no money. It seemed an obvious choice."

He considers this for a minute. "An obvious choice. You think so?"

"Someone I knew, a friend of a friend, went into it when she needed extra cash for school fees. I got in touch with her. She told me what to do."

"Which is?"

I lift my mouth into a shrug. "It's simple enough. You either sign up with an agency or go it alone—set up a website, get another mobile phone, wait for the calls."

"Build it and they will come."

I laugh. "Pretty much."

Paul closes his eyes briefly. Then downs the rest of his martini in one gulp, setting the glass on the coffee table between us. "So far, so predictable. But I can't help feeling there's a great deal more to it than that."

"More than being broke?"

He leans forward. "Come on, Stella. You strike me as a very resourceful woman. Surely you don't expect me to believe this was your only option?"

A stir of aggravation. What is it with clients? Not content to get inside your knickers, they want inside your head as well. For a moment I consider calling it a day. Heading back to the peace and stillness of my empty flat, and bugger the lost income.

But something about this man intrigues me. Not so much the way he looks as his overwhelming air of power and confidence. I feel strangely energized, with a sudden urge to break the deadlock between us.

I drain the rest of my glass, get up, and remove my jacket. Taking a few paces toward him, I unzip the back of my dress, letting it slip to the floor. I stand there, in boots, stockings, and underwear, waiting for some kind of reaction.

Paul doesn't move a muscle. Just watches me in that lazy way a lion eyes a nearby gazelle. Trying to decide whether or not he's hungry.

"I can leave if you like," I say, more to break the silence than anything else.

A twitch of his mouth, as if suppressing something. "No. That's not what I'd like at all."

"So what do you want?" I'm not usually this direct, but coyness will clearly get us nowhere.

Paul breathes in slowly. Considers my question. "It never pays to rush things, I've learned."

"I agree." I glance over at the clock on the mantelpiece. "But you only booked me for an hour."

"An oversight," he says. "I wasn't sure of my schedule."

"Okay. But perhaps we'd better get down to business."

At this he stands. Approaches me, raising his hand to my chin. I feel a kind of shock at his touch, a rush of desire that may have everything or nothing to do with the martini. I move closer, lifting my face up to his, and he bends to kiss me. A hard, forceful, almost angry kiss. Full of sex. Full of promise.

A buzz from the desk, where a mobile phone is vibrating energetically. That look again on Paul's face, the same annoyance as I glimpsed in the lobby—clearly this isn't a call he's expecting.

"One minute." He disappears into one of the adjoining rooms, shutting the door behind him. I hear him speaking in what sounds like Arabic.

I stand there for a minute, then move to the window, examining the line of elegant terraced mansions across the square. The kind of voluminous town houses that sell for twenty million or more. Down on the street, directly below me, a steady trickle of black cabs deposits and collects the hotel's guests.

On the other side of the door I can just make out Paul's voice, raised now. Terse. Irritated.

I check the clock again. Half past four. At this rate there will barely be time for anything except a quick kiss good-bye. I feel almost disappointed; I realize I was beginning to enjoy myself.

Crossing from the window to the desk, I examine a lovely art deco lamp in tiered glass, then sniff the adjacent yellow roses massed in a clear round vase, but they're scentless, purely for show. I run my hand over the dark polished surface of the desk, inlaid with a paler wood in delicate arches and swirls. It's a beautiful piece of furniture, probably original, carefully restored. On impulse I pull on the tiny gilt handle to the top drawer. It slides open silently.

Inside is a slim black wallet. Beneath it two passports: one maroon, one blue. English and American.

In the other room I hear Paul talking again. In French this time. Fast and urgent.

"*C'est moi.* Alex."

Alex? I grit my teeth. I'm not sure why this unnerves me, given I work under an alias myself. But it does.

I reach down to pick up one of the passports, but the tips of my fingers brush something cold and smooth. I pull them away, surprised, then bend to peer into the drawer.

Small, discreet. Mother-of-pearl handle and sort of vintage-looking.

But very much a gun.

What the fuck? Before I can decide what to do, the voice in the other room goes quiet. I shut the drawer quickly and take a couple of steps back from the desk, facing the door. But Paul . . . Alex doesn't emerge.

I move in closer, trying to catch what he's saying, but he's speaking fast and my French is a long way from fluent. *"Non, pas besoin . . . Je vous ai déjà tout expliqué, Philippe . . . parce que ce sont de vrais salauds, vous le savez bien . . . des salauds."*

Salauds. Bastards. I learned that word on a school trip to Boulogne.

"D'accord. Non . . . non, je comprends. Je prends le prochain vol pour Paris . . . oui . . . oui . . . à bientôt."

A pause. I step back from the door just as he emerges. Despite the urgency in his voice only moments ago, his face betrays no sign of agitation. Alex gazes at me, half-naked in the middle of the room, as if he's forgotten why I'm here.

"Get dressed."

I don't hide my irritation. It's one thing a client bailing out at the beginning of an appointment; quite another half an hour in. Then I think of the gun and decide to let it go; this has all gone a bit off-limits for me.

Alex picks up my dress and tosses it to me. "Change of plan. I've got to catch a plane. Sorry."

He goes over to the desk and opens the drawer. I freeze, but all he removes is his wallet. Hands me half a dozen fifties. Too many, but I'm not about to argue. I stuff them into my bag and pull on my clothes, avoiding his gaze as I make for the door.

"Stella." Alex's voice forces me to turn and look into his eyes.

"Yes."

He smiles, if you could call it that. Somehow more of a smirk. "It really was a pleasure to meet you at last."

FIVE

By the time I spot Anna over by the double doors, I've nearly finished my drink. I stand and wave. She meanders across to my table, bending to kiss my cheek, and I get a waft of perfume, probably one of those exclusive couture fragrances she gets at Liberty.

"Sorry I'm late." She sheds her coat to reveal a pale blue cashmere sweater and a pair of Dolce & Gabbana jeans that emphasize the already enviable length of her legs. "Had an appointment with my bank manager. It ran over."

I raise an eyebrow.

"Strictly financial." Anna laughs, then nods at my glass. "Another?"

"Just a fizzy water."

"Seriously?" She frowns and regards me steadily. "You look like you could use something stronger."

I relent. "A chianti, then. A small one."

She's gone for a couple of minutes, reappearing with my wine in one hand, a bottle of beer in the other.

"Thanks for coming at such short notice," I say, grabbing my drink.

"Pleasure." She sits down and flicks open the top on her Grolsch. "You seen that new agency, Eastern Alliance? Packed full of Russians and Lithuanians. None of them a day over fifteen by the look of them." Her expression turns morose. "I think I may have to drop my rates again. The whole mature English rose thing doesn't seem to hit the spot these days."

"It's the tail end of the recession," I reassure her. "It'll pick up."

Anna doesn't appear convinced. "Maybe." She drains an inch off her beer, then spreads her hands out on the table. A cluster of silver rings on each of her long fingers. "Anyway, what's up? You seemed a bit subdued when you rang."

"Just having a bad day." I shrug, suddenly reluctant to talk.

"A punter?"

I shake my head. Sigh and pull the envelope out of my pocket and push it across the table. She removes the single sheet of paper and flattens it on the table.

"Decree absolute?"

I nod.

She stares back down at the letter. "No wonder you're feeling low."

"Yep." I shift in my seat. It's also my dad's birthday, but that's something I'm determined to forget.

Anna leans forward and rests her hand on my arm. "Oh, Grace, honey, I didn't even know you were married."

"Not anymore."

"You okay?" Her hand tightens to a squeeze.

I nod again. In truth I'm not sure how I feel about the divorce. Sad. Guilty. Relieved. Of course I knew it was imminent, but somehow finding the letter on the mat this morning, scanning those sparse sentences that spell the end of my marriage, left me breath-less and hollow and in need of good company.

"I know what you're going through." Anna retracts her hand and runs it through her hair, revealing dark roots behind her ears. "I cried when mine arrived. Even though I hated the bastard."

"I don't hate him . . ." I let the words trail off. More like the other way round. I've given him plenty of reason to hate me. And I wonder, not for the first time this morning, how he feels about this. The letter spelling the end of his marriage.

Bloody jubilant, I imagine.

"It's a kind of death, I guess," says Anna. "Of what you'd once hoped for and believed in."

I manage a sorry excuse for a smile. "Thanks."

"For what?"

"For understanding."

She sniffs and tips her head back. Downs another inch. "God knows, you need plenty of that in this business."

Too true. I've known Anna since I went on the game. We met at my first duo session, and she took me under her wing, happy to embrace the role of mentor as well as friend. In a world as hard-nosed as the sex industry, I got lucky the day I bumped up against Anna.

"You'll be all right tomorrow," she advises. "It's like turning thirty—horrendous in the run-up, but a relief once it's over."

"Thanks," I repeat, grateful she doesn't ask me any more about my marriage. It's an unspoken rule between us that we don't pick over the wasteland of our previous lives. I know only the barest bones of her past: the job in IT, the husband, a couple of children—now living in Norfolk with her ex and his girlfriend—that Anna hardly ever gets to see.

At the bar I see two men glance over, then lean in to confer. The taller one stares back at Anna.

I give a discreet nod toward them. "I think you've pulled."

Anna turns and smirks openly. He looks away, embarrassed. "Come on," she says, grabbing her coat. "Let's sit outside. I need a fag."

I leave our food order at the bar and follow her out to the small beer garden, deserted except for a couple huddling in the corner under an outdoor gas heater. Anna sits at the nearest bench, fishes in her bag for her cigarettes.

"Here, treat yourself. You deserve one, today of all days." She holds up a neat honeycomb of filter tips. I shake my head.

Anna removes one and lights it. "Good girl," she exhales, twisting her head to avoid blowing smoke in my face. "Hang on in there."

We sit in silence for a minute, stunned by the fierce sunlight and frosty air. I stare up at the contrails high above our heads, the latticework of white lines against the blue winter sky. It makes me think of that man Alex, his urgent flight to Paris, and I wonder again about that encounter in the lobby. How did he know who I was? I'm certain I haven't met him before, not in any walk of life. I may not be great with names, but faces generally stick. And his was definitely not one I'd forget.

And the gun. I can't fathom how I feel about that either. Freaked? Not really. It's hardly as if I've never come across one before—or rather the aftermath.

Maybe it was legal. But who, these days, is allowed to carry firearms outside the forces? Spies? Somebody in the security services? Undercover police?

Anna's voice cuts through my thoughts. "You seen that guy again recently, the scriptwriter?" she asks, face raised as she exhales another pale cloud of smoke.

I shake my head again. "Last time we met he asked what I thought of his show. So I told him. It didn't go down too well."

"He can't have taken it that badly." She grins. "He was quite complimentary on PunterWeb. Gave you eight-point-five."

I hold up my hand to stop her. "Don't tell me any more. You know I don't look at those things."

It's true. I never read anything clients write on the Net. Escort reviews are one of the least pleasant sides of the business—piss someone off and there's half a dozen places where he can dress you down. Literally and figuratively.

And if that's not bad enough, some sites even have a ranking system, marking each escort on looks and performance. A great deal of cheating goes on—fake reviews from girls, fake reviews from pet clients, paid off with service in kind. A constant jostling for position that leads to a lot of bitchiness, bruised egos, and lost business.

"Don't take it so seriously," says Anna. "You know it's all just so much wank-fodder."

She's right, at least on one level. Reviews invariably include a blow-by-blow account of the "date." Less an accurate appraisal of the encounter than a piece of erotic fiction, the client casting himself in a starring role in his own little fantasy.

She downs the rest of her beer and snorts. "I did have one guy last week . . . you won't believe this."

"What happened?"

She colors slightly, hesitating.

I look at her. "Jesus, Anna, how bad was it?"

She finishes her cigarette. Stubs it out on the underside of the table and tosses the butt into a nearby bin. "He got me one of those burqa things to dress up in—you know, the big black tent with a slit for the eyes. Wanted me to wear it out with him—and only that, I mean. Took me to Greenwich Park. We walked round for half an hour till it was dusk, then he screwed me up against a tree."

"Jesus, Anna." I'm not sure whether to laugh or commiserate.

She sighs. "I keep worrying I'll burn in hell for all eternity. Or someone will issue a fatwa."

"Don't be daft."

"He wants to do it again next week. Offered me twice my usual rate. Says he'll take me shopping on Bond Street."

I picture Anna wandering round Fenwick, naked under a burqa. "You going to do it?"

Anna wrinkles up her nose. "Depends on the weather. I nearly froze my tits off in Greenwich. I couldn't stop shivering." She grimaces, a look that's one part humor and two parts fatigue. "Let's just say I didn't have to bother counting the money."

I smile. This was the best advice Anna ever gave me. If you start feeling anything for a client—and it *does* happen—you count the money. That always brings you back down to earth.

Despite the lightness in my friend's voice, I experience a niggle of discomfort. As if she's taken a step closer to an abyss we're both pretending isn't anywhere near. I try to imagine Anna working in an office, picking up her kids from school. Having comfy married sex with her husband.

I just can't picture it.

"I'm getting too old for all this," she sighs, catching my mood.

"You're only thirty-seven."

"Nearly thirty-eight," she corrects. "Christ, Grace, I don't even fancy myself anymore. I made myself masturbate the other day because I haven't come in months."

"Ah," I say, smiling again. "A pity wank."

"Honestly, I'm so sick of it all. Men and their dicks. Pretending to be impressed by them."

"You mean the men? Or their dicks?"

"Is there a difference?"

We snigger, enjoying the gallows humor, then fall quiet again, as if both avoiding something deeper, leaving silence the safest option. I listen to the overhead whine of jet engines banking around Heathrow. The background chatter from the pub, one man's voice carrying over the others, a sonic boom punctuated by the odd staccato laugh.

Inhaling, I look at Anna straight on. "Do you ever think about getting out?"

She lifts her shoulders, then lights another cigarette. As I wait for her answer I play with the packet, flipping it over and over, wondering why I even asked.

I guess the truth is I'm worried. Anna's been in the business for seven years now, which is at least five years too long to be functioning normally. Escorting is like radiation: fine in small doses, but prolonged exposure is highly toxic.

"I think about it," she says eventually. "But never seem to get further than that." She examines the end of the cigarette scissored between her fingers. "How about you, more to the point? What's your exit strategy?"

"More to the point?"

Anna squints into the sun. "I'm a lost cause, Grace, but you're not. You don't want to be stuck like me, dressing up in burqas for some pathetic little pervert."

What's your exit strategy?

My mind chews over the question. I haven't really considered it, even though I brought the subject up. That's another of my rules—never think much beyond the next week or two.

"Christ, we're like bloody refugees," Anna mutters.

"From what?" I look over and see her expression hovering close to sadness.

"Our former lives." She kicks at a bit of gravel and it skitters across the concrete paving. "Who said that? About the past being a different country?"

"'The past is a foreign country,'" I say. "L. P. Hartley."

"That's the one." She takes a final drag, sending a plume of smoke into the London air, where it disperses a little then hangs there as she stubs out the butt and chucks it into the bottom of her beer bottle. "Either way, one thing's for sure. There's definitely no going back."

SIX

My six o'clock smiles as he walks into my flat, though he's chewing the inside corner of his lip and it gives the expression a wry twist. He's cute. Not in that obviously pretty-boy sort of way; rather he has the kind of face that's quietly appealing.

Ben stands in my lounge, looking awkward, checking me out while pretending that's precisely not what he's doing. His eyes dart around the room, taking in the sofas, the coffee table, and the TV, the bookshelves and my little desk area in the nook by the kitchen. But most of all, flitting over me.

"Can I take your coat?" I ask. "It looks wet."

He glances down at his black overcoat as if he's only now realized it's been raining. Then shrugs it off and hands it to me. I hang it by the door, next to mine.

"Nice place," he says as I reappear.

"Thanks." Though in truth it's ordinary by anyone's standards.

One bedroom, a kitchen, a living room, and a bathroom. Décor, in the main, courtesy of IKEA.

"Handy for the tube. And the trains." He colors, as if embarrassed by his own banality. Runs a hand through dark hair that's graying a little at the edges.

I offer him a drink. He looks like he needs something to ease things along.

"Please," he says, clearly relieved.

"Beer or wine?"

"Red. If you've got it."

I nod. Grab a couple of glasses from the kitchen, and a bottle of Australian Shiraz. Open it and pour us both a glass. I seem to be making a habit of drinking on the job.

I size him up as I hand him his wine. Late thirties, early forties at a push. Beige chinos and a green polo shirt, topped by a black sweater. Your standard corporate smart-casual.

Roughly speaking, you can divide my clients into two types. The younger ones—up to, say, fifty—are usually after a no-strings shag. I'm one of life's little treats, alongside the occasional bottle of grand cru or lunch at Quaglino's.

Then there's the other kind, typically older, who want more; more than I could possibly offer. Most have hit that dog-end of marriage where boredom, irritation, or the hormonal ravages of menopause have worn libidos to a stub—along with all chance of physical affection or intimacy. They land on my doorstep thinking they're here for the sex, only to discover they're yearning for a connection far more than skin-deep.

This bloke, however, doesn't quite fit either category. Too young and easy on the eye to be looking for love in exactly the wrong place. Then again, he's booked two hours—the quick-fucks only ever book one. Most would plump for half if I offered it, but I leave that to my colleagues over in Soho.

Ben puts his glass down on the coffee table and sits in the arm-chair. Leans forward, elbows balanced on his knees, examining the books on my shelves. He's clearly uncomfortable, and I wonder if this is his first time with an escort.

"What's your verdict on this?" He leans over, pulls out a copy of a recent Man Booker nominee.

I shrug. "Underwhelming."

He laughs. "I've met her, actually. She lives up the road from me."

"Really? What's she like?"

"Oh, you know. Intense. Neurotic. Like most writers."

I laugh. "Like most whores, come to that."

He looks openly surprised. Shocked even. Then makes a visible effort to recover.

"What do you do?" I ask, trying not to smile at his discomfort.

"Ad exec."

"Ah, nice," I say, insincerely.

He grimaces. "Spending most of your waking hours feeding the demons of capitalism is not exactly something I'd describe as *nice*."

"Creative though."

"Only if you think schmoozing clients and flattering people you despise is creative."

"I'm probably not the right person to ask," I quip. Then realize how rude that sounds. I grit my teeth. *Jesus, Grace, shut it.*

But Ben looks me over with a grin. "I'll bet," he says, examining my face. "So what about you?"

"What about me?"

"I'm assuming this isn't all you do. Or did."

"Why would you assume that?"

"Your book choices give you away." He watches me as he waits for my response.

"This is what I do now," I say simply.

"Shame." He lets his eyes rest on mine. "Seems like rather a waste."

I lift an eyebrow in mock offense. "You reckon? I like to think I'm very good at what I do."

"I don't doubt it for a second."

I swallow a mouthful of wine, suddenly wary. This whole booking seems to be veering more into the territory of flirtation than straight fornication. I feel a bit out of my depth.

Ben, on the other hand, is gaining momentum. He replaces the book on the shelf and gets up and walks toward me. Takes my glass and puts it down on the table.

"You're not at all like I imagined."

He slips his left arm around my waist and pulls me toward him. With his right hand he moves my hair away from my face, clasping it against the back of my neck as he drops his head and places his lips on mine.

It's a deep, slow kiss. He tastes of wine and mint, his skin smelling dimly of soap. A warm ache flowers low in my abdomen, the stirrings of real desire. And with it the resurgence of the feeling that's haunted me ever since my encounter outside that hotel lift.

That somehow, for some reason I can't quite grasp, I'm beginning to lose my grip.

Afterward we lie in bed and finish the bottle. We've gone way overtime, but I've no one booked in after Ben, and am seized by a sudden sense of what-the-hell.

"So what's your name?" He props himself on his elbow and gazes down at me. From the corner of my eye I see the outline of his shoulders, his lean chest, and have to resist the urge to turn round and touch him.

"Stella."

"No, your real name."

"It's really Stella."

He cocks his head slightly and I'm stung with something. Guilt, maybe. That small dirty feeling a lie leaves inside you, like a smear.

"And yours?" I ask.

"Ben. It's really Ben."

I believe him. It's astonishing how few men bother to conceal their identity.

"This isn't at all what I expected," he says.

"What did you expect?"

He shrugs. "I don't know. Someone, something . . . more clinical, I suppose."

"Clinical? As in 'wham, bam, thank you, ma'am?'"

He laughs. "Yeah, I guess something like that."

"Well, two hours upgrades you to the full-on GFE."

"GFE?"

"Girlfriend experience," I explain. "It's a technical term we use in the trade."

"Girlfriend experience." He sniffs, scratches his cheek. "I'd say that pretty much sums it up."

"Minus the PMS and the arguments about whose turn it is to unload the dishwasher. And the bitching when you want to watch the match."

He laughs. "What makes you think I'd mind all that stuff?"

I raise my eyes to his. "Then why are you here?"

His cheeks flush a little. "Good question."

"Purely rhetorical. You don't have to tell me anything. That's another reason you pay me. I don't need any answers and you don't owe me any explanations."

He leans over and runs a finger down my nose in a gesture that feels too intimate. "I really don't know what to make of you."

"Me neither." I sit up, hugging my knees to my chest. "Best not to bother trying."

I sense his eyes fixed on my face. It makes me feel twitchy, like posing in front of a camera. All of a sudden I can't think how to arrange my features.

"I guess I didn't expect you to be so . . . so appealing." His voice sounds soft. Inviting.

"Anybody can be appealing for a couple of hours, Ben. It's keeping it up for thirty years that's tricky." I swing my legs over the side of the bed and turn my head toward him. To his credit he manages not to stare at my breasts. Instead his eyes linger on my face, as if posing a question.

I glance at the clock. "I'm afraid I have to go out in a while," I fib.

He checks the time. "Shit. Sorry. *Tempus fugit* and all that."

"No problem."

I put on my dressing gown while he pulls on his clothes, and see him to the door. He removes his wallet from his pocket. Hands me a wodge of crisp new bills, fresh from the cashpoint.

I see instantly he's overpaid. "My rate's two fifty an hour, not three hundred."

He looks at me. "I know. It's a tip. For services rendered so expertly."

For a moment I feel a stir of discomfort I can't identify. Disappointment? Debasement? I take a fifty-pound note and thrust it at him.

"Please. Consider it a down payment on next time," he insists.

"Okay. Well, thank you." I return his smile and accept the money. There's a good chance I'll see him again, though it's not guaranteed, whatever he says—there's nothing more fickle than a punter.

"My pleasure." He leans forward and kisses me on the cheek. "Till then."

SEVEN

What do you think?" asks the woman behind the mask.

I gaze at Elisa's half-obscured face. The mask is beautiful, delicate filigree studded with colored jewels, garlands of tiny gold flowers framing her eyes but leaving the mouth exposed. Long blond hair tumbling around her shoulders, all without the aid of extensions—she resembles no one so much as a youthful Brigitte Bardot—at least before the sun got to her.

"Exquisite," I say sincerely.

Elisa grins. "Isn't it? I picked it up in Venice. A client took me last year, to the *carnevale*." She pronounces the word with Italian flourish, rounding it off with a pout of her perfect lips.

"Here. You try this one." She hands me a black version. It's plainer, but foxy, elegantly shaped with little black feathers swooping out from the corners of the eyeholes. Elisa slips it over my face and stands back to assess the effect. "*Parfait.*"

I adjust it slightly and look around. Over in the far corner of the room, I see Janine pulling on a glossy black stocking and fixing it into her suspenders—no mean feat given the length of her acrylic nails. She's wearing an elaborate black and green corset, a semiopaque inner panel running from her breasts to her crotch allowing a veiled view of the diamond stud in her navel. Elbow-length black gloves set off her slender arms, and she's completely devoid of jewelry, save a pair of jet cluster earrings and her long auburn hair extensions.

I watch her straighten and squeeze her feet into six-inch black stilettos. Christian Louboutin, I notice, checking out the red soles.

"I feel a bit dowdy," I say, turning back to Elisa. I'm wearing a black basque, heavily boned with lacing at the back and adorned with little bows and ruffles. Just below my crotch the hem of a tiny lace skirt skims the tops of my thighs, both demure and tantalizing.

"Don't be ridiculous," she purrs, squeezing my arm. "You look delicious."

I adjust the skirt again in the mirror and try not to ogle her as she slides into her costume. A gorgeous Rigby & Peller dark blue bustier with matching panties, topped with a sheer Agent Provocateur kimono cinched tight round her tiny waist. The whole outfit must have cost over a grand—though I doubt, of course, that she paid for any of it herself.

Elisa is a rarity, more courtesan than call girl. A girl so genuinely lovely she can keep a stable of paying companions, all willing to supplement that income with expensive gifts. Rumor has it she's had at least three marriage proposals, as well as several offers to buy her out of the business.

But Elisa stubbornly resists any kind of exclusivity, insisting on working on her own terms. These parties are her pièce de résistance. Available only to select clients, they're legendary on the London circuit, all-night debauches with absolutely nothing off the menu.

Which is where I come in. In the world of high-end escorting,

I have a not-so-common aptitude—a ready willingness to take it up the arse.

Tonight's theme is vaudeville, and we're going big on burlesque. Janine has done our makeup: pale foundation and ruby-red lips, heavy sweeps of eyeliner à la Dita von Teese. And false eyelashes— Elisa had to help with mine and I'm still not used to them. I keep catching glimpses at the edge of my vision, a flutter of black wings.

Though I have to hand it to Janine—we look amazing.

I glance at the clock on the mantelpiece. Ten minutes before the arrival of the "gentlemen," as we're supposed to call them. It's a word that gets bandied about a lot at the top end of the business, along with "discreet" and "discerning"—all trying to gentrify a relationship that is, at bottom, as mutually exploitative as a twenty-quid blow job in the back of a car.

But in this case with far more salubrious surroundings.

Indeed, the large apartment in Canary Wharf that Elisa has hired—or more likely been lent—is sumptuous. Cherrywood floors and expensive minimalist furniture. Floor-to-ceiling windows with panoramic views across central London's nightscape. I can't even guess how much this place would cost to buy.

"Right, the five c's." Elisa holds up her left hand, counting off each finger. "Champagne, canapés, cake, condoms, coke. Check, check, check, check, and er"—she picks up and opens the silver cigar case housing the drugs—"check."

This is my fifth time at one of Elisa's "events," but I still feel a flutter of nerves as we count down the minutes until the men arrive. Part apprehension—you never can be sure what to expect—and part genuine excitement. I enjoy the parties. It's not only that the money is good—double what I'd make for a night working on my own—but they're fun too. The chance to dress up, go a bit over the top. And the camaraderie, winking and pulling occasional faces to each other when the clients aren't looking. Rather like being back at school.

"Right." Elisa tucks her phone into her bag, stashing it behind one of the leather sofas. "Remember, cover up and keep safe. Just because they're paying top dollar doesn't mean they can take liberties. And if anyone feels overwhelmed, don't forget the password."

"Jodhpurs," I repeat. "Hard to see how we might slip that into the conversation."

"Precisely," says Elisa. "Don't want anybody firing it off by accident."

I smile. Elisa's private education rarely shows, but occasionally her voice takes on a schoolmarmish tone that belies her ingénue appearance.

"Have you checked the bathroom?" she asks Janine.

Janine nods. "I put in the bath oils, the extra towels, and dressing gowns. And more condoms in the medicine cabinet. Oh, and Viagra, if anyone needs it."

"Good." Elisa inspects the lounge before dimming the overhead lighting. Large Jo Malone candles perfume the air with the scent of grapefruit and white jasmine, their flicker reflecting in the huge windows, echoing the more distant lights of the city. Janine adjusts the music, a muted sound track that hits exactly the right ambience of relaxed and sensual.

"Fabulous," Elisa concludes, and my nerves ease a little. She walks into the kitchen and brings back a bottle of champagne. Expertly pops the cork, pouring it into three narrow flutes.

"To pleasure," she toasts.

"To business," counters Janine.

"To both," I add with a smile.

We raise our glasses into the air, chink them together, and swallow a welcome draft of the Bollinger, just as the loud buzz of the intercom fills the room.

EIGHT

As soon as Elisa buzzes them up we swing into action. Janine drapes herself across the arm of a sofa, a huge black feather held archly across her cleavage, while I pose with my back to the window, framed by the lights of the city beyond. Elisa stands by the door, ready to meet and greet, her Venetian mask emphasizing her radiant smile.

First to appear is a tall, fleshy man with a face like a full moon. He kisses Elisa on the lips, then strides over to Janine, grabbing her by the waist and pulling her toward him in a tight embrace. I'm guessing this is Harry—banker and tonight's birthday boy. One of Janine's regulars.

"Oh, by the way, I've brought along another friend," he says, turning back to Elisa. "Don't worry. He'll cough up."

An almost imperceptible hitch in Elisa's smile, then it's gone. Ever the pro, there's no hint of her displeasure as the other men file into the room. But behind her effusive welcome I know she's

calculating if we'll have enough of everything. Not only supplies—
an extra cock means more work for everyone.

While Elisa meets and greets, I take in the guests. Two are wearing suits and uneasy expressions that suggest they've never done
anything like this before. Behind them, a third man comes into
view, sporting a navy blue shirt and dark trousers, and an air of
studied nonchalance, as if all this were nothing new.

A hitch in my throat. It's him. Alex. Aka Paul Franklin.

The man with two names, two passports, and one possibly illegal firearm.

He glances at me, his lips twitching as he registers my surprise.
No sign of it on his face, I notice. But then he knew I'd be here, I
realize. He knew that two weeks ago when we met at the hotel;
clearly he was checking me out.

But why? To make sure I was worth the expense?

My sense of anticipation curdles. I offer to take their coats, hanging them in one of the bedroom wardrobes. I feel wrong-footed,
thrown off-balance, ready to snatch the champagne Elisa offers me
on my return.

"To Harry," says Janine, raising her glass.

"Happy birthday," we chorus in unison.

Harry grins and downs his drink in a couple of mouthfuls. As
Janine pours him another, he plants his hand on her arse and gives it
a firm squeeze, his heavy face and neck already flushed. Probably oiled
himself up a bit beforehand, I think, concealing a shudder of distaste.

He lifts his champagne for a second toast. "To health, wealth,
and happiness," he booms.

"To health, wealth, and happiness," we echo.

I take another gulp and risk a quick glance at Alex. He's staring at me, his expression amused, challenging me to some kind
of response. I turn my back, grabbing a bottle for another round
of refills. Whatever game he's playing, I'm having none of it.

"Let me introduce everyone," says Harry, slumping onto one of the sofas. "This is my colleague Rob." He nods toward one of the men lowering himself into the armchair opposite. Rob reciprocates with a nervous flutter of his hand.

"Alex," Harry gestures. "We were at university together, once upon a time."

Alex doesn't respond. Just lifts his eyebrows a fraction.

"And James." Harry points to the other suited man by the window. "Another college chum, and by far the most illustrious among us."

James flashes his friend a warning look, but Harry seems oblivious, tipping back his head and pouring the rest of his drink down his throat. Janine perches on his lap, giggling as his hand snakes round her waist and lifts to squeeze her breast.

Elisa catches my eye and gives a discreet nod toward the window. I walk over to James, who has turned his back on everyone and is staring out across the illuminated London landscape.

"Amazing view, isn't it?"

He turns and smiles briefly.

"You seem preoccupied," I venture.

James takes a sip of his drink and I notice the wedding band on his finger. "I'm sorry. Work rather piling up at the moment."

"What do you do?"

A wariness crosses his features. I know immediately I've made a false move. Most clients love talking about their job; the more successful they are, the more they like to tell you about it. But James plainly doesn't want to stray anywhere close to the subject.

"I understand," I say quickly, before he's forced to make something up. "You're here to enjoy yourself, not talk business."

"Quite." He exhales audibly, glancing back at the others. Janine has her face suctioned to Harry's, while Elisa leans into Alex, her kimono parted just enough to give him a view of the ample swell of her breasts.

"The thing is, I've not really done anything like this before." James's eyes won't meet mine. "Been rather roped into this, it being Harry's fiftieth. Determined to see in his next half century with a bang."

"Or two," I crack, taking a step toward him and slipping my arm through his. "There's nothing to it. You simply relax and enjoy yourself."

He looks at me properly. "So you're Stella."

"You've done your homework."

"Always," he says, his eyes exploring my face. "Nice website, by the way. And your reviews—very impressive. Though I have to say the pictures Janine forwarded barely do you justice."

I make a mental note to get some new ones done. "I'm not particularly photogenic. My features are too angular."

He smiles. "Well, nor am I. Can't stand bloody photographs. Avoid the press like the plague."

The press? I pretend to overlook this admission.

"This really is quite something," he says, turning back to the view of the Thames below us, meandering its way through the capital. The BT Tower and Centre Point twinkle in the distance, the pale blue circle of the London Eye glowing like a halo. I take a few steps forward and press my face up to the glass, cupping my hands around my eyes to block out the light from the room. To the right of the Eye I can just make out City Hall and Tower Bridge, and the more distant towers of the City.

"That's Big Ben," James says, pointing to the left. "And Westminster, a bit further along."

We stare at it for a minute or two. "How very far away it all seems," he says finally. I smile, slipping my arm around his waist as he steps back from the window. He flinches momentarily, and I wonder if I've made another mistake, until he turns and kisses me on the mouth.

It's a nice kiss, but I feel uneasy. Behind us I sense Alex watching our every move.

"Come on." I nod toward one of the bedrooms.

James releases me. "If you don't mind, I'd like another drink first."

"Of course." I retrieve a bottle from the table and fill his glass. He swallows most of it in one go, then I lead him into the bedroom, resisting the urge to look back.

It's quick. James seems both eager and embarrassed, almost in a rush to get it over. I undo his trousers and drop my head to go down on him, but he pushes me onto the bed, removing the lower half of my costume with a decisive tug. I grab a condom and he nudges inside me, burying his face in my hair.

He emits a kind of whimper when he comes, like he's in pain. Or in shame. We lie there for several minutes in silence, then I get up and offer him one of the bathrobes. He shakes his head and pulls up his trousers. I retrieve my silk gown from the en suite, tidying myself up before we both go back into the lounge.

Things have warmed up in our absence. Anya Marina's "Whatever You Like" on the sound system, her beautiful husky voice getting everyone in the mood. A silver tube lies discarded on the coffee table, a smear of powder visible against the glass.

Janine sits astride Harry, who's gripping her hips and fucking her with an expression of leery concentration. Rob, clearly fascinated, is spread-eagled in the armchair opposite, an erection lifting his toweling dressing gown. I glance across at Alex and Elisa. She's leaning into him, talking. His hand fondles her breast as he listens, but he shows no signs of taking it any further. I look away before he notices me watching.

"Jesus Christ," James mutters behind me. He grabs one of the bottles and pours himself another drink. Downs it in one, then drops into the armchair and stares, dazed, at his companions.

"Stella." Harry withdraws from Janine and beckons me over.

"I hear you've got something of a party trick." As I approach, he clutches my dressing gown and pulls it clean away, spinning me round in the process. Grasping my hips, he pushes me onto all fours, his cock nudging my thigh.

"Wait." Janine reaches for a fresh condom and he rolls it on. I take a deep breath.

It's showtime.

A moment later Harry inserts himself inside me. I steady my breathing, willing myself to relax—tensing up is what makes anal sex painful. But as he starts to thrust I find myself wincing. I should have insisted on more lube—there's some on the condom, but far from enough to prevent this hurting.

Out of the corner of my eye I see Rob get up and whisper something in Elisa's ear. Glimpse Alex studying our little tableau with interest.

"Why not?" Elisa shrugs. "Stella's nothing if not accommodating."

Rob walks over. "Mind sharing?" he asks Harry.

Harry pauses, and grins as he grasps Rob's meaning. "A pleasure, old boy." He withdraws, pulling me upright so Rob can slide himself underneath. Rob opens his robe and I lower myself onto him.

Rob's large. Very large. I'm not at all sure this is going to work.

"As you were, Harry." Rob gives Harry a salacious wink. I feel Harry ease himself back inside me.

There's a groan from Rob as they both begin to move, falling into a necessary rhythm with each other. I close my eyes, but I sense the others watching. Even in our world, DP—double penetration— is not something you see every day.

"God almighty," James says from somewhere across the room. I can't tell if he's excited or appalled.

Rob groans again. His thrusts become more urgent and I know this won't be a long performance. I close my eyes and keep my breathing slow and steady, riding out the sensation of fullness inside me.

Go with it, Grace, I tell myself. *Just go with it.*

A bleep from somewhere in the room. I look up to see Elisa sitting on a leather pouf a few feet away, her mobile phone in her hand.

"Excuse me," she murmurs, catching my frown, and pops it back in her bag.

I'm hit by a rush of irritation. What the hell is she up to? Using the fact that everyone's distracted to do some sly texting? *Christ.*

Rob makes a whimpering sound as he comes. Harry follows right behind, his climax marked by nothing more than an indistinct grunt. Both pull out of me in unison, leaving me feeling curiously empty. Harry's sweat cooling on my back, making me desperate for a shower.

Elisa walks over, running her hand through my hair as she bends to whisper in my ear.

"Nice job, darling."

James leaves shortly after my party piece, muttering something about pressure of work. He goes up to Alex and says something out of earshot of the rest of us.

The atmosphere in the room seems to collapse with his departure. Harry sits back and lights a cigarette, smiling benignly. Rob, exhausted, wilts into the nearest armchair. Only Alex appears alert, chewing on a canapé and regarding everyone coolly with that calculating stare.

Janine and I tidy up, letting the men recover for a while. I go for a wee in one of the bathrooms. Check out my reflection in the mirror covering the whole of one wall. The woman gazing back at me appears remote, unfamiliar. I wipe away the smudge of mascara under my left eye and look away.

Back in the living room Elisa gives us the nod. Time to pick things up again.

"Come here, birthday boy," she croons at Harry, sinking to the floor in front of him and wrapping her lips round his cock.

Across the room Janine, stripped to stockings and suspenders, towers over Rob in her six-inch heels. "Wakey-wakey," she says, lifting her right foot and using the toe of her stilettos to push him flat on the sofa. He grins, beckons her forward. She straddles him, lowering herself onto his face.

"Oh God," Harry groans as he starts to get hard again, lacing his hands through Elisa's hair. I can see him pulling it by the roots. That has to hurt, but Elisa doesn't so much as flinch.

"You fucking beautiful bitch," he mumbles as she slides her mouth up and down his shaft, one hand cradling and caressing his balls as the other holds him steady.

I glance over at Alex, who's observing Elisa and Harry with his ironic semismile. He's barely touched any of us this evening, I realize; indeed, he's the only one in the room still fully dressed. I should go over to him, pick up where we left off back in Mayfair, but something in his manner deters me.

Leave it, Grace, I tell myself. Maybe he just likes to watch. After all, half the point of these parties is to cater to men's inner voyeur— a rare opportunity to see people fucking in the flesh.

So I help out Elisa instead, kneeling behind her and running my tongue down her spine. Harry stares at me over the top of her head, groaning even louder as I bring my hand round to cup her breast. Elisa wriggles appreciatively, but I know it's all for show. Just as I know exactly how far I can go.

No girls. That's Elisa's cardinal rule. Not because she doesn't like women, but because she does. "Men only" is her way of staying loyal to her girlfriend.

"Stop," commands Harry, and Elisa obediently removes her mouth. He gets up from the chair and motions her to sit in his place. With one foot on the floor and the other kneeling beside her, he takes his cock in his hand and starts to rub up and down. At the last moment he lifts himself higher and spurts over her face. A glob of semen lands on her cheek, another close to her left eye.

It's all I can do not to glare at him. The stupid bastard. Thinks he's the star in his own personal porno.

I hand Elisa a couple of tissues as he turns away. She dabs at her eye and I see her wince in pain. "Jodhpurs," she mouths at me as she looks up.

"Come on." I grab her hand and lead her to a bathroom, closing the door behind us. Elisa leans over the sink, splashing water over her face.

I feel for her. Nothing stings like semen in your eye.

She raises her head and reaches for some more tissues. "That fucking pig." She pats her skin dry, then looks at me, her expression more serious than I've ever seen it. "Don't worry. I'll make sure he pays for that."

I can't imagine how, but I applaud the sentiment. God only knows how Janine can put up with him.

Elisa peers in the mirror. Her eyeball looks sore and red and her makeup is ruined.

"Where's your bag?" I ask, then remember where she stashed it in the living room. I go and look behind the sofa. As I grasp the handle, her phone falls out onto the floor—I'm about to pick it up when Elisa's hand appears and grabs it.

"It's okay. I've got it."

She retreats into the bathroom, emerging five minutes later with her face fully restored. "Thank you," she says in a whisper, kissing me lightly on the cheek before glancing around at the remains of the party. "Once more unto the breach, dear friend."

NINE

The evening slides into the early hours. The Viagra has obviously worn off because Harry and Rob have collapsed on the sofa with Janine sprawling naked between them, all absorbed in the adult DVDs she brought with her. Good stuff, thank God. The delectable James Deen screwing a girl over a kitchen table, his eyes locked on hers as he whispers filth into her ear.

Harry fondles his penis as he stares at the screen, but it's limp and lifeless now, a portent of years to come. Rob looks glassy-eyed, close to sleep.

Deen flips the girl onto her stomach and I risk a look at Alex's face as he watches. Definitely not handsome, no, but there's a kind of remorseless energy about him, a cool, calculating intelligence that attracts and repels in equal measure.

As Deen lines himself up for the cum shot, Alex looks across at me in a way that tells me he's perfectly aware of my inspection. I turn away, retrieving the last of the empty champagne bottles and taking them to the kitchen. The clock above the sleek range cooker says 3:15 A.M.; with any luck we can wrap things up by six.

A second later Elisa appears, holding a plate of half-eaten canapés. I take them from her and tip them into a Tupperware box. No need for them to go to waste.

"Did you find out who he was?" she asks.

"Who?"

"The one that left. James."

I shrug. "No idea. Why?"

"Harry says he's in government."

"An MP?"

"Harry won't say."

I turn to face her. "Does it matter?"

"Of course not," Elisa laughs. "I'm being nosy, that's all."

"Look, is everything all right?" I keep my eyes fixed on her, alert for tells. Nonverbal leakage, as I was trained to call it.

She stares back at me, her expression a question mark.

"I noticed you messaging or something earlier. On your phone."

There. A slight flush in her cheeks before she looks away. "A bit of a family crisis. Sorry."

"But you're okay?"

She purses her lips a little, then smiles. "I'm fine. Really."

"Right."

She removes a couple of bottles of sparkling water from the fridge and takes them into the lounge. I follow with some clean glasses. Put them on the coffee table, then check the three bedrooms to make sure everything's still respectable. All look pristine—after all, most of the evening's action has taken place in the living room—but in the largest I spot a condom wrapper just underneath the bed.

I bend down to pick it up. As I straighten I catch sight of Alex in the doorway, observing me with the same kind of dispassionate curiosity he wore for the porn.

I stare back at him. He walks in, closing the door behind him.

"So, *Alex*," I say. "How was Paris?"

He sizes me up for a moment, then laughs. "Why? Did you miss me?"

When I don't respond, he takes another step forward. This man makes me very nervous, and it's not only that gun. There's something about him that feels calculated, almost rehearsed.

"So, the appointment the other week. What was that all about?"

Alex doesn't reply. Just holds my gaze.

"Checking me out, were you? Why? This party was booked a month ago."

Alex shrugs. "Simply curious. Thought it might be interesting to get to know you a bit beforehand." He moves closer, until he's only a few inches away. I can smell his aftershave, something subtle and musky. He looks right into my eyes, but doesn't attempt to touch me.

"I'm still interested," he says, "in hearing about you."

"Like I said, there's nothing to tell." I resist the temptation to step back, to put more distance between us.

"Stella . . ." His tongue dallies on my name as his hand darts out and grabs my wrist. I flinch and try to twist away, but his grip is firm as he pulls me to him. "Quite the little enigma."

He holds the back of my head firmly as his mouth presses itself against mine, his kiss rough and insistent. Then he pushes me on the bed, parting my gown, his lips moving to my breast. I stop resisting. My body responds to his touch like parched earth to rain, my skin prickling, my mind turning blank as deep water as he runs his hand down my belly and slips it between my legs.

"Wet already, Stella?" he says, his voice teasing. He hovers for an instant before pushing two fingers inside me. I feel myself contract around him as he leans over and kisses me hard on the mouth.

"Don't you get tired of all this?" he murmurs as he slides his fingers in and out, his thumb hovering over my clitoris.

"I—"

"Shhhhh . . ." He increases his pace. "Don't say a word. Put everything out of your mind."

His thumb presses harder, starts to circle, and my hips curve up to meet him. Another kiss, then he pulls his head back and locks eyes with mine, his look almost challenging, as he steps up the rhythm on my clit.

A warmth spreads through my abdomen, a hitch in my breathing.

"You," he says, with a small crook of his mouth, "are a very provocative woman."

I turn away from the intensity of his gaze, but he uses his free hand to pull my face back to his.

"Come on, Stella. Let it go." His voice is low, insistent, speaking to that unthinking part of me that has taken over, hungry, oblivious to anything but the exquisite sensation in my groin.

"I can't . . ." I gasp, but sense myself getting near.

"I think you can," he whispers, so close to my ear I can feel the moistness of his breath on my skin, and then I come with a cross between a yelp and a moan, Alex suspended above me, watching me subside. That perpetual half smile. A taunt. An invitation.

I lean forward and grasp his neck, pulling him toward me, parting my legs as my hand goes down to unzip his trousers.

But he pulls away. "No, Stella. Not here."

I look at him. "Why not?"

He just shakes his head. "Get up."

The night is wearing into early morning, though it's still dark outside. Harry and Rob have tired of porn and now CNN runs soundlessly from the screen on the wall. Janine is picking at a tag on her nail, mentally on sabbatical now that no one is paying her any attention.

"*Shit.*"

Harry grabs the remote and turns up the volume. We all stare at the TV. A reporter in a gray trench coat stands in front of the

Houses of Parliament, speaking fast into a handheld microphone, reeling off details of some defense contract. Before I can catch what it's all about, Alex gets up and seizes the remote, blanking the screen.

"What the—" Harry blurts, but shuts up when he sees the frown on Alex's face. Even so, his features are rigid with excitement. He punches the air, belly fat wobbling with the force of the movement.

"Fucking yessssss!"

Alex's expression gives nothing away.

"He did it," Harry exclaims loudly. "*He actually fucking did it.*"

"Who?" asks Elisa, looking from one to the other. "Did what?

Harry eyes her and sniggers. "We could tell you, darling, but then we'd have to kill you."

Elisa smiles, but there's frost in it. Harry doesn't pay any attention.

"I can't believe the bastard didn't say anything all evening. Not a fucking thing!" He looks around and spots a half-empty bottle of whisky. Gets up and gathers together a collection of glasses. "Come on, girls, let's party."

Elisa and Janine both accept a Scotch. Janine downs hers with a wince—clearly she's more of a champagne girl.

"This calls for emergency supplies." Harry digs in his pocket and pulls out another bag of white powder. He offers it to Alex, who shakes his head. Janine does a line, then Rob. He waves it at Elisa and me.

I excuse myself. "Too much to do today."

"What?" Harry snorts. "Get your fanny waxed?"

I let myself stare at him for an instant too long, but he's too high to notice.

"Well, I'm gonna get totally wankered." Harry wipes his nose and leans back into the sofa, a beatific smile across his lunar face. "Being as I'm now a damned sight richer than I was this time yesterday."

He looks over at Alex. "And you, mate. What have you just made? Huh?"

Alex maintains his impassive expression.

"Thought so." Harry grins.

Janine sits on the side of the sofa. She looks first at Harry, then Alex. "Sounds like you're both very lucky boys."

Alex's mouth tics, as if repressing the impulse to say something snide.

"Naughty boys, more like," drawls Harry with a snort of laughter. "We're golden, darling, we can't lose. We're fucking untouchable."

"Untouchable?" Janine leans toward him, giving him a premium view of her cleavage, while slipping a hand inside his dressing gown. "Surely not?"

"You've no idea, sweetheart." Harry downs the rest of his Scotch and pulls her onto his lap. Yanking a breast from her corset, he pinches her nipple between his thumb and forefinger.

"You've got no fucking idea at all."

TEN

As soon as Rachel walks in I realize I've made a mistake. Everything about the place—the central circular bar, the runway floor lighting, the clumps of live bamboo—seems silly and frivolous juxtaposed against her heavy brown mac and large practical handbag, the strap slung across her chest like a bandolier.

Rachel takes in the crowd of twenty-something media types and City traders as she wriggles out from under her bag and coat, ignoring the hovering waitress anxious to relegate them to the cloakroom. Underneath she wears a gray trouser suit, the jacket straining over the bust. Her cheeks have a ruddy glow untempered by makeup.

There's a dip in the corner of her mouth that might be disapproval. Or disdain. She slings her things over the back of the chair and sits with a heavy sigh, leaning on the table and pressing the heels of her hands into her eyes.

"Glad you could make it." I offer her a welcoming smile.

Rachel sniffs. "I couldn't find it. I went round the block twice—
in the end I had to go in and ask at the pizza place on the corner."
She nods across at the plate glass entrance to the restaurant. "Would
it kill them to put up a sign? Or is that too unhip?"

She turns back and stares at the bamboo thicket a few feet away
from us. "What's today's special? Panda steaks?"

"We could go back to the pizza restaurant if you prefer."

Her cheeks grow redder and she shakes her head. She picks up
her menu and scans through the options. Another twitch of the
mouth as she notes the prices.

"It's my treat," I insist.

She chews her lip. Doesn't argue.

The waitress glides over. I order a glass of Prosecco then look
at Rachel. "San Pellegrino."

"Prosecco for me too," she tells the waitress, then sees me frowning and laughs.

"It's okay. I've stopped breast-feeding. Finally."

Her phone bleeps from somewhere in her bag. She retrieves it
and reads the message. Starts to text something back.

I glance around as I wait for her to finish. A man over by the
bar catches my eye and smiles. I check him out briefly. Tall, slim
build, but not really my type. I turn back to Rachel, who's stashing
her mobile away again, lips pursed in apology.

"Sorry, just checking in with Tim."

She squints at the other diners, running a self-conscious hand
over her windblown hair.

"So, how did it go?" I prompt.

"It nearly didn't go at all. Therese has got a cold and couldn't
go to nursery, and by the time Tim arranged to work from home,
I'd missed the train. I barely made the meeting."

"And?"

Rachel shrugs. "It went okay."

"You sure? You don't sound very certain."

"Oh, they want me back, all right. Even offered me more money."

"So what's the problem?"

She groans. "It's not that I don't want to go back to work—I'm more than ready to do something other than trail after the kids all day. It's just that I'm not sure I want to go back *there*."

Rachel went into employment law thinking it would be a quiet backwater after the cut and thrust of the bar. Little realizing that hell hath no fury like an employee scorned.

"But the money's good," she sighs. "We need a bigger house now Theo's growing up—they can't share a room forever, and you know Tim's job is always hanging in the balance." She scratches the tip of her nose. "They made a second bloke in his department redundant last week."

I give her a sympathetic look and for the first time since she arrived her features relax into a smile. The waitress returns with the wine and takes our order. Rachel seizes her glass, swallowing almost half in one go, then grunts in appreciation.

"Christ, I've been dying for a drink for nearly three years."

I eye the inch or so left. "I'll get you another."

"Better not." She puts her glass back down. "It'll go straight to my head, and I must catch the eight-thirty train."

I dig my teeth into my lips, trying to hide my disappointment. I'd been hoping Rachel would keep the whole evening free—I can't remember the last time we got to hang out together. But I know she's making an effort as it is.

"So, how's things?" She sits back, scrutinizes my face.

"Fine. Good."

Rachel stares at me a bit longer, then down at the tablecloth. I can see she's struggling for something neutral to say. She loses the fight. "You're still . . ."

I sigh. "Yes."

She chews the inside of her lip. Raises her eyes back to mine. "Grace—"

"Rachel, let's not do this again, shall we? Let's not go over this anymore. I'm okay. Really."

She fiddles with the stem of her glass, twirling it in her fingers so the little bubbles spin and swirl. "I know, Grace. But Jesus, I . . ."

I snort.

She looks at me quizzically. Almost offended.

"We're like some Victorian pastiche," I say. "The mother and the fallen woman. It seems you're always trying to save me or something."

Rachel's smile is reluctant. "I'm not trying to save you, Grace. I'm simply trying to . . ." She stops, as if she no longer knows what to say. "I just can't believe you're doing this. Not after everything . . ." Her voice lapses into silence.

Not after everything.

I stare at my oldest friend, wondering how to respond. Wondering if it ever occurs to her that I'm doing this precisely *because* of everything. I consider trying to explain. How the way I am now is the only way I can live with what came before.

I close my eyes briefly, and there he is. Michael. The first time we met, the look he gave me—cocky, knowing, full of challenge. A smile that said there was nothing I could do for him, but I was welcome to try.

Christ, to think I imagined I could help. Hard to believe I was ever such a fool.

"Grace?"

I lift my gaze back to my friend. See out of the corner of my eye that the man at the bar still has his head turned in my direction. "How's Tim?" I ask, pointedly changing the subject. "Finished his shed yet?"

Rachel grins, allowing me this one, the alcohol finally lifting her mood. "Nearly. Another few years and it'll be great."

"Men and their caves, eh?"

"You should come and have a look." Something a little offhand in her tone.

"I will," I insist, at the same time knowing I've said this once too often for Rachel to take it seriously. I try to recall the last time I was there. Right after Therese was born. Over two years, I realize with a lurch of guilt.

The waitress appears with a plate in each hand, bending her knees as she places them in front of us. Rachel examines her salad.

"Is that all you're going to have?" I ask.

She grimaces. "I'm trying to lose some weight. I can hardly get into my old work clothes and I can't afford new stuff." She picks over the green leaves, flicking something to the side of her plate. "Christ, I hate fucking capers."

I lean over, spear a couple with my fork, and pop them in my mouth. Replace them with a few of my basil gnocchi.

Rachel looks sheepish but grateful. "Hang on . . ." She fishes into her bag and pulls out an envelope. "Before I forget. I've got this for you."

"It's a bit late for Christmas cards," I say, a subtle dig. She refused to send any this year—said it was a waste of paper.

"Just open it."

I slide a finger under the tab to break the seal and pull out a heavily embossed piece of white card.

"She wasn't sure where to send it so she gave it to me," Rachel says as I examine the elaborately curlicued script. An invitation to Jane's wedding. Jane Transom—our old flatmate at university.

"So Clive finally got round to asking her, then?"

"I think she ended up asking him," Rachel laughs. "After eight years living together, he had the good sense not to refuse."

"Are you going?"

Her mirth subsides into a frown. "Of course. We're leaving the kids with Mum."

I scan the invitation. A church in rural Hertfordshire with the reception at Shaldcott Manor. The full works, by the look of it. I check the date—only a couple of weeks away. "Not much notice, is it?" I say.

Rachel's cheeks flush and I read between the lines. Clearly Jane thought twice before inviting me. "I'm not sure I can . . ." I begin, but no plausible excuse follows in its wake.

Rachel eyes me with a serious expression. "C'mon, Grace, you should come."

I swallow. Picture all the people who'll be there. Everyone who'll know me and what . . . I pull my mind away.

"You will come, won't you?" Rachel's tone is more insistent. "Jane will be disappointed if you don't. Really."

She would? Somehow I find that hard to believe. Not after what happened. After all, no one except Rachel has bothered to keep in touch since our university days.

"I'll try." I put the card back into the envelope and slip it into my bag. Steer the conversation into safer waters. But the meal feels rushed; Rachel checking the time regularly. It seems no time at all before she stands and drags on her coat, reaching in her bag for her purse.

I shake my head. "Like I said. My treat."

Rachel gives me a grateful smile. "And I meant what I said, Grace. Come and see us soon; get away from here for a few days. It'll do you good." A meaningful look as she slings the strap of her bag over her head.

"I promise," I say, trying to convince myself I mean it, and stand to give her a hug. She clutches me tightly, then steps back. Raises a gloved hand to my face.

"We still love you, you know."

She holds her hand there for a moment. I lean forward and squeeze her to me again, blinking.

"Take care," Rachel says with emphasis as she turns to leave.

I watch her retreat into the London night. Sit down and finish my glass, wondering why I feel so abandoned. The waitress approaches with the bill. I give her my credit card, and as she moves away I see the man from the bar hovering behind her.

"I wanted to ask if you'd like to join me for a drink." His smile the right side of hopeful. Up close he looks more attractive, a faint stubble line lending an appealing ruggedness to his features.

I weigh up my options. A night alone in front of the telly—or accept his offer. Suddenly the siren call of the sofa doesn't seem so sweet.

ELEVEN

I'm there again. In that dismal flat, cold gray sky barely visible through naked windows. Beneath me the bare mattress, one spring digging into my shoulder as the weight of his body pins me down. The stale sour smell of the air in the room, the musky scent of skin and sweat as he pushes into me, hard and relentless, hurting, and I'm wondering how I can possibly be here again, after everything, how I could have repeated that mistake, and I'm crying with shame because I'm here again and it's terrible, always so terrible, and now I know I'm never, ever going to be able to leave . . .

I wake with a gasp. Disoriented, my cheeks damp with tears. I raise my head and look around, heart racing.

Where am I?

Dark curtains, the gap between revealing the faintest sliver of orange streetlight. Enough to see I'm in a double bed, half covered by the duvet. Beside me a man, asleep, face turned away.

Memory seeps in. The guy from the restaurant. Not Michael,

I realize with a rush of relief, the dregs of my nightmare lingering in some recess of my mind. I slow my breathing.

Calm down, Grace. It's not him, and you're not there. It's over.

Lifting my head again, I peer back toward the window. What time is it? I wonder. Not yet light, so five, maybe six? I calculate my hours of sleep—no more than four, at the most. Oh God.

I lie still, unmoving, letting the minutes slip by. Somewhere outside, I make out the faint sound of birdsong. The first rumble of traffic. Inside, closer, an intermittent clunking noise as the heating kicks in.

Not that early, then. Seven, perhaps?

The man beside me stirs. Mutters something from a dream. I strain to remember his name; he must have told me. I wonder which one I gave him—Stella or Grace?

I lift the duvet carefully. I can see only his shoulders, the curve of the spine down to the dark cleft of his arse. For a moment I'm tempted to wake him, to have him embrace me, kiss away my morning breath. Let him run a hand between my thighs before slipping inside me and fucking all the bad thoughts out of my head.

But he doesn't move. Doesn't wake. How come men can always bloody sleep?

Christ, I need a cigarette.

I stare up at the ceiling, a tide of anxiety threatening to overwhelm me. I have to get up. I slide my legs over the side of the bed, but even the effort of sitting ignites my hangover, leaving me dizzy and nauseous.

Too much of everything, I acknowledge, flashing back to the night before. To the bar. To the club. The coke, the pot. The fumbled hasty sex when we finally tumbled into bed.

Too fucking much of everything. And always the price to pay in the morning.

Tears well again. I blink them away. *No point, Grace*, I tell myself as I rise unsteadily to my feet. No fucking point at all.

I don't turn on the light in the bathroom, reluctant now to wake him. Unable yet to bear the strain of communication. Groping for the loo, I lower the seat and pee—there's not much, probably beer-brown with dehydration. I daren't flush afterward. I pull on the dressing gown hanging on the back of the door and turn the tap on low. Splash water on my face, thankful it's too dark to catch sight of myself in the mirror.

A heave in my stomach. I lean on the sink, breathing hard.

Oh, please, don't let me be sick.

Gradually the nausea ebbs away. I locate the kitchen and close the door behind me. Switch on the light. The room is tiny—compact, an estate agent would say. A line of units, a fridge, and a stove.

My spirits lift a little when I spot the expensive coffeemaker. I open a few cupboards, find half a packet of ground arabica. Fill the machine and stand there, watching it dribble into the flask, its busy gurgling somehow a small shred of comfort. Pour myself a cup, then reconsider.

Give him a chance, Grace.

I fill a second mug and take it into the bedroom, placing it on his bedside table. The man whose name I still can't remember blinks, opens his eyes. His complexion is blotchy, his stubble more pronounced. But he's not bad, even in the harsh daylight now per-colating into the room.

"I made you some coffee."

He mumbles "thanks," pulls himself up into a semireclining position. Looks at me briefly before shutting his eyes again. "You okay?"

"Fine," I lie. "Thank you."

I stand there for a few seconds. Graphic designer, I remember now. Recently broken up from a long-term relationship. My body recalls his mouth on my nipple, hot and eager. The feel of him inside me, the little gasp he made when he came.

"You're welcome to use the shower," he says, not opening his eyes.

My cue to leave.

I stare at him briefly, reevaluating the night before. Definitely a rebound fuck.

I dress, not bothering with the shower. Find my bag in the living room, by the side of the sofa. Hunt through it, fingers groping into every corner of the lining. *Please, God.* I turn up three ibuprofen. Go back into the kitchen and pour myself another inch of coffee and swallow them one by one.

It's then I see the calendar on the wall. And the date. The fourteenth of February.

Happy fucking Valentine, Grace.

Swilling my mug under the tap, I dry it with a tea towel and replace it on the shelf. Like I was never here at all. Then pull on my coat and let myself out, closing the door to the flat softly behind me.

I don't bother with good-bye.

TWELVE

God, I've missed you."

Roy traces a finger from the hollow of my breastbone down to my belly button, where it pauses, waiting for my response.

"It's been a while." I keep my voice noncommittal.

He smiles, but his eyes betray his disappointment. Poor old Roy. Always hoping for more. My gaze flicks to the card on my chest of drawers. A cutesy teddy bear holding a red heart-shaped balloon with BE MY VALENTINE printed across the front.

Jesus. A shift of guilt inside me. I hate feeling I'm leading someone on, even when I'm not. And I have made it clear, as firmly and kindly as I can, that this is just what it is.

"Issues at home." Roy clears his throat. "Big fuss about my daughter's wedding. I couldn't get away till it was all over."

Roy lives somewhere in the Home Counties. The kind of place where women like me exist only in the pages of the *Daily Mail*. I'm his treat, his dirty little secret, possibly his sole indiscretion in an otherwise ordinary, irreproachable life.

"Did it go well?" I ask.

He gazes at me. He's had a recent haircut, I notice. It makes his bald patch more pronounced.

"Your daughter's wedding," I prompt.

"Ah. Yes. You know, the usual." He flushes slightly and looks away, as if he's made some kind of faux pas.

"You're not keen on him, then? Your son-in-law?"

He presses his thin lips into a line. "No, it's not that. He's a nice enough chap, a doctor. Neurologist, I think—something like that. It's more that . . . you know . . . you so desperately want them to be happy and . . ."

He pauses. Regroups. "The whole marriage thing isn't easy."

I turn onto my back. My sense of smell seems heightened somehow, and Roy's aftershave is almost unbearably strong. I study the ceiling, still feeling a little queasy.

"Yes, I know. I was married once."

"You were?" Roy's expression is incredulous. I wonder briefly if I should be insulted.

"Seven years," I say.

Why am I even telling him this? I close my eyes. It must be the dregs of my hangover. Or last night's encounter, already leaving the stain of regret.

"Seven years," he repeats.

I reopen my eyes and turn to face Roy. He still looks faintly shocked. Or perhaps merely surprised.

Too much detail, I scold myself, aware I can't afford to get complacent. Clients don't like having their idea of you shattered—even clients as devoted as Roy. Most prefer to believe you have absolutely nothing in common with their wives.

"So what happened?" he asks, and I can tell by his tone that he really wants to know. And seeing he cares somehow makes me feel worse.

"I screwed it up." I try to sound upbeat. Obviously fail miserably, because his expression turns sympathetic, his hand reaching across to mine.

"It takes two, though, Stella, to screw up a marriage."

I return his gaze. "Not in this case."

I say it quickly but it's too late. My mind seizes on an image of my husband's face after the police had dropped me home, his appalled, shell-shocked expression when I broke down and told him what had happened.

A good marriage. A sane and useful life. Wiped out in one afternoon.

I blink hard, squeezing away the memory. See Roy open his mouth to say something, then close it again. Knowing not to push things too far.

"So," I say, as brightly as I can manage, "how's it going at Twickers?" It's our joke, rugby being the standard excuse Roy gives for being here; though I do wonder how he makes this stick out of season.

"I'm much more interested in the state of play here," he chuckles, his hand lowering itself to my breast, his face taking on an intense look that tells me he's had enough of conversation.

I manage a surreptitious glance at the clock on the bedside table. Only ten to three. Oh God, another two hours and ten minutes to go. Which might be fine with a man not well into his sixties. A man still up for doing it a couple of times in a row. But even with the aid of the little blue pills the GP prescribes for Roy, twice would be a stretch too far.

So we need to make this one last. My heart sinks. All I want right now is to let my head droop onto the pillow and sleep off the aftermath of last night.

Consequences, Grace. There're always consequences.

I turn to Roy and smile, but he doesn't notice. He's distracting himself with my nipple, twirling it in his fingers like a radio dial. I can't even be bothered to pretend it's erotic, just let him fiddle away while my thoughts drift to that place in my head where no one can follow.

A narrow bed in a bright whitewashed room.

A single stone cottage.

An island surrounded by sea.

Nothing to see beyond except grass and cliff, rock and sky. Nothing to hear but the wind, and the steady, rhythmic pounding of waves on the boulders below.

THIRTEEN

The doctor peers up at me from behind the speculum. "Rather a lot of inflammation up round your cervix, Miss Thomas. Looks like you may have picked up a mild infection."

Infection? My mind leaps to HIV. I take a calming breath and remind myself she said "mild."

She drops the plastic speculum into the waste bin and pulls off her latex gloves. "Probably trichomoniasis, but we'll run a check for chlamydia too. Any other symptoms?"

"Such as?"

"Painful intercourse. Unusual vaginal discharge."

I shake my head, wishing I could get out of these stirrups. It's hard to discuss anything with your legs up in the air.

"So this was simply a routine checkup? Nothing in particular you're concerned about."

I shake my head again. "So, what causes it? This tricho . . ."

"Trichomoniasis. Unprotected sex," says the doctor, her tone peremptory.

"But I always use condoms. I mean always . . ." I stop. It's true. I do always use condoms . . . with clients.

Shit. The man from the restaurant. I can't remember clearly enough what we did.

"It only takes once," she says wearily. I feel shame, hard and heavy in my stomach. How could I have been so stupid?

"How about oral?" Guilt congeals the feeling in my belly as I think of other clients I might have exposed. "Can you pass it on that way?"

The doctor shakes her head. "Only penetrative sex. Or shared sex toys." She releases my legs and waits for me to heave myself into a sitting position. "Do you need a pregnancy test as well?"

"I'm on the pill. Belt and braces." People imagine what escorts fear most is violence from clients; my worst nightmare is one getting me pregnant.

"You on any other medication?"

"Just an inhaler. For my asthma."

She scribbles a prescription and hands it to me. "Antibiotics. Broad spectrum. Single dose. No alcohol and no sex for a week."

I take the piece of paper and stuff it into my handbag. "Thanks."

She calls me back once I've dressed. "If you need more condoms, you can pick some up free at reception."

"Don't worry," I say, my smile sheepish. "I won't be making that mistake again."

FOURTEEN

have to cancel two appointments while I wait for the antibiotics to do their thing. One with a regular who I know plans meticulously for our meetings. The other a dinner date with a Finnish man who sounded nice on the phone.

I calculate my little foray into Civvy Street has cost me well over twelve hundred quid. *That'll teach you, Grace.*

Still, I use the fallow time productively. Go through my bank statements, pay all my bills. Get in a few sessions at the gym and persuade my hairdresser to squeeze me in for a trim. Actually take myself off to the cinema, luxuriating in the dark of a matinee, watching Lars von Trier.

On my last afternoon in purdah I'm updating my website, mixing things up a bit. A couple of new photographs, my face subtly obscured. A quick tweak of the text. I like to keep it sharp, snappy. Nothing cheesy; no erotic poetry or lurid accounts of my sexual fantasies.

Five e-mails arrive while I'm fiddling around online. One from

Stacy at the crisis center to see if I can do an extra shift on Friday. Answer—yes. One from a client I've seen a couple of times, an engineer for a large oil company, down from Aberdeen for a meeting next week. Another yes. A request for face pics—I pick out three and mail them back.

The man inquiring about role play—the usual stuff, maid and master, boss and secretary—I refer on to Anna. God knows, getting through an appointment with a straight face can be hard enough at the best of times.

The last is from Ben, asking if I could meet up tomorrow, in Gloucestershire of all places. I check it out on Google Maps. A nice country house hotel, but looks a bugger to get to without a car.

I ponder it for several minutes. I usually refuse out-of-town appointments. The travel is a hassle, and you're not paid for the time it takes. Besides, I've got the wedding in a few days' time. Plenty of country house there.

On the other hand. I'm pleased Ben wants to book me again.

I'll decide later, I think, stretching out the stiffness in my back. My stomach is growly, but I don't feel hungry. The lingering effects of the antibiotics, maybe. I consider going out for a walk. Pick up something light for supper, then come back and read for a while, get an early night. I'm about to shut down my laptop when another e-mail pops into my inbox.

I open it up, assuming it's from a client. But it's from a woman.

Hi,

I'm sorry I don't know your real name. Amanda, my girlfriend—I think you know her as Elisa—always called you Stella. I'm not even sure I've got the right person, but you're the only Stella I've found working in this part of London.

Anyway, I was wondering if you'd heard from her at all? She left the flat yesterday in the afternoon and hasn't been back

since. I've tried her mobile but she never picks up. I'm getting a
bit worried and trying everyone who might have seen her recently.

Thanks, Kristen

I stare at the screen. Elisa has disappeared?

My first thought is she must have gone off on a long appointment and failed to tell her girlfriend. Elisa regularly has two- or
even three-day bookings from clients who want her all to themselves. It would explain why she's not answering her mobile.

It doesn't seem likely though. Elisa might play up the ditzy
blonde to punters, but underneath she's meticulous; she wouldn't
forget to tell Kristen.

So she must have some other reason. Something she doesn't
want her to find out. An affair, perhaps? Another girl on the side?

But I'm not convinced of that either. Elisa seems devoted to
her girlfriend. She's never said much about Kristen, granted—just
her name—but she was always mentioning little things: stuff they
were going to do together, places they'd been. She told me once
about a birthday treat she'd been planning for ages, a surprise
weekend in Madrid, staying at one of the city's most luxurious
hotels.

Besides, it's not her style somehow. If Elisa—Amanda—has
tired of Kristen, I feel sure she'd deal with it up front rather than
sneak around behind her back.

I open up the reply box, my fingers hovering over the keys. I'm
about to say I can't think of anything, when I remember the party.
Elisa tinkering with her phone, texting or whatever in the middle
of the action. I was annoyed. And surprised. She was usually so
professional.

What was it she'd said when I asked her? Some kind of family
crisis. Could that have something to do with her disappearance?

It's all I can come up with so I type it out quickly. Say I'm sorry

I can't be of more help, but I'm sure it will be okay. That Elisa is bound to turn up soon.

I go back and change the name to Amanda before I press Send. Amanda, I repeat to myself firmly, trying to fix it in my head. By mutual agreement we call each other by our working names, so we don't slip up in front of clients. It's difficult to adjust.

I abandon the idea of a walk. Make myself a decaf tea instead and find a packet of biscuits in the back of the cupboard, the ones with the coffee icing. Only a little stale. I nibble one while I run a bath. I already showered before the clinic appointment this morning, but I've an urge for the soothing comfort of hot water. I pour in a capful of Tisserand floral soak, strip off, sink down, leaving only my face exposed.

Could anything have actually happened to Amanda? I wonder. I'm sure I'm being silly, that Kristen has probably overlooked a note or got her wires crossed perhaps. But I can't quite shake the feeling of disquiet.

I close my eyes and inhale the scent of oranges and lavender, an echo of summer, of somewhere more pastoral. I breathe slowly, trying to relax, but my mind has built up its own momentum, determined to run this to ground.

In all honesty, I've never worried much about what I do. Statistically, prostitutes may well be more at risk of rape and physical abuse, but that's more of a concern for girls working the street. I take the usual precautions. Don't answer withheld numbers. Always call clients back on their mobiles to confirm an appointment, and insist on a real, verifiable name before going to a private residence.

And in three years nothing has happened to make even this caution feel warranted. Sure, some clients can be a bit pushy, wanting to try something off-limits or dispense with the condom, but nobody has ever really crossed the line. Most are polite, gentle, even charming—treating us better, I suspect, than their own wives or girlfriends.

No, the things that bother me most are far more prosaic. Whether an appointment will go well. Whether my shaving rash will flare up or I'll get an asthma attack halfway through.

So why, now, am I so uneasy about Amanda? It's not like I know her that well. We've worked together only, what, half a dozen times? And we've never met up socially.

I sit up and soak a washcloth. Press it to my face. It was the anxiety in Kristen's e-mail, I realize, the fear underpinning every sentence. For the first time it hits me just how difficult it must be to love people like us. I always assumed the jealousy would be the hardest thing; now, I can see, it may well be the worry.

But there's a niggle at the back of my mind, a detail I never even thought to mention to Kristen. That moment at the party, in the kitchen, when I asked Elisa—Amanda—what she was doing with her mobile. I remember the flush in her cheeks. The way her eyes wouldn't quite meet mine.

A family crisis, she said. Yet in the ten hours we spent together that night she showed no sign of being anxious or preoccupied. She seemed upbeat, cheerful even—apart from that little incident with Harry and the facial.

I pull the damp cloth off my face and wipe it with a towel. Release the plug and lie there, unmoving, while the water sucks and drains around me.

Amanda. The more I consider it, the more my certainty grows that she was lying about those texts. However badly I've misread things in the past, I couldn't miss a reaction as obvious as that.

No, I decide. There was definitely something else going on. Though what, of course, I'll probably never know.

FIFTEEN

Nice place."

I slip off my coat and drop it on a chair, walk over to the hotel window, and examine the view across the wide lawn to the distant lake. The crowd of birds massing on the water, white against steel gray.

"Work's paying," Ben says. "I've got a client conference tomorrow. You don't mind coming all the way out here?"

I shake my head. "It's nice to get out of town for a while. Remind myself that there's life outside the capital."

Ben smiles. "I know what you mean."

He stands over by the desk, dressed in a white shirt and dark trousers. His hair glossy, recently washed. I look away. Attractive clients make me uncomfortable, like I've got more to prove.

"I've been thinking about you," he says.

"Good thoughts?" My voice comes out too bright, its tone somehow false.

"Very."

I smile, but there's not enough heart in it. In truth I feel odd, wobbly. Something in Kristen's e-mail yesterday has me rattled. Or maybe I'm just getting too old for all this.

"So," says Ben, looking like someone struggling to get into his stride, "how's things with you?"

"Fine. Same old."

He studies me for a few seconds. "You seem tired, if you don't mind me saying."

I flush, turning self-conscious. "Sorry. Probably a bit of a rush job with my makeup. I'll knock fifty pounds off."

Something flashes across his face. I can't tell if it's hurt or irritation. "Don't be ridiculous, Stella. I wasn't complaining. I'm concerned about you, that's all."

"Okay. Sorry." I cross the room to meet him. "Enough talk." I reach out to unbutton his shirt, but his hand comes up to stop me.

"Slow down."

I laugh. "That's not something I'm used to hearing."

Ben keeps hold of my hand. "I thought we might take a walk. Over to the lake."

I stare at him. *Seriously?*

Then remind myself he's paying. And a tidy sum too. Enough money to entice me into a two-hour train and a twenty-minute taxi ride. "Sure. That would be lovely."

Thank God I had the forethought to bring a spare pair of boots. Flat ones, so I don't have to teeter around the Gloucestershire countryside in black stilettos. Though now I'm thinking this pencil skirt wasn't such a great idea.

"Here," says Ben, noticing me shivering in my thin jacket. He takes his scarf and wraps it twice round my neck. Stands back and laughs.

"Piss off," I say, then laugh myself.

We trudge down to the lake, taking the path anticlockwise around the perimeter, past the copse of leafless beech and a dense thicket of reeds with their ceaseless swishing and rustling. The sky is overcast, but the trees and surrounding fields have taken on that luminous glow you see only in the dead of winter.

"Fresh air." Ben inhales deeply, head into the breeze. I notice how the pale light emphasizes the flecks of gray in his eyes. "Every time I leave London I wonder how on earth I can ever go back."

I sniff, the wind making my nose run. I should have brought some tissues. "I can't imagine living anywhere else."

He thrusts his hands into his pockets and we walk toward the far corner of the lake. As we approach the birds I see they are swans. Seven of them. Bobbing around on the water, heads turned away as if mildly offended by our presence.

"Where did you grow up?" Ben asks suddenly.

I pause, taken aback by the question. Consider what to say. I've never constructed a cover story going that far back.

"Surrey," I say, opting for truth. What harm could it do? "A little village near Godalming."

"Nice."

"Deadly," I reply. "I was so bored most of the time I thought I might actually die."

"Really?" He laughs. "Didn't you have friends? Siblings?"

I shake my head. "I'm an only child. I had friends at school, but they lived miles away, so I didn't get to meet up with them much outside class."

"So what did you do?"

"Read. A lot."

"Didn't your parents take you out? Family trips? Walks? Whatever?"

"Parent," I say. "There was only my dad. And trips out weren't exactly his sort of thing."

Ben looks at me. "What happened to your mum?"

"She died when I was fifteen."

"How?" He stops, turning so he can see all of my face.

"Cancer." I shrug. "What else does anyone die of?"

"Shit. I'm sorry. That's rough."

"Not really. We were well-off. Nice house. Good education. People have it a lot worse."

Ben falls silent for a minute. "How about your father? Is he still alive?"

"Yes."

"You see much of him?"

"No," I say, swallowing down my natural response, but Ben reads it in my face. "Mind my own business, right?"

"We should get back." My voice edgy, its tone a tad too sharp. *He's not simply paying for sex, Grace*, I remind myself—*he's paying you to be pleasant.*

We pick up our pace, rounding the far end of the lake. There's a swan on the path, pecking at the grass along the bank. It turns to face me as I pass, flapping its wings and emitting a long, low hiss.

Fuck you, I think, giving it a cool, hard stare.

Ben orders room service while I warm up in the bath. Tea cakes and hot chocolate. A plateful of buttery shortbread. All served on dainty rose-covered china with pale yellow linen napkins.

The red-haired girl who carries it in beams at the pair of us as she sets the tray on the coffee table. She thinks we're here on some kind of romantic minibreak, I realize, feeling awkward and cross. This appointment is taking on a life of its own. Again.

You should have said no, Grace. You should have told him it was too far to come.

I glance at the clock. Half past four. Two hours gone and we haven't even fucked. What the hell is he waiting for? Maybe he's changed his mind, I think gloomily. Perhaps I'm wearing thin on him already.

"So, is there anyone?" Ben asks, out of the blue. "I mean, anybody special?"

I'm so ambushed by the question, I don't answer. Just take a long sip of my hot chocolate, sweet and strong.

"Sorry." He grabs one of the tea cakes and covers it in butter. "None of my business again. I get it."

I evade his gaze, unsettled by the unexpected atmosphere of intimacy between us. Maybe I should cut my losses and leave, before this goes any further. Ask him for enough money to cover my train fare and a taxi back to the station.

"Christ," Ben says suddenly, putting down his plate. "I'm sorry, Stella. I don't know what's got into me. Can we just start again?"

I look at him. See in his face that he's as unnerved by all this as I am. I nod and he gets up and grabs my hand and pulls me into the bedroom. Moments later we're screwing, good and deep and hard and I let the sex erase everything until my mind feels blank and still as the silt at the bottom of the lake.

Then we do it again. And this time I don't think of Alex at all.

Afterward I lock myself in a cubicle in the ladies' loo on the ground floor. Take out the envelope and break the seal, pulling out the little wad of fifties. They're perfectly aligned, fresh from the cashpoint machine.

I stare at them for a minute, then lift them to my nose, inhaling that particular scent of brand-new notes. I count them carefully, one by one, focusing on the way they feel in my hand, their crispness, their pristine newness. I inspect the red swirl and sweep of the lettering, the grainy images of the Bank of England and a younger queen. Turn one over to view Boulton and Watt, the industrial steam pioneers.

Power and money, I think, examining their austere faces before stuffing them back in the envelope. Power and money.

The rest is just detail.

I count it again. It's all there, plus a tip. Twenty notes.

One thousand quid exactly.

SIXTEEN

I survive the bone-aching chill in the church—why would anyone get married in February, for God's sake?—and that ubiquitous bloody reading on love from Corinthians. I hold it together through the wedding vows, those big white lies most of us can never hope to keep, and maintain a gracious smile as we exit the church, half the other women teetering in fuck-me stilettos that make them look like their rates are considerably lower than mine.

I chat to Tim in the car ride up to the manor, then make affable small talk with a farmer called Alan, a rather stolid cousin of Jane's sitting on my left at our table. He's clearly single, and I can't help wondering if it's a setup, Rachel in cahoots with Jane to sort me out with somebody safe and wholesome. Someone to save me.

Still, after a glass of champagne I'm content to listen to his plans for a llama farm in Wales. Rachel is checking her phone, nervous about leaving the kids with her mother for the day, while Tim peruses the other guests, on the lookout for faces from our old university crowd. I'm just thinking I might get through this whole ordeal relatively unscathed when I hear a plummy male voice behind me.

"Stella?"

I turn to see a face I hoped I'd never encounter again. Smug and piggy, dark hair cropped hard and tight, like topiary. A smile crawling across his meaty lips as he takes in my appalled expression.

Christ, how come I didn't spot him earlier?

"Hello, Max," I say, trying to keep my voice steady as Rachel whips round to stare at us both. "Fancy seeing you here."

"Yes, Stella. Quite a surprise." His smile morphs into a smirk. "Didn't really have you down as the wedding type, I must admit."

Rachel's astonished look hardens into anger. "And you are?"

Max regards her pleasantly. "An old acquaintance of Stella's," he replies without the slightest show of embarrassment.

Rachel swallows. Puts down her phone. Tim looks confused for a moment, then stares into his watercress and goat's cheese starter. Clearly it's just dawned on him what's going on.

Glancing toward the space Max vacated, Rachel spots a woman in a blue dress, staring in our direction. "Well, it's been nice meeting you." Her tone clipped, dismissive, heavy with emphasis. "But I'm sure you need to return to your *wife*."

"My wife?" Max follows her gaze and laughs. "Goodness, no, she's not my wife. Only my plus-one." He turns back to me. "If I'd known you were coming, Stella, I'd have hooked up with you instead." Max looks at me meaningfully. "We could have come to some kind of arrangement."

I don't grace this with an answer, but Rachel presses her lips together, then beckons him over. He takes a step forward, inclining his head to hers.

"Fuck off," she says in a voice just low enough not to alarm the other guests.

Max straightens. Studies her for a second or two, then turns on his heels and walks away.

"Excuse me." Ignoring Alan's puzzled expression, I get up and head to the loos, locking myself in the stall at the end. I lower the lid of the toilet and sit down, sinking my head into my hands. I'm gritting my teeth so hard my jaw aches.

The fucking shit.

I saw him only once, but it was enough. Max was the sort of client that left you with a bad taste in your mouth—and not simply from sucking his dick. It wasn't anything in particular, more the way he looked at you, with a kind of contempt, or how he held you, a tad too firm. The way he pushed your head into his crotch while you blew him, as if trying to make you gag.

Max had you counting the minutes until he left. The type of client you double-lock the door behind. The kind you let go to voice mail the next time he calls.

Outside, the door to the loos opens with a squeak. I hold my breath.

"Grace?"

I exhale slowly.

"Grace, come on. I know you're in there."

I exit the stall. Rachel is leaning against a porcelain sink, wearing an expression that makes my insides shrivel. "Jesus, Grace, don't you see how awful this is?" she says, her lips puckered with anger. "I mean, what a fucking mess you've got yourself into?"

I don't bother to answer. What the hell does she think I'm doing in here? Her eyes fix on mine. I've never seen her look at me quite this way before. Like she's given up.

"I'm not sure I can handle this anymore," she says quietly.

"Rachel, I'm sorry. I had absolutely no idea he would be here. How could I?"

"But don't you see?" she hisses. "This could happen anywhere. Anytime. I mean, how can you live like this?"

I haven't a choice, I want to say. I can only live like this. I stare across the gulf growing between us, knowing I haven't words enough to bridge it. And knowing that's my fault. There's nothing unreasonable, after all, in what my best friend just said; she is saying it because she still cares, not because she's stopped.

Rachel is the first to look away, her eyes shining. "It's as if you're in free fall, Grace. Five years and no sign yet of hitting the ground. I'm sick of holding my breath and waiting for the moment of impact. All of us, everyone who loves you, we can only watch, powerless to do anything. And it's horrible, Grace. Horrible."

I feel my face grow hot. My chest tight. "Can we not do this right now?" I say, despising the pleading tone that's crept into my voice. "Please."

Rachel bites her lip. Looks at me a little longer. "I'll see you outside."

No sign of Max when I reclaim my seat; nor the girl in blue. Perhaps they've left, I think with a rush of relief. Maybe Rachel actually shamed him into going.

Alan, once so full of conversation, doesn't return my tentative smile. Probably wondering why I introduced myself as Grace, yet apparently answer to Stella. I sit through the speeches, trying to look cheerful despite feeling more alone than I can ever remember. Tim glances over occasionally; Rachel acts as if I'm not even here.

I should have hired a car, I think miserably. Or booked a taxi. Instead I'll have to wait for them to leave and endure the silent treatment all the way back to the station.

A round of applause and some raucous whoops mark the end of the best man's contribution. Jane and Clive rise and walk over to cut the cake. I watch his hand encircle hers as she holds the knife and I feel a surge of claustrophobia.

I wait till the formal bit is over, then get up and make my way toward the patio doors, desperate for fresh air and solitude. But halfway there I see Jane wave at me, sitting beside a woman I recognize instantly: Alice Morgan, from my psychology course. And next to her Jim Brunton and Bill Frewin, both in our year at college.

I make myself go over.

"Grace." Jane smiles. "Good to see you. You remember everyone, of course?"

I dig out my friendliest expression. "How could I forget?"

They all laugh, though it's not remotely funny, and I realize they're nervous. Embarrassed, even.

A swell of panic churns my stomach. Has Rachel told them what I'm doing? I've never asked her not to, always assumed she'd keep it to herself. After all, she's my oldest friend. But there's definitely something in their manner. Bill can barely meet my eyes and Alice's voice, when she speaks, sounds too bright.

"So how's things, Grace? None of us have seen you in ages."

I swallow, trying to relax the muscles in my face. "Great. Fine. How about you?"

She laughs unnecessarily. Holds up her hand so I can view the duo of platinum rings, one sporting a sizable diamond. "You know, hitched. Babies. The usual."

"You got married, didn't you?" asks Jim. "To that bloke in the year below us?"

There's an uncomfortable silence. I have a feeling someone just kicked Jim's foot under the table.

"I was," I say. "Not now."

No one speaks. Their expressions become more awkward. They know, I realize. Not about the escorting, perhaps, but about what happened before. Of course they know, I think, my cheeks beginning to burn. Even if no one told them, it was in all the regional papers; even made several of the nationals.

Instantly I'm back in that airless courtroom, sitting in the witness stand, being cross-examined by Michael's barrister. Everyone staring at me, like I'm the one on trial.

Isn't it true, Ms. Thomas, that your own involvement with Mr. Farrish rather negates the testimony you've just given us?

The implication being that I was to blame. That it was my fault she died.

"Grace," asks Alice, looking concerned. "Are you feeling okay?"

"Excuse me," I mumble. I turn away before I can see their surprise segue into relief, and make a bolt for the exit.

Outside, twilight is rapidly fading into night. I pull my jacket tight and crunch across the gravel patio to the gardens beyond. Bare earth in the borders, but farther, up in the grass around the trees, I can just make out several long drifts of snowdrops, tiny white jewels glowing against their backdrop of green.

I lean against a stone birdbath, taking deep gulps of cold air, waiting for the panic to subside. Behind me, faint but audible, the band kicks off with a smooth, jazzy version of "Unforgettable." Through the large leaded windows I see Clive leading Jane onto the dance floor. From this distance, the whole thing looks quite magical. The grand room with its chandeliers. The elegant floral bouquets. The candles flickering on the tables.

And I find myself genuinely hoping they make it. That all this will count for something.

Though it never did for me.

"Grace?"

I jump and turn. Tim. I actually sigh with relief. He makes his way toward me, shivering in his shirt. "You okay?"

I nod.

"I don't get the feeling you're enjoying this very much." He thrusts his hands into his trouser pockets for warmth.

"Not much," I admit.

"That man . . . earlier . . . I take it he's somebody you've met. You know, in your work."

I nod again.

"Seems like a right prick."

I look up at Tim and the sympathy on his face makes my eyes sting. I dig my nails into my palms, forcing the tears to recede as Tim places a consoling arm around my shoulder. "Sod's law, eh . . ." He puts on a Humphrey Bogart voice. "Of all the weddings in all the towns in all the world, he walks into this one."

I laugh and rest my head against his chest. I may not have much faith left in marriage, but I have plenty in Rachel and Tim.

"Rachel's fine," he says, preempting my question. "She worries, that's all."

I sniff and run the heel of my hand across my cheek. "I know. But she's right. I am a mess."

Tim gives me a squeeze. "I don't see a mess, Grace. Simply someone who's had a very tough time. Don't be so hard on yourself."

"Thanks," I say.

"Rachel just can't bear the thought of you being so alone," he adds tentatively.

I drop my gaze. And find myself, for some reason, thinking of Ben. He's probably seeing some other girl right now. Men with a taste for escorts rarely stick to one—they're paying for variety, after all.

I inhale, forcing my mind away. Tim looks back toward the lights and the music. "Do you want to go soon?" he asks.

"God, please." I flash him a grateful smile. "Thank you."

Inside I spot Jane and Clive in the corner, eating a piece of wedding cake. I pick my way through the crowd on the dance floor to say good-bye, but before I reach them I'm ambushed by an outstretched arm.

Max. His lips pulled into a condescending smile. "Dance?" he asks, standing too close.

I glance around. No sign of the girl in blue. "No, thanks."

"But I insist."

I glare at him. "You have no right to insist on anything. Just piss off and leave me alone." I go to walk past but he stands in my way.

"Come on, Stella. Try to be nice." Max slides his hand into his jacket. Removes his wallet and pulls out a twenty-pound note. "That cover a dance?"

I take a step forward. Stick my face up close to his. "Shove it up your arse, you pathetic little creep."

His jaw tightens as he considers his next move, then Max grabs my arm, pinching it in his fat fingers. "You know, Stell-la . . ." he sneers, stretching both syllables of my nom de guerre. "Or should I say Grace? Either way, you really should be more careful. I imagine you wouldn't want everyone here knowing what you've been up to, would you?"

"Nor, I imagine, would you," I retort.

He laughs. "Don't bet on it, sweetheart. I'm not married. And I believe that old double standard is still very much alive—men get off far more lightly in most people's books."

I narrow my eyes and hold his gaze.

"So how about that dance?" he asks again.

I count to five and smile. Let my features soften, lifting my left hand to his shoulder as if accepting his offer. With my right I locate his balls through the thin fabric of his suit and squeeze—just hard enough to render him immobile.

Max's eyes bulge as I put my mouth up to his ear.

"Dance with you?" I hiss over the boom of the music. "I'd rather fucking die."

It's gone midnight by the time I walk into the warmth of my flat. I inhale deeply, savoring the stillness, the silence, the ineffable sweetness of being entirely, gloriously alone. I search in my bag for my phone, intending to turn it off, but find a text from Anna, sent earlier this afternoon. I forgot I put the alert tone on mute.

"Check your e-mail. Now."

I fire up my laptop and open her message. Inside is a single Web link. I click on it and find I'm facing a report from the local evening news. I stare at the photograph, then the headline, and my breath dies in my throat.

PROSTITUTE FOUND DEAD
IN BAYSWATER HOTEL ROOM

Christ, no. I avert my eyes from the screen for a few seconds, listening to the thump of my pulse in my ears.

Oh fuck. Fuck, fuck, fuck.

I force myself to look back at the picture of Amanda, her face smiling, half turned away from the camera. It looks like a private snapshot, taken at a family gathering, perhaps, or an evening out with friends. She looks happy and relaxed. Off the clock.

Tears prick my eyes. I get up and grab my inhaler. Take a couple of puffs and wait for my breathing to slow before sitting back down at my desk. I read through the report, only half taking it in.

> . . . woman found dead yesterday in a hotel room in Bayswater, after being reported missing several days ago. Police identified the body as Amanda Mansfield, a 31-year-old prostitute known to be working in the London area. They are treating her death as suspicious and are appealing for any witnesses who saw her on the night of the 24th.

Amanda is dead.

I say it soundlessly, my lips forming the words, trying them for size. It feels impossible. Inconceivable.

All that beauty. All that life.

I read the report again, slowly this time, sentence by sentence. Think back to Kristen's e-mail. The worry in the lines. My own bland reassurance.

Oh God. The urge for a cigarette strong-arms its way into my consciousness, as tangible as hunger. It's all I can do not to grab my coat and head off to the twenty-four-hour store on the corner.

I Google Amanda's name. Several hits, all of them news reports, none adding much to what I've just read. Except one, the *South London Echo*, which quotes a source at the Metropolitan Police saying the body had been "molested" around the time of death.

I lean back and close my eyes, feeling cold, almost shivery. Molested. In a hotel room. The inference is obvious.

Amanda was murdered by a client.

SEVENTEEN

Anna shivers, thrusting her hands deep into the pockets of her military-style coat. She looks tired, her skin a grayish pallor in the low winter sunlight. A hint of redness around her eyes. "Have you heard anything more since yesterday?"

I shake my head.

"It's all over the Net," she says. "There's a huge thread on PunterWeb about it."

"I'll bet."

"Mostly speculation, of course. And a lot of hysteria. Joanne, you know, that girl who used to work with me at the agency, she's going to take a minder to every appointment."

"Actually into the room?"

Anna rolls her eyes. Manages a smile. "Wouldn't that be every man's dream job?" She sniffs, pulling up the collar of her coat against the wind blowing along the embankment. There's a fierce bite to it, a nip of cold from somewhere Siberian.

"Jesus, poor Elisa," she says. "I keep remembering the time

we went to see a Jewish guy, over in that place in Harrington Gardens."

"The Bentley?"

"Yes, that's the one. He told her to kneel on all fours and bark. Like a bloody dog."

"You're kidding. Did she agree?"

"Like hell!" Anna snorts. "She flat refused. Told him it was against her religion."

I can't help but laugh. "I didn't realize you knew her that well."

"I didn't. Not really. I only worked with her a couple of times. She was a bit out of my league."

"She was a bit out of everyone's league," I say, and Anna smiles. Tips her head back and lets the wind fan out her hair. "You did those parties together, didn't you?"

"A few."

She stops. Leans on the wall and gazes out at the river. The water looks dark and slatey, the surface rippling in the breeze. A splay of cables suspending the Albert Bridge over the motley collection of boats moored along the pier.

"What do you think happened?" she asks, pinning back her hair with one hand to stop it blowing around her face.

"I guess she ran into the wrong guy." A chill inside as I finally articulate what neither of us wants to admit.

"A client?" Anna chews her lip. It looks sore, chapped.

"I suppose so. After all, she was found in a hotel room."

Anna doesn't speak, just stares out across the water.

"I heard from her," I say, suddenly. "Her girlfriend, I mean. She e-mailed me after Elisa disappeared. Asking if I had any idea where she might be."

Anna turns to look at me. "When was that?"

"Wednesday, I think. She said Ama— . . . Elisa had vanished without a word the day before."

Anna thinks for a minute, grabbing at a stray bit of hair that's flapping in the breeze. "So she'd been missing, what . . . three days when they found her?"

I nod.

"And her girlfriend didn't know where she'd gone?" Anna turns back to the view across the Thames. "God only knows what she was up to."

I grimace. Poor Kristen.

"Come on." Anna links her arm through mine and we start walking again, heading toward Chelsea Bridge. "It makes you think though, doesn't it?"

"How do you mean?"

"About getting out." She half closes her eyes, staring into the sun. "I was mulling over what you asked before. Maybe it's time to call it a day. Things are starting to get to me." Anna gives me a rueful smile. "I had a bloke last week ask me to pretend I was his wife's best friend. So I did. Told him he was a cheat and a liar."

I laugh again. "We all have those days."

"Yeah, but I can't afford to start alienating clients like that. He left without paying. And he'll probably post a shitty review."

"Any ideas what you'd do? If you stop, I mean."

"Not really. I've considered setting up an agency, but I can't stand the idea of managing a bunch of sullen Lithuanians."

"Stick to English girls, then."

Anna sniffs. "Still a nightmare. Everyone trying to rip you off, making deals with clients behind your back. I should know—I was with my agency for three years before I went indie."

"What about your old job? Didn't you work for some IT firm?"

"Telecoms. I was in corporate training."

"Couldn't you go back to that?"

"I doubt it." Anna pulls a face. "If nothing else, I'm way out of date. I'd have to retrain."

"So retrain."

"I've considered it, but . . ."

"But what?"

Anna doesn't say anything for over a minute. Then stops and turns to face me.

"Okay, here's the thing." She sniffs again and scratches her nose with the tip of her nail. "I've got myself into debt. Quite a lot of debt, actually—I can barely meet the mortgage payments as it is. I could sell my flat and use the equity to pay off what I owe, but then I'd have nowhere to live. And no income."

She glances over the Thames toward Battersea Park as I take this in. Her face looks older suddenly, more fragile. I exhale slowly and cast caution to the wind.

"So, how much do you owe?"

Her eyes flick back to mine.

"I'm sorry," I say quickly. "None of my business."

"No, it's fine." Anna takes a deep breath. "Just shy of thirty thousand."

"Thirty grand?" Too late to hide the shock on my face. "Jesus, Anna, what—"

I see the look on hers and shut up. Neither of us speaks for what feels like ages. My mind spins around her revelation.

Thirty thousand pounds. Christ.

I mean, I know Anna has expensive habits, especially when it comes to clothes; I've seen the stuff she wears, and the bank of wardrobes lining her spare room. Even so, that's one fuck of a lot of money. Business must have been worse than she's been letting on.

"So what are you going to do?" I venture.

She kicks at a stone on the pavement. "No idea."

"You could always sell off some things," I say cautiously, gauging her reaction. "Get a lodger maybe. While you retrain."

Anna grimaces. "It still wouldn't be enough. I'd need at least twenty-five thousand to pay the tuition fees and live on in London for a year."

I reflect on this for a minute or two. "You ever thought about moving further afield?"

She sighs. A long, slow sound just audible over the hum of wind and traffic. "Yeah, I've thought about it—for ten seconds or so. That's how long before I realize I'd go insane rotting away in the suburbs."

"It doesn't have to be Chipping Norton, for heaven's sake. What's wrong with Brighton? Or Bristol?"

"Barely any cheaper than London these days."

I swing my eyes to the river. I'm getting the sense I'm not helping.

Another silence, then Anna tugs briefly on my arm. "I know I asked you this before, but what about you? What's your escape plan?"

"This is it."

Anna raises her eyebrows and gives me an intense look. "Come on, Grace. You don't want to still be doing this when you're fifty."

I pull a face.

"I'm not joking," she says. "You remember Helen? I saw a review on her the other day, and frankly it was less than kind. She must be pushing forty-seven now."

"And no doubt still pretending she's thirty-five."

Anna grins. "No doubt."

She picks up her pace, stretching out her long legs in what look like designer biker boots. I can't help wondering how much further they've taken her into the red.

"Seriously, Grace, what *are* you going to do?"

I feel a flush of something hot and sour. Why does everyone keep asking me this?

"I've no idea," I snap, more sharply than intended. "I'm not ready to jack it in yet."

She ignores my obvious irritation. "You need to think about it. Hard. Too long at this malarkey and you end up losing your soul."

Or your life, I think, my stomach rolling as I remember Amanda.

We arrive at the junction with Chelsea Bridge and Grosvenor Road. Anna looks up toward Knightsbridge. "I'd better go. I've got an appointment this afternoon with that bloke you referred to me."

"The role-play guy?"

"Yeah. We're doing the secretary thing first. I'm going to his office for an 'interview' and I need to get a pair of fake glasses. All I can find is those cheap reading ones they sell everywhere, but they make me dizzy." She giggles. "Mind you, at least they'd make his dick look bigger."

"He's going to screw you in his office?"

Anna shrugs. "I guess so."

"What about the other staff? Won't they catch on?"

"Who knows? Maybe that's the attraction—you know these bloody exhibitionists. Anyway, what do I care? It's not my job on the line if we get caught."

I manage a smile, but underneath it I feel impossibly tired. A dull sort of weariness, like the shine has worn off everything. I find myself considering Amanda's parents, how they must know now what it was she did for a living. How it probably killed her.

And wonder if they're aware of Kristen. Or was she another of Amanda's secrets?

Hell, I think. *Kristen*. It hits me how bad she must be feeling right now. "Hey," I say to Anna. "Do you know where she lived? Amanda . . . Elisa, I mean."

She releases my arm. "Not sure. Over toward Chiswick, I seem to remember. Why'd you ask?"

"I thought I might go round and see her girlfriend. Check she's coping. I e-mailed her yesterday when I heard, but I've had nothing back."

Anna considers this as she buttons up her coat. "Try Janine," she suggests. "I'm pretty certain she knows. She used to hang out with them occasionally."

"Thanks."

She leans forward and gives me a hug, a little longer and tighter than usual. Then stands back and examines my features. "Can I give you some advice, Grace?"

"Okay."

"Don't get involved. I'm sure you mean well, but honestly, I think you're better off staying out of it."

She's right. I know that.

But somehow this feels like something I have to do. The least I can do. For Amanda. For Kristen.

And maybe for myself.

EIGHTEEN

MONDAY, 2 MARCH

Kristen's flat is in a two-story terraced house in a narrow side road just off Chiswick Common. Pale London brick, a big bay window surrounded by a small, paved garden, the front door freshly painted in high-gloss navy blue. The window box under the bay is filled with ivy and spring bulbs, while a pair of dwarf conifers stand like sentries at each side of the porch.

Smart, yes, but somehow lacking the glamor I always associated with Elisa. It's almost impossible to imagine her in a setting this prosaic.

I study the tags alongside the doorbells. SHELTON, D in neat script by the lower one; above it MANSFIELD/GRAINGER in black type.

Amanda Mansfield. Such an ordinary name.

I press the top bell once. There's no sound that I can hear, but a minute later the door swings open and I find myself looking at a girl with light brown hair pulled back in a short ponytail. Her face bare of makeup, her eyes puffy and dark.

"Kristen?"

She squints into the sunlight. "Yes?"

"My name's Stella. You contacted me about Amanda?"

A blank look.

"I e-mailed you the other day when I . . . when I heard. But you probably haven't had a chance to respond." She carries on staring at me as I gabble. "I just wanted to check you're okay. If there's anything I can do or . . ."

I stop, feeling suddenly foolish. Anna was right. It was a mistake to come.

Kristen turns abruptly and walks back through the hallway. I pause in the entrance, then assume this is an invitation. I follow her up the stairs and find her waiting at the top, holding the door.

The flat isn't large, but a skylight floods the lounge with light and the white walls are clean and fresh. A couple of giant canvases add big splashes of color, and the outsize L-shaped sofa, which should make the room appear smaller, somehow gives it a more generous feel.

"It's nice of you to come." Her Scottish accent is soft—Edinburgh maybe, or somewhere farther north—but her voice has the slow, heavy tone of someone still in shock. She attempts a smile, but it's like her features have forgotten how; the corners of her mouth turn up for a second, then subside.

We examine each other for a moment. She's midheight—barely taller than me. Pretty, but not spectacularly so. That said, there's a quality, a certain vibrancy about her that I could imagine Amanda found alluring.

"I hope you don't mind me barging round like this," I begin. "I was—"

Without warning, Kristen bursts into tears. A snuffling, anguished howl, her arms hanging by her sides as if broken. I hesitate, then step forward and give her a hug. She lets me hold her for a few seconds before pulling away.

"I'm sorry," she chokes, swiping at her face with the back of her hand. "I'm so exhausted. I can't sleep and I've just got back from the police station. They've been asking me questions for hours."

"Surely they don't imagine that you . . ."

She frowns. "I don't think so, not really. They wanted to go over everything about Amanda—her work—you know. They've already been round the flat, taken her computer, her personal phone, other stuff." She sighs. "They took my laptop too—that's why I never got your e-mail. I've no idea when I'll get it back."

"Why not? They can't keep it, can they?"

"They can, at least for as long as they need it for the investigation. I asked." Kristen looks out the window, chewing her lip. Then turns back to me. "Do you want a cup of coffee or tea?"

I shake my head. "I'm fine. Really. I only popped round to see if you were all right. And to tell you how terribly sorry I am. Amanda was lovely, truly one of a kind."

Kristen's mouth starts to tremble. She sinks onto the enormous sofa. I lower myself into the leather beanbag opposite.

"We bought this place together three years ago," she says, her voice quivering. "We were doing it up before we got married."

"Married?" My voice betrays my surprise, and Kristen looks at me.

"We'd set a date. June next year, our seven-year anniversary."

"Oh." I can't think what else to say.

"She was going to stop, you know, stop working." She's talking faster now, the earlier lethargy in her voice superseded by a kind of manic energy. "We had an agreement, you see, that she'd carry on till the wedding. By then she planned to have saved up enough for us to set up a business together." Tears start to roll down her cheeks again.

"Doing what?"

"Graphic design. I'm an artist and Amanda's going to classes in Quark," she says, seemingly unaware that she's straying into the present tense. "So she can handle the layout side of things."

I take this in. "I'm so sorry."

Kristen stares at me for several moments. "Do you want something to drink, Stella? Tea? Coffee?" she says, forgetting she's already asked.

"No, honestly, I'm fine," I repeat. "And please, call me Grace. My real name is Grace."

She drops her head into her hands, running her fingers through her hair before looking back up at me. "I don't suppose you have any idea who she might have been seeing that day?"

I shake my head again. "None. We never talked about work that much. Only the things we did together . . ." I pause, suddenly embarrassed. "You know, like the parties."

Kristen nods. "The thing is, there wasn't anything on her computer—I checked, before the police took it. She always kept a record of appointments, their duration, that sort of stuff, but there was no mention of this one—in fact, she had nothing down at all for the day she disappeared. Or for the next few days. We'd been toying with the idea of going somewhere for the weekend and she was keeping her diary clear."

"She must have got a call. Went straight out without making a note of it."

Kristen screws up her face. "She wouldn't. Amanda was always so thorough with things like that."

I keep my expression neutral. What can I say? Maybe Amanda didn't want Kristen knowing about this one. Most escorts in long-term relationships deceive their partners on some level—too much honesty being as corrosive as too little.

"What do the police think?"

"The obvious." She shrugs. "That Amanda met up with a client in a hotel and he screwed her, then strangled her."

"That's how she died?"

"Apparently. Death by asphyxiation, they called it."

I shudder. An image of Amanda's long neck surrounded by her silk kimono.

Kristen leans her head in her hands, elbows on her knees. "That's what I don't understand—she was always so careful. Religious about security, calling them back on their mobile, checking them out beforehand. And she told me about every appointment, always— who she was seeing, their number, where they were meeting, for how long. She never forgot."

Her fingers work at the furrows on her brow, kneading and massaging. "But this time, nothing . . . she simply upped and left without a word."

"Were you at work?"

She shakes her head. "I'm freelance, I work from home, but I went out to pick up some stuff for supper and when I got back there was no sign of her. I assumed she'd gone for a run or some- thing, over in the park, but when she didn't return after an hour I called her. Her work mobile and her personal one—they were both off."

"You must have been frantic."

She nods. "When it got to around half seven, I rang the police, but they weren't interested. She hadn't been missing twenty-four hours."

"Did you tell them what she did? Her work, I mean."

"Not then. I was worried about telling them, about them know- ing. But I did later, the next day, when she still hadn't come back."

"What did they do?"

Kristen pulls a face. "Nothing, I suspect. I imagine as far as they were concerned she was a prostitute and going AWOL was par for the course."

"And then they found her."

"Yes. In a crappy three-star hotel on Westbourne Grove, can

you believe?" Kristen looks at me, bewildered. "As if Amanda would be seen dead in a place like that."

I grimace at the irony, but she appears not to notice. "Like I said, it doesn't make sense."

"No, I can see it doesn't," I admit. "I mean, if she went out to meet this guy, how come he waited three days to kill her? And how come they only checked into the hotel the night before?"

"Precisely."

"So the police have no other theories?"

"I honestly don't know; they haven't exactly told me. They just say they're pursuing 'various lines of inquiry.'" She laughs, presumably at the cliché, then stares out the window at the darkening sky. Clouds seem to have massed out of nowhere, obscuring the sun. The flat feels chillier, the walls less brilliant white than cold gray.

Several tears inch down Kristen's cheeks. We both ignore them.

"So who registered the room she was found in?" I ask. "I mean, that should give them some clues."

"She did, apparently. They said she paid for it up front, on her credit card."

"*She* paid for it?" I don't bother to hide my astonishment.

Kristen nods miserably. "That's another thing that doesn't make sense. Why the hell would Amanda pay to meet up with a client?"

"Perhaps he said he'd give her the money," I suggest, but the instant the words leave my mouth I realize how stupid they are. No escort would fork out for a room on the promise of a punter.

Christ, I think, my stomach growing heavy. Maybe Amanda was fooling around. Yet somehow I can't bring myself to believe it.

"But that's not the only thing," Kristen continues. "I asked to see her bag. I wanted to know what was in it. They weren't keen, but eventually they showed me the contents, though they were in plastic bags and I couldn't touch them or anything. It was all there— her work phone, her personal one, her makeup, her client kit—"

"Her client kit?"

"She always carried it in the side pocket, so she wouldn't forget. It wasn't much, only a small bottle of Astroglide, and five condoms in a silk purse."

I remember it now. Green silk, with sprays of pink cherry blossom. Exquisite. Probably a gift from a client.

"And that was the thing," Kristen says, reaching round and pulling a tissue from a box on a little lamp table. "All the condoms were there. I checked."

I look at her. "I'm sorry—I'm not following."

"They said they found evidence that she'd had sex, but no semen, only lubricant, so whoever it was used a condom. But there were five left."

"Five condoms?" I'm beginning to feel a bit thick. What does she mean?

Kristen catches my puzzled expression. "Oh, sorry, I assumed you knew. Amanda always took five condoms along to every appointment. It was one of her things. You know what a control freak she could be." She laughs, gloomily. "I always said she had a touch of OCD."

"So hang on a minute, you're saying none of them were used?" She nods.

"Perhaps he brought his own?"

Kristen shakes her head. "She always insisted on using this particular brand. She ordered them from the U.S. Said they were the only ones that didn't make her sore."

I run my teeth across the top of my tongue. Come to the only other conclusion I can think of.

"Perhaps she went bareback, Kristen. It happens. Some clients will pay a lot extra for the privilege."

I say this as gently as I can. But not gently enough. Kristen gives me a fierce look. "No, Stella—"

"Grace," I repeat.

"Like I said, there was no semen."

"He may have pulled out . . ." Come on her, I nearly add. Plenty of men are into that too.

"No, you don't understand. There was no DNA at all, the police said." Kristen's tone is emphatic, her eyes glistening. "Just traces of a spermicide they use on condoms."

"Okay."

"Besides, Amanda wouldn't ever do that—go bareback, I mean. She was totally fucking paranoid about catching something—or getting pregnant."

"Pregnant?"

"She didn't use contraception," she explains with exaggerated patience. "We didn't need the pill, did we? That's how I know she'd *never* take that kind of risk."

I stare back at her, at the intense expression hardening her soft features.

"So you're saying that . . . what . . . she was raped?"

Kristen presses her lips together before speaking. "She carried an alarm, in her bag, but she hadn't used it. And there were no signs of a struggle, the detective said, no bruises or marks."

I let this sink in. She's right; it doesn't make sense. "Have you said all this to the police?"

She nods, then snorts, gritting her teeth in disgust. "They said it could be somebody else. Perhaps a lover."

"But you told them about you and her? That she doesn't like men?"

"Of course. I reckon that was one reason they came here, to check out whether I was telling the truth, that we weren't just flatmates or something, that I hadn't simply made it up." She gives a short bark of a laugh. "You know, when it comes down to it, it's surprisingly hard to prove you're someone's partner."

I press my lips together as I mull this over. "So what's your theory, Kristen? About what happened?"

Her face relaxes into desolation. "I haven't a clue, Grace. I go over it and over it, round and round. And her father keeps phoning and yelling at me because of course her family didn't know anything. Nothing at all, not about me . . . or what she did."

Secrets, I think, examining the bare wood floor. I wonder whether to bring up again what happened at the party. The texting, the so-called family crisis. But it feels too insubstantial now, too inconsequential against the weight of Kristen's revelations.

When I look up again, she's crying again, soundlessly, her hands squeezed between her knees. "I can't sleep, Grace. I keep seeing her face, keep imagining what it must have been like for her . . ."

"You mustn't." I lean forward and touch her arm.

She lifts her eyes, rimmed red with grief. "Her parents are insisting on organizing the funeral. But the police won't even say when they're going to give her back . . ." Her voice cracks. "Her body, I mean."

"Jesus . . ." I squeeze her arm. "What a fucking mess."

She gazes into my face, as if searching for something she's lost. "I loved her, Grace. Really loved her. I realize that Amanda isn't . . . wasn't perfect, that she probably did stuff I'm best off never knowing, but I trusted her."

She blinks, twice, raising her eyes to the ceiling then dropping them back to me. "And I know she loved me, Grace. I *know* she wouldn't do anything to hurt me."

"I believe you," I say. And I do.

NINETEEN

"You seem preoccupied."

"I do?" I resurrect my smile and aim it squarely at Joe, a hefty middle-aged lawyer from Cincinnati with a rapidly receding hairline. "Sorry, I was wondering if I should change my mind. About dessert, I mean. I'm feeling rather stuffed."

It's a stupid fib and we both know it. Truth is I tuned out of Joe's monologue on contract law a full half hour ago. Was almost looking forward to the sex—inasmuch as I wouldn't have to sit here any longer pretending I give a shit about his latest wrangle with Time Warner.

Though, evidently, I haven't been doing a very good job of it.

"My fault." His smile is rueful. "Shouldn't bring my work home with me."

"Amen to that." I pick up my glass and disguise my sarcasm with a toast. "Here's to a healthy work-life balance."

He smiles, taking a slug of premier cru and relaxing into his seat. "So, tell me what's really on your mind."

I ratch him up a notch in my estimation—not quite as self-absorbed as I assumed.

"Do you see a lot of girls? Like me, I mean."

He looks briefly taken aback. "A few. Only when I'm over here—I can't risk it at home."

I nod.

"Why do you ask?"

Stop it, Grace.

"Did you ever meet one called Elisa?"

He frowns. "No, I don't think so."

I lean back to allow the waiter to serve the desserts. "Okay. I'm sure you'd remember if you had."

Joe picks up a spoon and tucks into his chocolate and Grand Marnier mousse, garnished with a delicate little spiral of spun sugar. "This got anything to do with that girl they found in Bayswater?"

Too late to stop my look of surprise. "How do you know about that?"

"It's all over the Net. I saw something on it when I was checking you out."

He swallows another mouthful of mousse. Washes it down with more wine. "She a friend of yours?"

"Not exactly. We worked together a few times."

"Hmmm . . ." He chews on the sugar, his mouth revolving like a washing machine. "I imagine this must have you pretty freaked out?"

I shift my gaze to his. And realize he's right.

"Well, if it's any consolation, it wasn't me. I was in L.A. when it happened, and I can prove it."

I attempt a laugh. "I wasn't for a minute suggesting . . ."

"I'm sure you weren't. Just thought I'd put it on record."

He finishes his dessert. Glances over at my peach and almond sorbet, slowly melting onto the immaculate white china.

"You gonna eat that?"

I hand him my plate.

It doesn't last long. We strip and he pulls me across his considerable girth. I bob up and down until he comes, a drawn-out sibilant sound extending to a sigh. As it subsides, I realize I've forgotten to fake my own climax. I fake a smile instead as I dismount, making a discreet check of the time on his bedside clock.

An hour to go. Perhaps he'll revive and take another run at it. Or maybe not. Which makes this, what, eight hundred quid for three minutes of pleasure?

But that would be missing the point. The Michelin-starred restaurant is the point. The wine, the food, the studied elegance of the dining room, is the point. And the chance to bore the pants off someone who otherwise wouldn't look at you twice.

Joe drapes an arm over me, heavy as ballast. I let my head sink into the feather pillow. Close my eyes for a moment and conjure up an image of Alex, trying to revive my appetite for seconds. But this particular stimulus to desire feels too worn now, and my mind drifts home to my flat. A bath. The book on my bedside table.

I open my eyes. And almost groan. I've fallen asleep.

Fuck.

I roll toward the shadowy bulk of my client, praying nothing gave me away.

"I should sue you," he says. The room lights are dimmed and I can't make out if he's serious.

"I'm so sorry." I consider making some excuse, but realize it's pointless.

"Breach of contract," he laughs. "I don't remember anything about downtime in your terms and conditions."

I lean across and kiss him. "I'll stay a bit longer if you like."

"Go home," he says, looking at me. "Get to bed."

My smile is genuinely contrite. "Sorry, really. It's inexcusable."

He gets up. Hands me the money. I stuff it into my handbag and pull on my clothes, pausing by the door. "Thank you for a lovely evening."

"Likewise," says Joe. "But seriously, Stella, get some more sleep."

I'm wide-awake by the time I arrive home, my mind too restless for reading. I check my e-mails. Nothing much. A couple from clients, another from a Web designer touting for business.

And one from Kristen, about the funeral, her mobile number tagged to the end. It's in four days' time.

I make a note in my diary and turn on the TV. Flick to the news, hoping for an update on Amanda. Several channels picked up the story in the days following her death, but I haven't seen much since—either there's nothing new to say or the press has simply lost interest.

I sit through the usual economic doom and gloom. The endless conflict in the Middle East. More instances of tax evasion by major corporations. The perpetual sense that everything's going to hell. *The shadow let loose in the world.*

Where did I hear that? My brain worries at it for a minute or two. My therapist, I suddenly remember, the one who supervised my training: a committed Jungian with a penchant for rummaging about in other people's unconscious minds. "None of us escapes our shadow," she'd say. "Just take a look around you."

She was right. And I should have looked harder.

I'm about to hit the off switch when I see a face I recognize. Not Amanda's. That man. James. The nervous guy from the party, the one who left early.

He's hurrying away from a building, flanked by several men in dark suits. The House of Commons, I realize, the distinctive Gothic architecture looming into view. The camera trails him to a waiting car, then cuts to a nearby reporter clutching an umbrella and a microphone.

"Edward Hardy, parliamentary under secretary of state for defense equipment and support, appeared yesterday before the parliamentary select committee on government arms procurement—"

Edward Hardy.

"—where he defended his department from accusations of corruption . . ."

The picture zooms in on Hardy as he ducks into a black limousine, then switches to the news studio and the face of a woman in her fifties. "Shadow Defense Minister Jane Goodall," the caption reads at the bottom.

"Hardy insists his department followed all the guidelines, but there are still a lot of unanswered questions that need to be addressed," she says with calculated indignation. "He's simply echoing the assurances offered by the defense secretary in the Commons last week when asked about the leaked information on the Abstar contract . . ."

The scene changes again. A cartoon this time. *South Park*. Kenny holding a firecracker that explodes, blowing him to pieces. *Shit*. I've been gripping the remote so tight I must have hit the channel button. I try to flick back, but when I find the right program the news has moved on to a feature on NHS redundancies.

"*Fuck*."

I grab my laptop. Type Hardy's name and "arms inquiry" into the search engine. It rewards me with dozens of hits. I click on the first. It doesn't take long to get the gist. Leaked e-mails suggested that senior politicians have received kickbacks from several large international defense firms in return for favorable treatment in the tendering process.

I think back to that night at the party. Rack my brain for details. But all I can remember is Harry's boast.

We're golden, darling, we can't lose. We're fucking untouchable.

TWENTY

WEDNESDAY, 11 MARCH

Despite the delays on the Northern Line, I arrive half an hour early. Even so, as I walk up the long drive to the crematorium, I can see people already clustering outside. Tight little groups, some standing in silence, wearing their funeral faces. Others conversing as if this were any ordinary social event, a chance to catch up with family and friends.

I glance around. There's no one I recognize, so I hover in the garden to the side of the main entrance.

Several black limousines pull up in front of the building. A man with a tight-clipped gray beard climbs out of the first car, turning to extend his hand to the woman emerging behind him.

My heart almost stops. Pale blond hair. That tall, balletic frame. I walk back toward the entrance to get a closer look.

Amanda's mother. It has to be.

She looks over, catches me staring. Offers a tight-lipped smile as she turns away, and I wonder again if I should have come. Is it too obvious how I know . . . knew her daughter? I've dressed down, of course. Dispensed with all but the lightest makeup. But I still feel exposed somehow, as if something indefinable gives me away.

"Grace?"

I turn to see Kristen, bundled up in a black trench coat with dark trousers underneath. She looks smaller than I remember, more fragile. Beside her stands a slightly older woman holding an umbrella over both their heads, even though the rain stopped a good ten minutes ago.

"This is my sister, Ruth," says Kristen, putting an arm on her shoulder. "Ruth, this is Grace. Remember I told you about her?"

I feel myself flush, but Ruth's smile is warm as she extends her hand. "Pleased to meet you."

I squeeze hers firmly, grateful for the gesture. "How are you?" I ask Kristen.

"I'm okay." She nods, but I see tears looming as she looks away.

"She wanted a proper funeral." Ruth leans in, lowering her voice. "But the coroner won't release the body. It being evidence, you know . . . the inquiry."

"Is there any news? On the case?"

Ruth shakes her head. "But then again, no one tells us anything."

She turns and puts her arm around her sister, nodding toward the line of people shuffling into the building. "I think we should go in."

I follow them through the foyer into the main chapel. It's exactly like the one I remember from my mother's funeral. High white walls, long blue curtains blocking all natural light. Bland, inclusive, anonymous—the kind of place that almost makes you wish you were dead yourself.

At the front, up where the coffin should be, several wreaths are propped upright; between them, on what looks like an easel, is a large photo of Amanda. Not taken recently—sometime in her late teens, probably, her cheeks fuller and her hair shorter, less styled. She's wearing a white summer dress, smiling shyly at the camera. Surrounded by those circles of flowers, with their white lilies and pale yellow daffodils, Amanda's face looks fresh, lovely. Impossibly innocent.

Which is entirely the point, I realize. This whole thing is going to be a whitewash.

Kristen and Ruth take seats toward the back, away from the main throng of mourners. Well away from Amanda's family too, I note with a swell of sympathy.

I sit behind them and slightly to the left, in the farthest corner of the chapel—a good vantage point to survey the other funeral-goers. There must be upward of eighty or 90, more drifting in as the recorded organ music drones on. Many are older, clearly friends of the family, a number going up to greet Amanda's parents before taking a seat. Here and there, several groups about Amanda's age, huddled together, talking quickly. People from her school, perhaps, or university.

Near the back I spot a couple of lone males. One stares intently at the order of service, doing his best to look inconspicuous. The other keeps his gaze fixed forward, ignoring everyone around him.

Former clients, I'm guessing.

The one closest to me, with his salt-and-pepper hair and hand-some features, seems faintly familiar. Finally I place him—the host of that TV show, the one that does a weekly review of social media. He glances toward me, sensing my scrutiny. I avert my eyes. Study the back of Kristen's head, hatless now, bent over, her gaze firmly fixed on the floor.

At that moment the vicar appears in full regalia—dog collar, white robe, purple sash. I cringe. Granted, I didn't know Amanda that well, but I'm fairly sure she hadn't a religious bone in her body.

The music ends abruptly, and the vicar clears his throat, opening a leather folder and balancing it in his right hand.

"We're gathered here today to commemorate the passing of Amanda Sonya Mansfield, beloved daughter of Janet and Tom Mansfield." He glances at his notes, his hands twitching. He looks apprehensive, almost nervous.

He knows, I think. About who . . . what she was. After all the news reports, how could he not?

"No one who met Amanda could have failed to appreciate her many outstanding qualities—her warmth, her humor, her intelligence. And, indeed, her beauty."

Every head turns to study the photograph. The luminous Amanda smiles back at us, demure and virtuous. The vicar looks faintly embarrassed, as if conscious of having strayed onto shifting sands. He embarks on a résumé of her childhood, the muscles in his face relaxing as he finds himself on firmer ground. Amanda emerges as sweet and diligent. Something of a star at school. Top grades and an accomplished violinist, a scholarship to a music conservatory overthrown in favor of studying politics at university.

He describes her first job with a management consultancy, her promotion within a year. Her subsequent engagement to another of the firm's highfliers.

Then nothing. A discreet veil is drawn over what followed, like her life ended seven years not several weeks ago. It's as if what Amanda did next—and did so consummately well—simply never happened. Where's Elisa in all this? I wonder. Playful, wicked, irreverent Elisa.

Someone coughs. I start to crave a cigarette. *Fucking churches*, I think, glancing around at the plain wooden cross hung discreetly at the back. Weddings, funerals—why does no one ever tell the truth in these places?

The vicar invites us to stand and sing, and I grasp the order of service, trying to focus on the words of the hymn.

*I am waiting for the dawning
Of the bright and blessed day,
When the darksome night of sorrow
Shall have vanished far away.*

Is this what it will be like at my funeral? I ask myself. *Everybody ashamed, everybody playing dumb?*

Those, that is, who bother to go.

I swallow. It's impossibly warm in here. Much too hot for the black wool dress and coat I chose, mindful of the cold at Jane's wedding. Sweat prickles my skin. My throat feels raspy and dry, but I nearly smile at the irony—the chill of a wedding, the warmth of death.

Far beyond this vale of tears . . .

My voice breaks midverse, and I know I'm going to cry. *Not in here,* I think, desperately, knowing that's ridiculous. Where better?

I don't care. I get up and head for the exit. See Kristen's head turning toward me, the question mark on her face.

"You okay, miss?" asks a young male usher as I charge through the foyer and out the main entrance. Hurrying round the side of the building, I lean back on the red brick, closing my eyes against the daylight, against the tears. If I start now I'll never stop.

I open my eyes again, blinking. Grope for a tissue in my pocket.

It's then I notice the man. Standing near the car park, gazing right at me. Not that I can be entirely certain. He's wearing sunglasses, the shiny, reflective kind, despite a sky both soggy and overcast.

Something in the angles of his face, his stance, his sense of aloofness, reminds me of Alex, and I feel an involuntary rush of anticipation. Then he turns his head and the resemblance ends. But the way he looked straight at me was odd somehow. Blatant. Evaluating.

I glance toward the chapel. Still the faint hum of music inside.

I should go back, I think, remembering Kristen, remembering that, however difficult this is for me, it must be a thousand times worse for her. What will she make of me rushing out like that?

But I can't. I just can't face it.

I look back toward the man, but he's gone. Vanished. I scan the car park, the little flower garden, down the drive—but there's no trace of him.

What the fuck?

He must have got into a car, I tell myself, but it still creeps me out. I turned away only for a second.

I examine the line of cars. All appear empty, except a black BMW with tinted windows I can't see into. I consider walking up and peering inside, then come to my senses. What would I say, even if he were there? Loitering in the car park of a crematorium is hardly a crime.

Christ, Grace, just pull yourself together.

"Enough," I decide out loud, taking a deep breath. I'm going home. I'll call Kristen in a day or two to apologize for bolting, then put this right behind me.

After all, I've done my bit. What I could. No need for me to do any more.

TWENTY-ONE

My sense of disquiet starts the moment I open the door. Nothing I can put my finger on, simply a feeling that something isn't quite right.

My client, however, looks relaxed enough. Midfifties, buzz-cut hair, the air of someone at ease in his own skin. Gives a brief smile before he walks into my flat, shedding his coat before I can even ask to take it.

He offers little in the way of small talk. I'm guessing this man is an experienced punter, doesn't like to waste a minute of his booking with preliminaries. So I lead him straight into the bedroom, trying to pull myself together as we undress. Why do I feel so edgy? Was it just yesterday's funeral?

The man lies belly-down on the bed. I take the hint and straddle him. Squatting over his buttocks, I work his shoulders with my fingers. My hands are trembling, I realize, and make a conscious effort to relax, pressing my thumbs into his muscles. They're taut, resisting, surprisingly firm for his age; I have to squeeze hard to make any impression.

The body beneath me settles into the duvet as I use the heel of my palm to knead each shoulder blade, bending in to apply the right amount of pressure.

And that's when it hits me. An aroma so subtle it's taken my conscious mind several minutes to catch up.

His aftershave.

I pull back, swallowing back a wave of revulsion. My client rolls over, interpreting my withdrawal as a signal to move on.

It's not him, I repeat silently to myself. *He's not Michael.*

I smile briefly, then force myself to stroke his chest and belly, my eyes following my hands as they're drawn inexorably to a thick line of scar tissue, running diagonally from his left hip to the tip of his pubic hair.

My client reads the question in my fingers. "Argentina," he says, his voice matter-of-fact. "Stanley. Up near Two Sisters."

I trace the history on his stomach, silver toned and shinier than the surrounding skin. A souvenir from the Malvinas.

"Bayonet," he adds.

I look right at him. Try not to inhale too deeply.

"Does it bother you?" he asks.

"What?" I say, thinking he means his aftershave.

"That I killed somebody." There's no challenge in his voice, merely inquiry.

"I've met others," I evade.

"Soldiers?"

I shake my head. His gaze lingers, gauging my response, but he doesn't pursue it. Knows it's none of his business. I glance back down at his belly. "Must have hurt."

He considers this. "Yes . . . no. It's difficult to remember. The fear's always there, but when the adrenaline kicks in, you don't notice. Or the pain."

"So you saw him?" I ask, curiosity overcoming my growing sense of unease. "The man that did this?"

"Barely." His voice slows, deepens, as his mind sinks back to the past. "It was very dark. But I heard him. 'Forgive me,' he said, in English. Right before he stuck it in."

A pause where neither of us speaks.

"And then?"

His mouth twitches. "And then I put my gun to his head and blew it off."

I flinch despite myself. They must have been closer than we are now, I realize, imagining that visceral contact, that thrust. Like sex.

I picture that foreign soldier shivering in the dark on that bleak, windswept island, suddenly face-to-face with the man beneath me. That fleeting, bewildering moment where his whole life shrank to a choice that was no choice at all—to kill or be killed.

"What's it like?"

My client looks at me inquiringly.

"Killing someone."

He smiles at my question, lifts his eyes to the ceiling. "It shakes you up the first time, but you get used to it."

Could I do it? I wonder. Could I hold a gun to somebody's head and pull the trigger? It would be so easy, I suspect, crossing that line. One small step and there you are, on the other side.

A hand on my breast breaks into my thoughts. My client sits up and kisses me, tentatively at first, then with undisguised enthusiasm. I close my eyes but find Michael waiting for me in the darkness, and snap them open again.

"You okay?" He pulls away to look at my face. "You seem kind of edgy."

"I'm fine," I swallow. "Just a slight headache. It'll pass in a minute."

He smiles and touches my hair, then rolls me onto my back. Turns to get a condom and ease it over himself. Then looms back in again, smothering me in another embrace as he slides himself on top of me, a hand between my legs to guide himself inside.

The scent is unbearably strong. The same Michael wore—sweet and musky, mixed with the waxy, slightly sweaty smell of male skin. And as he enters me I'm back there. Back in that flat on that bare lumpy mattress. I'm back in my nightmares and it's him fucking me and I push him away, out of my mind, but I'm spiraling down and it's Amanda's face I see now, Amanda in that hotel room, that man screwing her, his hands around her neck and that dreadful, excruciating moment where I can't breathe . . .

I can't fucking breathe . . .

I shove aside the body above me and sit up with a gasp. A pain in my chest, suddenly desperately tight. Grab my inhaler from the bedside table, firing a stream of mist into the back of my mouth as I'm seized by a jagged fit of coughing.

Oh God.

The world spins. I'm bent double in the effort to breathe. Long seconds before the ache in my lungs begins to ease.

"Can I do anything?" My client's voice, concerned.

I shake my head again. "Sorry," I manage to say, but it comes out more as a whisper. "I'm afraid I can't do this today."

He doesn't reply. I look away so I don't have to see his pissed-off expression, forcing myself to inhale and exhale, slowly, carefully, waiting for the tightness in my chest to subside. I hear sounds of dressing, the slight rasp of fabric on skin. A moment later a brief jangle of car keys as he pulls on his jacket in the lounge, then the clunk of the door as he shuts it behind him.

Lines from that Yeats poem rise up from the backwaters of my mind. *Things fall apart . . . the center cannot hold.*

I force my eyes open, inhaling deeply. I should have taken the day off, I think. I hadn't realized all this was getting to me so much. Tears prick at me again, as I remember that gruesome, untruthful service.

This time I let myself cry.

TWENTY-TWO

Hello?" Kristen picks up after a couple of rings, her tone tentative, anxious.

"Hi, it's Grace," I say. "I'm just calling to apologize for leaving so suddenly the other day. I—"

"Oh, Grace," Kristen cuts in with a loud sigh. Almost a groan. A pause where I wonder if she's angry with me, then she clears her throat. "Sorry. I assumed you were the police."

"The police? Why?"

"I called them nearly an hour ago. I'm still waiting for them to get back to me."

"About Amanda?"

"No . . . it's the flat." I hear Kristen hesitate. "I've been staying with Ruth since the funeral. I just got in and found the place has been broken into. Completely trashed."

"You've been *burgled*?"

Don't get involved, Grace.

"I've no idea what they've taken. It's all such a mess."

Her voice cracks with emotion.

Oh fuck. I mentally scan my agenda. Nothing else till six this evening. "Would you like me to come over?"

Kristen sounds hesitant. "Don't worry. I don't want to put you to any . . ."

"It's no trouble, really. I'd be glad to help."

Silence for a moment, then relief in her tone. "Would you mind, Grace? I'm scared . . ." She breaks off, as if too confused to even finish the thought. "Ruth has to go to work, and there's no one . . ."

Don't do it, Grace.

"I'll jump in a taxi. I'll be there in half an hour."

I'm so taken aback I can't speak. Even from the corridor I can see the chaos. The swath of coats and scarves scattered around the hallway; beyond, a further tide of debris strewn across the living room floor.

"Jesus . . ." I gasp as I pick my way inside.

Kristen looks exhausted. The shadows under her eyes have deepened to hollows, the lids scalded from crying.

I stand in the middle of the flat and survey the damage.

What the hell?

The once neat little lounge now looks like the aftermath of a battle. Everything has been pulled off the shelves and thrown over the floor. Ornaments lie smashed, books and DVDs litter the rugs, some lying on their spines, words, pictures, shiny discs exposed like guts. A box of photographs has spilled its contents in an arc across the left side of the room. Images of Kristen and Amanda smile up at me, eerily, an ironic commentary on the surrounding devastation.

I spin round. The beautiful sofa is upended, its cushions slashed and the material peeled away, gaping wounds revealing white foamy entrails. Underneath, the backing fabric has been ripped right off, exposing the wood and metal skeleton within.

To the left of the ruined sofa, in the corner where Kristen kept her desk, bank statements and utility bills lie sprinkled like giant confetti, every file opened and emptied, the beige carpet almost entirely obscured.

Christ. This looks more like an act of terrorism than a burglary. *Why did they have to make such a bloody mess?*

"The bedroom?" I ask.

Kristen nods. "The same. They didn't spare a thing. Not even the clothes."

"Have the police been?"

She shakes her head. "Not yet. The detective handling Amanda's case wants to see it, but she can't come before three."

"Why a detective? I thought they sent in the uniforms to deal with burglaries."

Kristen shrugs. "I don't know. I guess they have to check it isn't connected to the murder."

I look at her. "Do you think it is? Connected to Amanda, I mean?"

"I don't see how," Kristen sighs. "It's not as if burglaries are exactly rare round here. The man who lives above the corner shop got broken into several months ago. Crack addicts, he reckons. This is probably the same lot."

I stare around me. "But why would they do this?" I sweep my gaze across the carnage. "And how did they know you were out? You work from home, don't you?"

She nods. "I've hardly left the flat since Amanda died. I guess they must have known about the funeral."

"I still don't get why they'd waste the place like this. It's unbelievable."

Kristen looks around, her eyes glistening. "The worst is the stuff I had left—of hers, I mean."

"What did they take?"

"A bit of money we kept in a pot in the kitchen. Our jewelry . . . well, mainly hers. I didn't really have much worth stealing, only a few things she gave me." She runs her hands through her hair, which is loose today, disheveled and in need of a wash. "To be honest, I'm not sure. I'm not supposed to touch anything, not until the police have been over the place. So it's hard to say exactly what's missing."

She starts crying in earnest, tears spilling down her cheeks.

"Here." I hand her a tissue from my bag. She wipes her eyes, then presses it to her lips, trying to hold in a wail of anguish. I step forward and fold her into my arms. This time she doesn't pull away, her head sinking onto my shoulder. We stand there for several minutes until the crying subsides.

"Sorry," she whispers, her voice choked with emotion.

"Oh God, Kristen, I'm the one who's sorry. This is awful. The last thing you need after . . ." I stop and stare at her helplessly.

She meets my eyes briefly, then looks away, her gaze unfocused.

"Do you want a cup of tea? I haven't any coffee, it's all on the floor, but I've salvaged a few tea bags if you don't mind having it black. A couple of mugs are still intact and I think the kettle's okay."

"Listen. You make the tea. I'll pop down to the corner shop and get some milk."

She gives me a grateful smile. "Thanks, Grace. That would be great."

While I'm there I pick up everything I can think of. Milk. More coffee. Another packet of tea bags, a loaf of bread, and a pack of biscuits. A reasonably moist-looking carrot cake. A few cans of soup and some dried pasta and Bolognese sauce. Enough to keep Kristen going until she can leave the flat.

On the way back I stop outside the house. Put down the two shopping bags and check over the door and the frame. I rarely dealt with burglars—even serial housebreakers don't end up in maximum-security prisons, not unless they progress to more violent crime. But I remember the profile well enough: poor, young, male, usually from an unstable home with a single mother. Often living nearby. Opportunistic rather than organized. And commonly under the influence of alcohol or drugs at the time of the offense.

Generally not well equipped, however. No skeleton keys or sophisticated electronic gadgets. Most burglars prefer to enter through inadequately secured doors or windows, and that invariably leaves telltale signs like scrapes or scratches. Smashed glass or cracks in the frame where they used a jimmy.

Only I can't see any sign of forced entry. The area around the lock looks normal; pristine even, the paintwork glossy and smooth. I glance over the bay window of the downstairs flat; everything seems intact.

I let myself in with the keys Kristen gave me. Check the internal door to the flat. Again, no signs of it having been levered or forced.

"Any idea how they got in?" I ask as I hand Kristen the shopping bags.

She sighs. "I've no clue. There's a Yale lock and a mortise. You have to have both for the insurance."

I chew the inside of my lip. "Where are you going to go for the next few days, Kristen? You can't stay here with it like this." I consider inviting her to my place, but it would be tricky with the in-calls.

"Don't worry. I rang my sister while you were out. I can stay with her until we've cleared all this up."

I feel relieved. The idea of Kristen alone here tonight troubles me. I'm not sure the people who did this were vandals or druggies high on crack. After all, they broke into a well-secured property without leaving a trace.

They clearly knew what they were doing.

It doesn't add up, I think as I take the tube back home. Why make the effort to get in so cleanly, then trash the place? It's almost as if . . .

My mind flashes to the man waiting . . . no, *watching* outside the crematorium. The cool, appraising way he regarded me, as if determining something.

You're getting paranoid, Grace, says a more sensible voice in my head. *Cognitive distortions. You don't need eleven years in psychology to know that isn't good.*

But somehow, as I reach my station and rise back up into the London daylight, I can't shake off the feeling that something about this isn't right at all.

TWENTY-THREE

What the fuck am I doing here?

I stare at the bland cream paintwork, the fake oak paneling around the reception area, trying not to think about the last time I was in a police station.

That interview. I jerk my mind away from the memory, but there's already a constriction in my breathing. A tension too close to panic. *The body always remembers*, the therapist in my head repeats; *the mind forgets, but the body always remembers.*

Another five minutes idles by. My stomach is light and jittery, the urge for a cigarette growing stronger. I remember the first I ever had—afterward, outside the station—and the face of the detective offering it, the way he couldn't quite look me in the eye.

I'd never smoked before, not even tried one at school, but I held the cigarette in my fingers and let him light it. I'd have taken anything at that moment—crack, smack, Prozac—whatever might distract me from what I'd just done.

"She won't be a minute." The voice of the duty officer pulls me back. He looks over and gives me a perfunctory smile. Returns his gaze to his computer screen.

Cigarettes. That acrid taste of smoke and chemicals, so vile and yet so addictive. It took nearly five years to kick the habit, to reach the point where I no longer need nicotine to get me through the day. Though God knows, there are times I still crave it like air.

Like now. *The body always remembers.*

My phone vibrates in my pocket. I check the screen. *Alex.*

I stand up and make for the door.

"Stella Wilson?" I stop and turn around. A slim woman with short dark hair walks up and offers her hand. Stuffing my mobile back in my pocket, I reach out and shake it.

"Detective Inspector Shaw," she says. "Annette Shaw."

About forty, I reckon, dressed in ordinary clothes. Her voice has that tone of quiet authority I once aspired to. She studies my face so intently that for a moment I'm wondering if she might somehow be connected to what happened back then.

Don't be ridiculous, I tell myself as she leads me down the corridor. It was another time, another place entirely. And she has no idea of my real name.

We enter a small interview room. Not the usual setup, the clinical desk and chairs and tape recorder you get when things turn serious. This is four cheap armchairs gathered around a mug-stained coffee table. The put-you-at-your-ease room. I used to use one myself.

She sits in the chair facing the door, indicating the one opposite. "Okay, Ms. Wilson . . ."

"Stella."

"Right, Stella. Thank you for ringing this morning. So what have you got to tell me?"

I clear my throat. Remind myself why I'm here. "Can I ask you a few things first?"

She looks at me. Nods. Her eyes are brown, the creases around them barely visible.

"I just wanted to ascertain how far you'd got with the case."

"Amanda Mansfield's murder?"

"Yes."

DI Shaw presses her lips together, assessing me again. "You know we can't disclose any details, Stella."

"Have you got any suspects?"

She doesn't answer. I take that as a no.

"There are . . . things I think perhaps you should be considering. And maybe you already are. I don't know."

She cocks her head. "Such as?"

I take a deep breath. "You believe Amanda was killed by a client, right? During an appointment? But I'm sure she wasn't."

"And why's that?"

"Because I used to work with her. And it doesn't fit."

"You worked with her? You're an escort?"

I nod, holding her gaze.

"Did you two *work* together much?" Subtle, but unmistakable, her intonation.

"Six, maybe seven times. A couple of duos. The rest were parties."

She stares back at me for a few seconds, her expression unreadable. "So tell me what you're thinking, Stella."

I'm feeling increasingly nervous. Inhale again as I gather my thoughts. "Amanda was always very hot on security. Made sure she had a valid mobile number for a client, that sort of thing. Kristen—her girlfriend—said Amanda always told her where she was going and how long she'd be away. But not this time." I pause, swallow, wishing I'd been offered a cup of tea. "So I was wondering, were they on her laptop? On her work phone?"

The detective sizes me up. Considering how much to tell me. "There's nothing on either that might suggest the identity of her attacker, no."

"She kept details of all her appointments on her computer, right?"

She nods.

"And this one, at the hotel, it wasn't on there?"

Another barely detectable nod.

"So why do you think that was?"

She shrugs. "Maybe it was a late booking and she didn't have time for the usual checks. Or maybe she couldn't be bothered."

"I don't think so."

"Do you always bother, Stella? Aren't there times some man rings on the off chance and you forget? Or decide to take a gamble?"

I force myself to regard her as coolly as she's looking at me. "We're not talking about me, are we?"

"I'm not sure what we're talking about, Stella. Or quite sure why you're here."

That makes two of us, I think, hesitating. Then remind myself exactly why I have dragged my sorry arse into this claustrophobic little room.

"I don't believe it was a client who killed Amanda."

"You don't?"

"It doesn't make sense. The lack of information about the appointment. The fact she didn't say anything to her girlfriend. And the hotel."

"What about the hotel?"

"Kristen said she paid for it herself, on her credit card. I mean, why the hell would she do that? Clients book the room, not the other way round. Not to mention that it's hardly the sort of place Amanda usually worked in."

DI Shaw lifts an eyebrow.

"Amanda was very much a five-star girl. Four at the outside. And any client who could afford her fees wouldn't stay in a hotel like that either."

Nothing from the detective. I know what she's doing. It's a standard interview technique—maintain a steady silence and the interviewee will blurt things out to fill the gaps.

But right now I don't care. "And why the delay? Kristen said she went missing on the Tuesday afternoon, yet she wasn't discovered until the Friday. Surely if she'd been off with somebody for three days she'd have mentioned it to her partner? And why was the hotel booked for only one night? If she was on such a long booking, why did she check in the evening before?"

Still no response.

I press on. "Why weren't there any condoms missing? You found five in her bag—am I right?"

DI Shaw makes no move.

"Kristen said she always carried five. Always. It was like a habit . . . no, a talisman, a ritual. Always five."

"So she got careless. Taking risks goes with the territory, doesn't it, Stella? In your business?"

I fix my eyes on hers. "Not really. How many women go out to a bar and get drunk and go off with some bloke they've only just met? How many bother to check out his name first, or get his phone number? How many tell someone exactly where they're going and for how long? Have *you* ever had a one-night stand?"

Silence.

"That's pretty risky behavior, wouldn't you say? Yet it happens all the time. We're not idiots, Detective Shaw, those of us who prefer to be paid for our trouble. We aren't all feeding a drug habit or controlled by pimps. Some of us probably had a better education than you."

She doesn't turn a hair at this. Just keeps her gaze locked on mine.

"And when it comes to it, Detective, rape, assault, murder—how many of these are committed by men the victim actually knows? By boyfriends or husbands, ex-boyfriends or ex-husbands? It doesn't make the headlines, does it, that routine domestic abuse? But if a woman's on the game and gets knocked off, that's big news."

A half smile creeps across Annette Shaw's lips. "Okay, Stella, fair point. So you tell me, what do you imagine happened to Amanda?"

I pause. Choose the right words. "I reckon whatever brought her into contact with this man, it wasn't about sex."

The detective raises her eyebrows. "So why did she have the condoms with her?"

"Kristen said she kept them in her handbag, in a special case. She never took them out."

"Fine," she muses. "Let's say she met up with her killer for other reasons. I agree, that could explain the lapse in her usual procedure. So how come we found her naked on a hotel room bed?"

I hesitate. "I don't know. Perhaps he lured her back for some reason. Or maybe he killed her first and dumped her there." Though as soon as I suggest this, I realize how difficult that would be. Especially as she paid for the room.

"Or perhaps they were having an affair," suggests DI Shaw with a wry smile.

"Is that the line you're taking? That he was her lover?" I feel a lurch of concern for Kristen.

"It would make sense."

"But why meet in a hotel?"

She shrugs. "Perhaps he was married."

I consider this for a second, then shake my head. "I don't reckon that's it."

"Why not?"

"She was gay."

"She was gay, but she made a career out of screwing men?"

"Yes."

"How can you be so sure? That she wasn't bisexual, I mean."

"We worked together. But only on appointments where the client didn't want the usual show."

"The usual show?"

"You know, the girl-on-girl stuff. The whole lesbian routine turns a lot of men on."

Another smile. "Maybe she just didn't fancy you?"

I grit my teeth. "I doubt she fancied her clients much either." I rub my hands against my jeans. They feel sticky, like they need a good wash. "No. Amanda was always strict about the lesbian stuff—with everyone, not just me. It was a no-go area with her because she loved Kristen. That was their deal—Amanda could fuck men because her girlfriend knew she didn't enjoy it."

"You're making a big assumption here."

I look at her. "How do you mean?"

"You're assuming her attacker was male."

"But . . ." I stop. She's right. I've been assuming exactly that. "Would a woman have the strength? To strangle somebody, I mean."

DI Shaw shrugs. "It's possible. Though there would probably be more signs of a struggle."

"She wasn't drugged? Or drunk?"

The detective shakes her head.

I drop my gaze. Study the pattern of stains on the carpet under the table. Looks almost like blood, after someone had tried to clean it away, but is more likely just coffee or tea. "But Kristen said there was evidence Amanda had sex right before she died."

Shaw nods.

"Though no semen, right? No DNA?"

She nods again.

"That's odd, isn't it? I mean, surely if you fuck someone, you leave your DNA in hair or skin or something. But all you found was traces of somebody using a condom?"

No reply.

"And you don't believe her killer was a woman?" I persist.

"We haven't entirely ruled it out. But no, probably not."

I run my teeth over my bottom lip. Consider this some more. "All right, so if this man were her lover, how did they arrange to meet? Even if afterward he wiped the call log on her mobile—I'm assuming you can access her records with the phone company."

Annette Shaw doesn't confirm or deny this. I exhale slowly. "So let me guess, there's nothing linking her with the hotel?"

"All I can say is we're looking into it."

"It wasn't a client. It doesn't make any sense. And I really don't believe she had a lover—man or woman."

"So who then?" she asks. "You sound like you've given this an awful lot of thought, Stella. What's your theory? Who *do* you think killed Amanda Mansfield?"

I gaze at her, uncertain. Realize I have absolutely no idea.

DI Shaw picks up a pen and makes a note on the little pad resting on her lap. There's a minute or so where neither of us speaks, then she leans forward and rests her elbows on the table, splaying her fingers and steepling the tips together.

"What I don't get, Stella, is exactly why you're here. You say you knew Amanda, but you also told me you only worked with her half a dozen times. You said you didn't socialize with her. That you'd never met Kristen before Amanda died. So I guess what interests me right now is why this interests you so much."

"Kristen is very distressed." I swallow. "I can't turn my back on her. And—"

I stop.

"And what?"

"I just want to find out what happened to Amanda."

"Yes, Stella, I understand that. That much is clear. But what I want to understand is why this is so important to you."

My mind flashes back to Michael's girlfriend, the disgust on her face after I'd given my testimony. The certain knowledge that I'd blown everything. Let someone off the hook who most definitely should have been on it.

Never again. I can't ever let anything like that happen again. Not if there's any way I can stop it.

I squeeze my eyes shut, then open them and stare at the detective. Come to a decision. "There's something else. Something I can't formulate. It's . . . more of a feeling."

"Tell me."

"We did a party, Amanda and I and another girl. A few weeks before she died. There were four men. I'd never met any of them before and neither had Amanda. This guy, a banker, it was his fiftieth—the other girl arranged it all because he was a regular client."

I clear my throat again. "Nothing happened. I mean, apart from the usual sort of thing—lots of sex, booze, a bit of coke. But afterward one man, the banker, started talking, implying they'd pulled off some deal. Made a lot of money."

"What kind of deal?"

"I'm not sure, but whatever it was, it was big. And then I saw one of them on TV the other night and . . ." *Fuck, I'm beginning to sound incoherent.* I swallow. Try to muster my thoughts into something intelligible.

The detective eyes me thoughtfully. Inhales and screws up the tip of her nose. "Can you give me more details? Their names, that kind of thing?"

I shake my head. "Only one for definite. The others went by Christian names, and they may not be their own."

"Tell me anyway."

"Harry, he was the banker, and Rob—I think he worked with him." I hesitate, pressing my lips together. "The other one was called Alex."

She writes them down. "And the one you're sure about?"

"I saw him on the news the other night. I recognized him at once. He said his name was James, but it was Edward Hardy."

"Edward Hardy?" Her expression a question mark.

"He's the"—I strain to remember his exact title—"the parliamentary under secretary of state for defense."

A ripple passes across the detective's impenetrably calm exterior. Finally I have made some kind of impression.

"Are you certain of this, Stella? You're confident it was him?"

I nod.

"So how do you think this is connected with Amanda's death?"

"I don't . . . not exactly. It's more of a hunch." Christ, what on earth am I saying? But I may as well get it all out now. I take a deep breath. "At the funeral . . . I mean the memorial service, there was somebody outside. I don't know, I just had a sense that he was nothing to do with the mourners. He looked . . . like he was watching the place."

"Watching? For what?"

"I've no idea," I admit.

DI Shaw sighs. I'm losing credibility by the minute, I realize, and wonder if it might help if I told her what I used to do. Decide it would probably make things worse.

"The burglary," I say suddenly. "You checked it out?"

She nods as she scribbles a note on her pad. "Briefly."

"Any idea how they got in?"

She raises her head quickly, her look sharp. "We're not sure. Why?"

"It's just that it didn't seem like something a bunch of addicts would do."

"Is that what you think?" The detective purses her lips. "What about this other girl you did the party with? She'd have the details and numbers of these men, I assume?"

"I'm not sure. I guess so."

"Can you tell me how I might contact her?"

"Her number's on her website. It's Janine—Google her under London escorts." I pause. "So you'll look into this, right?"

The detective thinks for a minute, her index finger tapping the end of her pen. "Let me recap. You're saying this politician, this

Edward Hardy, may have something to do with Amanda's murder? That's quite a leap, Stella."

I bite my lip. "I don't know, but . . ." I stop. Hear how ridiculous I sound. Textbook inflation and paranoia. Jesus, I hadn't realized quite how much all this has rattled me.

Her eyes consider me carefully. Then her features soften as she voices my own thoughts. "I think you're scared, Stella. You're frightened. Someone in the business gets killed like this and it's going to make a lot of people feel vulnerable."

"But you'll look into it?"

"We check out every lead we're given." She closes her pad.

"And you'll let me know?" I give her one of my cards with my number on it.

"I'm guessing this isn't your real name either," she says, glancing at it.

I shake my head.

"Are you willing to tell me what it is?"

I hesitate. Realize I have no choice if I want her to take me seriously. "Grace. Grace Thomas."

She looks at me. "Thank you. I can't promise anything, but if there proves to be any substance to this, rest assured I'll be in touch."

Leading me back to the entrance, she offers her hand. "In the meantime, take care of yourself, okay?"

Her grip on me lingers, and there's a warning in her eyes. "I mean it, Grace. Be careful."

TWENTY-FOUR

He's standing outside the entrance when I emerge from Shepherd's Bush tube station into the pale sunlight. I don't spot him at first. I'm too busy wondering which hotel we're heading to; nowhere decent near here that I can think of.

"Stella." I spin round at the sound of his voice, so firm, so self-assured. Like nothing in the world could ever touch him.

"Alex."

He leans forward and kisses me on the cheek. I expect us to head to Holland Park. Instead he marches toward the giant monolith of the Westfield shopping center, hands thrust deep into the pockets of his black coat.

"Really?" I ask as we pass House of Fraser and into the mall proper.

Alex just smiles.

I try again. "Why the hell are we going here?"

"What can I say? I like to shop."

I frown. "You do?" Somehow I doubt it. Clearly he gets a kick out of stringing me along.

We glide past Valentino and Ted Baker, then he turns abruptly into Prada, grabbing my elbow to steer me through the plate glass doors. I stand there, feeling awkward. I always hate the cultish atmosphere of these places, the rarefied air of high fashion taking itself way too seriously. Though Anna would be right at home.

As Alex seems to be. Ignoring the shop assistant beelining toward us, he flicks through a rail of garments and holds up a knee-length silk skirt in front of me. It's about my size. And my style, a beautiful tartan check etched in black and muted shades of brown.

I can't see the price tag, but it has to be a couple of appointments' worth.

"Suits you," he says. "Try it on."

I shake my head.

Alex shrugs, glances round. "Well, pick something you like."

I purse my lips and inadvertently catch the shop assistant's eye. She's openly regarding me, an unreadable expression on her flawlessly made-up face.

I have a feeling she's got me sussed.

"What are we doing here?" I ask plainly.

Alex grins. "Living up to all the clichés?"

I let myself smile. "No chance. You don't look anything like Richard Gere."

He crosses to another railing, starts fingering a lilac silk blouse. I follow him. Decide to be blunt.

"Alex, what's this about?"

He releases the blouse. Faces me. "Okay, what would you rather do?"

I glare at him. "I don't know. You booked the bloody appointment."

Alex glances over at the assistant, then steers me out the shop into the main concourse. I stare up at the roof of this great glass palace, at the light bouncing off the myriad shopfronts in a dizzying display of brightness and color.

"This place is insane," I mutter. "A fucking cathedral to consumption."

Alex eyes me with amusement. "You sound as if you could do with a drink." He leads me up the escalator to the next level and finds us a seat in an Italian restaurant. I feel slightly deflated; evidently this isn't going to be a standard appointment. So what is it? Some kind of test? Or does he enjoy spending several hundred quid an hour simply to wind me up?

"Wine?" asks Alex.

I nod.

He orders a couple of glasses of Rioja and glances at the menu. The usual pasta and pizza.

"You hungry?"

I shake my head. "Some olives would be nice." I stare around me at the swarm of shoppers, most clutching carrier bags splashed with logos. "Honestly?" I say. "I'd never have imagined this was your style."

"No?"

"More Bond Street or Faubourg Saint-Honoré, I'd have said."

Alex inhales, wrinkles his nose. "I enjoy the anonymity."

Yes, I realize, looking back at all the people cruising the walkways. It's much easier to get lost in a crowd. But why not meet in a hotel room? I wonder, if he doesn't want us seen together?

Unless, of course, he doesn't want *anyone* knowing where he is.

I force the thought from my mind. Decide he's not the only one who can play games. "Actually, I was somewhat surprised to hear from you."

"Why?" Alex raises an eyebrow and settles back in his seat.

I shrug. Answer with another question. "I'm assuming you heard about Amanda?"

His face twitches minutely. But he doesn't speak.

"Amanda Mansfield," I say, "but you knew her as Elisa. The girl from the party."

His eyes linger on my face. "I know who you're talking about, Stella. I read the reports in the papers."

I wait for him to expand. Nothing follows.

"Well?" I nudge, as the olives arrive along with the wine. I take a gulp. Let my eyes close for a second or two.

How should I play this?

"What do you want me to say, Stella?" His tone abrupt. "It's unfortunate. I was very sorry to hear it."

Unfortunate. I savor the word. It tastes sour in my mouth.

"Very unfortunate," he repeats. "She was quite a girl."

I exhale slowly. "So you know nothing about what happened to her?"

No tells this time. Alex's features remain immobile. "Like I said, only what I read in the papers."

I study him. His expression is unreadable. I have no idea whether he's lying or not. I wonder how far I can push this.

"Do you?" he asks, before I can decide what tack to take.

"Do I what?"

"Have any idea what happened to her?"

I think carefully before I reply. Suspecting I'm close to some sort of brink. "I saw him on TV."

"Saw who?"

"Your friend Hardy. Edward Hardy."

No reaction.

"Something to do with a select committee investigation," I add, observing his reaction, but there's nothing. It's like talking to one of the mannequins downstairs.

"Stella, I've really no idea what you're getting at." Alex sighs as if this conversation is starting to bore him. I suppress the impulse to drop the whole thing. After all, this isn't a standard appointment—

none of the usual rules apply. And what's the worst that can happen? He doesn't pay me?

"It's just that I'm curious. What Harry said. I got the impression you were all in on some kind of deal."

Alex's face stiffens, his eyebrows narrowing with irritation. I get a sense of something beginning to shift inside him. "Stella, you're going to have to take my word for this. There is nothing here to concern you. Nothing at all."

There's a chill in his tone that unnerves me. And convinces me to stop. If I push this any further, he's going to walk away.

I press my lips together. Take another gulp of wine to swallow down my frustration. "So why are we here, then?" I ask. "If we're not going to fuck, or talk about Amanda, why exactly did you want to meet?"

He leans back in his chair. Looks around at the other diners, considering something. Closing his eyes briefly, he exhales, turning back to me.

"I have a proposal."

I raise an eyebrow. "How very romantic. And such a lovely setting."

He doesn't smile. "Listen to me, Stella. Carefully. What I have in mind should appeal to you much more than that."

I don't reply. Spike an olive on a toothpick and chew it slowly, watching him choose his next words.

He leans forward, grabs my hand. My skin tingles at the unexpected contact. "I'd like to offer you a more exclusive arrangement."

"Oh, right." I force a smile. "And I'm guessing this one doesn't come with a ring."

"I'm being serious, Stella. I'm asking you to drop your other work. You will, of course, be more than adequately compensated."

I stare at him for a few seconds, then laugh. "What? You want me to become your paid mistress?"

Alex's mouth pouts at the corners. "I guess you could describe it as that, though it's a trifle old-fashioned, wouldn't you say? I view it more as a business arrangement—a mutually beneficial business arrangement."

He takes his first sip of wine, unable to hide the grimace that follows.

I inhale. He is being serious, I realize, and in that instant I have an urge to get up and walk away. This is insane. Me. Him. This bizarre standoff between us. But I stay put; I want to hear him out.

"There's a caveat," he adds.

"What?"

"I'd like you out of London."

"Out of London," I echo, revealing my surprise. "Why?"

He shrugs. "It's not convenient for me."

"Not convenient? London? Then where is?"

"New York. Paris. Pick a city. Just not London."

I snort. "You're having me on, right?"

His lips narrow with annoyance. "Did nobody tell you, Stella, not to look a gift horse in the mouth?"

"About a thousand times," I say. "But I'm stubborn that way."

Alex looks down at the table. Rubs the skin between his brows before raising his eyes to mine. "No, Stella. I'm not 'having you on.' I'm making you an offer I very much hope you won't refuse. An offer that is as much in your interests as mine, if not more."

If not more. There's something in that I don't like. It's almost a threat—or a warning.

"But why?" I ask. "Why me? Why now? I mean, we haven't even fucked, not properly. You barely even know me."

"Why not you?" he exhales. "I like you, a lot. You intrigue me. I happen to find you rather appealing. And why now? Why not? My life is very complicated. I don't have the kind of time or motivation to get involved in a romantic relationship. On the other hand, I want someone I can get to know. Variety may be the spice of life, but too much tends to dull the palate, I've found."

"So you'd prefer something more bland? More regular?"

He laughs. "Somehow I doubt you'd ever be bland, Stella. I'm sure you'd have an infinite number of ways to keep me on my toes."

I smile, but unease settles back around me like a fog. "Wouldn't you rather have somebody, I don't know . . . younger? More glamorous?" I think of Amanda. How much more suited to this kind of arrangement she'd have been. Or Anna even; Anna would jump at an opportunity like this.

Alex leans forward and pinches the end of my chin between his thumb and forefinger. It's a peculiarly intimate gesture and I feel the heat rise to my cheeks.

"It's not all about that." His eyes flick down to my breasts, then he taps the side of my head with his finger. "I like what's in here, Stella. Your mind, your spirit, call it what you will. I admire the way you see the world, how you move within it."

"But we've only met, what, twice before?" I protest again, pulling away. "As I said, you don't know a single thing about me."

Alex looks nonplussed. Again that sense that he'd like to contradict me, that he can somehow see right into my head and my heart. "I *know* enough, Stella, to know I want to get to know you much better."

I sit back, lost for words. Then actually consider it. I mean, what have I got to lose? What, after all, is there to keep me here?

The thought depresses me. How little ties me to my own life. How easily I could turn my back on it.

"You're crazy," is all I can think to say. "This is the craziest thing I've ever heard."

Alex leans back. Evaluating me. "Is there someone else? Someone special you don't want to leave behind?"

I examine his face. "You mean a boyfriend?"

"Or another client. You must have met some you like—and who like you."

Despite myself, I think of Ben; though I haven't heard from him in weeks.

"As far as clients are concerned, we're consumables. Like this wine." I hold up my half-empty glass for emphasis. "You don't date them. It never works out. And it's a waste of money."

"Never?"

"Not if you've got any sense," I say a little too bitterly, remembering that girl Anna knew who married a client and was six months pregnant with his baby when she discovered he was back screwing other escorts.

"So you've never been tempted," probes Alex. "Not even once?"

Christ, where is he going with this? Is he jealous or just winding me up?

"Not even once."

"But you must fancy some of them, right?"

"I fancy lots of people, Alex, but that doesn't mean I want a relationship with all of them."

He smiles. "And if you get to screw them on a regular basis and get paid for it, I guess that's really having your cake and eating it."

"Exactly."

Alex watches me, eyes narrowed in thought, while I drink the rest of my wine. Then leans over and grabs my hand and I find myself remembering that gun. Has he got it on him right now? Why the fuck *does* he have one, anyway?

"You've never told me what it is you do," I say, holding his gaze.

He looks at me without speaking. "Does it matter?"

I shrug. Withdraw my hand.

"If I'm not bothered about your profession, I can't imagine why you'd worry about mine."

"Touché," I say, dropping the subject. Somehow I know I'm not going to get anything like a straight answer.

"You see, every time you open your mouth you reveal yourself, Stella. It's one of your best features. And one of your greatest faults."

"How do you mean?"

"Just think it over, will you? Take a few days. And . . ." He pauses.

"And what?"

"And do me a favor, please. Keep a low profile."

I frown. "Would you care to explain?"

"Stay out of trouble, mind your own business."

I feel myself tense. "Mind my own business?"

Alex shakes his head. "Never mind. Consider my offer. Let me know by the end of the week."

He stands, retrieves his wallet, and chucks a twenty-pound note on the table.

"Isn't there something you've forgotten?" I say as he pulls on his jacket.

Alex cocks an eyebrow. Reaches inside his breast pocket and hands me the white envelope.

I push it back at him. "No," I hiss, a little too vehemently. "That's not what I meant. If I said yes to your little proposal, how much are you planning to compensate me for that?"

He frowns down at the floor, then raises his eyes to mine. There's something there. Something genuine.

"Whatever it takes, Stella. Whatever it takes."

TWENTY-FIVE

Rachel doesn't ask any questions when I ring and suggest I catch the next train down to Sussex. Doesn't even mention the suddenness of my visit when she picks me up from the station. Just gives me a look that tells me she's seen right through my cheerful expression to the miserable core of me.

"Come on." She holds open the passenger's door and nods at me to get in. "Tim's got supper on and I'm starving."

I glance in the car. Therese is asleep, strapped into the baby seat in the back, her head slumped to one side and a pacifier trailing from her mouth. She looks huge compared to when I last saw her.

"She only stopped crying a minute ago," Rachel says as I climb into the front. "I reckon she's got another tooth coming through."

"Where's Theo?"

"With Tim. They've been off to get him a new pair of shoes. Now he won't take them off. I foresee tears at bedtime."

I pull on my seat belt, then turn to Rachel. She looks tired, the skin beneath her eyes almost violet in tone. But she gazes back at me as if she's thinking the same thing.

"How's London?" she asks, in lieu of inquiring what I'm actually doing here.

"Busy. I just needed to escape. Thanks for putting me up."

The truth is I need air. Space. Time to reflect. The walls of my flat felt like they were closing in around me. Street noise sounded louder, more intrusive; even the ubiquitous shriek of sirens kept making me jump.

Alex's offer has unnerved me nearly as much as Amanda's death. Threatened to topple what little security I thought I had. Yet I seem unable to dismiss it out of hand.

"Anytime." Rachel smiles, squeezing my hand. "You know that goes without saying."

The drive back to the house takes half an hour. We stop off at the out-of-town supermarket to pick up some salad to go with Tim's lasagne. A tub of stuffed giant green olives and a loaf of fresh ciabatta. I insist on paying, throwing in a couple of bottles of decent red wine, mindful of how tight things have been since Rachel gave up work.

"What a sight for sore eyes." Tim practically snatches the bottles from my hands as I step through the door.

"Me, or the wine?"

Tim pretends to weigh it up. "Both." He laughs and kisses me on the cheek, while Theo hangs back in the doorway, eyeing me suspiciously.

"You remember Grace, don't you?" Rachel nudges.

Theo gives a solemn nod. Then steps one foot forward, ostentatiously. I duly look down. They're red leather, two straps with Velcro fastenings and a small boat logo on the toes.

"Hey, nice shoes, kiddo."

Theo beams. "They're new."

"So I see. Jolly smart."

I reach into my handbag and pull out the comics I picked up at Victoria station. His eyes brighten as I hand them over, and he skips into the lounge. I turn to Therese, now humped onto Rachel's hip, and give her the giant wax crayons. She grabs them, turning the packet over and over in her fat little fingers, examining it intently.

"Say 'thank you.'" Rachel nuzzles her face into her daughter's.

"Tank oo," gurgles Therese, her eyes never leaving the crayons.

Tim feeds the kids first and Rachel puts them to bed, reappearing twenty minutes later looking more exhausted than they were. I hand her a glass of wine.

"I think Therese might have finally gone to sleep." She holds up crossed fingers and takes a mouthful. Her shoulders slump with relief. "God, I needed that."

Tim places the bread in the oven to warm, then tips the salad leaves into a bowl and adds a few chopped tomatoes.

"Did you decide about Rowland Marshalls?" I ask Rachel as she joins me at the kitchen table.

She swirls the wine around, watching the streaks of alcohol slither back down the inside of the glass.

"Not yet. They've given me till April to make up my mind." She takes another long mouthful. "Meanwhile, I'm considering setting up on my own."

"Great idea. There's nothing like being self-employed."

Rachel shoots me a frown and I laugh. "Truly. You have far more control over your own life."

"As a matter of fact," she says, "I've had an idea."

I raise an eyebrow. She's giving me one of her meaningful looks.

"What's that?"

Rachel sits back in her chair, twirling the stem of her glass between her thumb and forefinger. I sense her weighing her next words carefully.

"Actually I was wondering if you fancied working with me?" She fixes my gaze with hers. "You know, forming a partnership."

I stare back at her. Behind me I can hear Tim busying himself with plates and cutlery.

"But I don't know anything about employment law."

"Well, I was thinking more of offering a broad range of services to local firms. Not simply legal advice, things like occupational psychology too." She watches my face for my reaction.

"I was a *forensic* psychologist, Rachel, dealing with convicts and criminals. It had nothing whatsoever to do with the workplace."

She presses her lips together and pushes on. "I'm aware of that, Grace. But you've already got your basic psychology degree and plenty of experience, so it's only a question of doing a master's in the occupational bit. I've looked into it. It doesn't seem that different from what you were doing before—only dealing with a different set of people."

Out of the corner of my eye I see Tim shoot her a warning glance. I feel my jaw begin to tighten and I lower my gaze to the table.

"Grace, it's only an idea, something that crossed my mind, that's all. A suggestion."

I swallow my response. Try to force myself to appear less angry than I feel.

"Just say you'll think about it, okay?"

I take a slug of Bordeaux and look out into the darkness beyond the patio doors. The silence weighs heavy in the room.

"Anyway," cuts in Tim, his voice a little too breezy, "I've got some news. I've been promoted. Regional manager."

I swing round, avoiding Rachel's eyes, and give him a grateful smile.

"Congratulations," I say, getting out of my seat and hugging him hard. "You should have said something earlier. I'd have bought champagne."

TWENTY-SIX

We take the kids to Colsham Bay on Sunday. The rain has retreated, bringing sunshine and a throng of day-trippers to the little resort, crowding the pubs and cafés along the seafront. Theo insists on going to the amusement arcade over by the pier. We spend nearly ten quid on the penny falls, emerging with a motley collection of plastic key rings and a hideous miniature plaster model of a kitten.

Tim queues for fish and chips and we eat them sitting on the low wall between the beach and the harbor, ignoring the loitering gangs of seagulls. I nibble my food, savoring the pungent flavor of vinegar and salt. Why do chips always taste so much better by the sea?

Three bowlegged Jack Russells approach, towing an older woman bundled in a huge brown coat. Seconds later they spot a nearby spaniel and launch into such a volley of barking that Therese bursts into tears in her buggy.

"Bad dogs!" she screams as Rachel tries to comfort her.

Tim grabs the plaster kitten out of his pocket and dangles it in front of her face. Therese snatches it from his hand, her sobs drying up instantly.

"If only everything were so easily sorted," Rachel sighs as she gazes at her daughter.

I smile as I watch an older couple admiring the dinghies and fishing boats moored in the harbor. Beyond them, families huddle in the shelter of the breakwaters, kids charging around on the sand. I pick at my fish with the wooden fork, trying to quash a rising sense of discomfort. It's all so innocent. So bloody picture-perfect. I feel suddenly twitchy and restless.

Only twenty-four hours out of London and I'm almost longing for its roughness and anonymity, the grunginess of life lived among so many.

An image of Kristen looms in my mind, standing in the wreckage of her life, her dead lover's face gazing up at her from the photographs scattered across the floor. Is she at the flat now? I wonder. Picking up the pieces? I feel a swell of guilt—I should have offered to go back, to help clean the place up.

Then I remember her sister. And Anna's warning. *Don't get involved.*

"So," says Rachel as Tim takes the kids off to the little carousel by the pier. "Why are you here?"

I crunch a piece of batter. "That doesn't sound very welcoming."

Rachel turns to look at me. "You know what I mean. What's up?"

For a moment I'm tempted to tell her. About Amanda. About the police station. About the party and seeing Hardy on TV. About the nagging sense that there's something I'm missing.

But how can I? Rachel doesn't know anything about the parties and I have no intention of filling her in. Escorting is one thing; full-on orgies would be a step too far for a woman who's been happily partnered up since university. As for Amanda's death, I might as well inform my friend that I'm expecting to be murdered any day now; she worries too much as it is.

"Okay, I get it." Rachel balls her chip wrapper and tosses it neatly into a nearby bin. "You don't want to tell me—or can't. And you're right, I'm probably better off not knowing."

"It's not . . ." I begin, but can't see any way through the maze. "It's complicated."

"Not a bloke, then? You've not met someone?"

I shake my head.

Rachel sighs. Nudges at a pile of sand with the toe of her boot. "I don't like how things have become between us. You cagey, me disapproving. It's as if we got stuck somewhere along the way."

"It's a difficult situation. I understand that—and your point of view."

She squints at me. "Do you, Grace? I sometimes wonder if you feel we've all abandoned you somehow."

"Why would I think that?"

Rachel shrugs. "I don't know. I just get the sense you don't realize how much people still care about you. Despite . . ." She stops. Leans forward, both hands in her coat pockets. "It's as if . . . well, maybe it's more like you've abandoned yourself in some way."

I don't say anything. A gust of wind blows sand in my eye. It stings but I don't want to wipe it away because I know Rachel will think I'm upset.

She turns to me. "I understand what you've been doing, and why you've been doing it, better than you give me credit for. I'm no psychologist, granted. I don't have your insight into things, but I can see why you felt the need to get away and bury yourself in all that. But I think it's time, Grace, time to put it all behind you. *Everything*, I mean—not simply your work."

I make myself return her gaze. I see a few strands of gray standing up from the bulk of her brown hair.

"You can't keep running from the past," she says, with such gentleness I have to swallow. "You can't allow what he did to ruin the rest of your life."

She doesn't say his name. Thank God.

"Listen to me." Rachel leans in, her tone fiercer. "What happened, *happened*, Grace. You *have* to let it go." She grabs my hand. "Most of all, my love, you've got to stop punishing yourself."

She's squeezing my fingers urgently, punctuating the flow of her words. "I don't doubt for a minute that you're great at what you do now. I can even accept that you might enjoy it. But I think you need to find something more positive to do with your life. You were good at your job before, despite what happened—you know you were."

I shake my head again, turning away so she can't see my eyes gleaming.

"I meant what I said," Rachel continues. "About setting up together. You don't have to leave London, your flat. I could get offices somewhere like Brighton and you could commute. You could even do a lot of work from home."

I clear my throat. "You've really thought this through, haven't you?"

She nods. "I honestly believe it could work, Grace." She squeezes my hand even harder. "Please say you'll consider it. Properly, I mean."

I think about it. And Alex's offer. Two different escape routes. Two very different outcomes.

"I already have," I sigh, pulling my hand away. "And the answer is no." To both, I decide, right at that moment.

Rachel's expression is first shocked, then offended.

"Why?"

I grit my teeth and fight to keep the exasperation from my voice. "Think about it, Rachel, think hard. It's out there. People know what happened. They know what I did. You reckon that sort of thing doesn't stick?"

"Grace, listen, you made one mistake. All right, it was a big mistake, but that doesn't define your whole—"

"It wasn't one mistake, though, was it? It was a whole catalog of mistakes. Somebody *died*, Rachel. You can't just walk away from something like that. You live with it. Every fucking day of your life, you live with it."

I'm almost shouting now. A couple over by the breakwater turn and stare.

"But it wasn't your fault, Grace. Whatever you believe."

I lose the battle. Tears well and threaten to tip down my face. "Fuck off, Rachel. You've no idea what's going on in my life, and your interfering is just making it worse."

My best friend looks shaken. Slapped. Her voice trembles as she gets to her feet.

"No, Grace, I'm not the one who's making it worse. And I can't stand it anymore. I can't sit by and watch you destroy yourself any longer." She glares at me. "You imagine I can't see the state you're in? And no, I don't want to know what kind of crap you've got yourself mixed up in this time. But I'm trying to throw you a lifeline, and it kills me that you fling it right back in my face."

She frowns and looks away. When she turns back I read what's coming before the words even leave her mouth.

"I've had it, Grace. *Finito*. If you want to wallow in shit for the rest of your life, I no longer want any part of it."

Rachel gets up, pulls her coat around her. She gives me a lingering look, her lips trembling with emotion, then turns and walks away, fast, her hair blowing out behind her as she heads toward the pier.

I stare after her, paralyzed by a rush of panic. Should I catch her up? Apologize? Tell her she's right and I'll give the job idea some genuine thought?

But I just sit there. Shivering. Weighed down by something I can't name.

Moments later Rachel disappears behind the bandstand.

I let her go.

TWENTY-SEVEN

He picks me up near Waterloo Bridge, in a government-issue black sedan. I climb in the back behind the driver and we pull off into the traffic, heading past the mainline train station and out toward Newington.

It was surprisingly easy to get hold of Edward Hardy. A few seconds on Google furnished me with his website, an e-mail address, a phone number for his office. A quick call to leave a message with his secretary.

"Just say it's Stella," I tell her when she asks for my name.

He sits here now beside me in raincoat and formal suit, clearly come straight from the Commons. For a moment or two neither of us speaks; we just stare at the back of his driver's head. I feel inhibited by his presence. Wonder if Hardy does too.

"So," he says, finally breaking the silence. "How can I help you today?" His eyes flick briefly to mine. I want to face him, but it's awkward in a car. I'm conscious of the driver's gaze reflecting back at me in the rearview mirror.

"I wanted to ask you something."

Hardy's eyebrows contract into a frown. He waits for me to go on.

"About Amanda Mansfield."

"Amanda Mansfield?" His tone tries to suggest he doesn't know who I mean, but the contraction in his jaw tells me otherwise.

"Elisa," I say simply. "The girl from the party."

"Ah." He inhales, then leans forward in his seat. "Drop us on the corner, Jake. By the postbox."

The car pulls over at the junction. I climb out after Hardy, who goes round to the driver's window and says something I don't pick up. The car slides back into the road and turns right.

"Let's walk," says Hardy. "I could do with some fresh air."

I follow him down a side street into an ordinary residential area flanked by nondescript blocks of redbrick flats. We keep going until we come to a rather pretty garden, a few scraps of lawn, a pond in the center, surrounded by emerging foliage. A series of rural-style cottages in the background. I pause to read the sign on the cast-iron gate: RED CROSS GARDEN, SOUTHWARK.

"Can we sit?" I nod at a nearby bench, hoping the recent shower hasn't left it too wet.

Hardy strides over, checks the surface of the wood, and lowers himself onto it. I settle on his near side, my back turned toward the entrance. For a second the clouds part and I feel the warmth of the sun on my face.

"So what do you want to know?" he asks. "About Amanda Mansfield?"

"You mean, apart from the fact that she's dead? Or to be more precise, murdered." I say the word slowly and see Hardy flush.

"Yes, I'm aware of that. I was very sorry to hear it."

Didn't Alex say much the same? The party line, I think, examining Hardy's face. His eyes avoid mine, flicking around the gardens. There's no one here apart from an old man over in the far corner, bending and poking at something with a walking stick.

"A nasty business," Hardy adds suddenly. "But I'm sure the police are on top of it. I don't see any need for you to worry."

"I'm not worried. Not exactly. It's more that I'm confused." I give him a tentative little smile.

"Confused?"

"Well, it's just that nothing about her death makes sense," I say.

"How so?"

I run through the reasons I gave DI Shaw. Hardy remains silent while I explain about the hotel, the condoms, the lapse in Amanda's usual procedure.

"It does sound odd," he concedes when I've finished. "But this is clearly something for the police."

"I've already spoken to them. And her girlfriend has told them all this too."

I watch his reaction as I mention Kristen, but his face shows no hint of surprise—despite the fact that none of the papers mentioned that Amanda was a lesbian.

"The thing is, I'm not sure they *are* taking it seriously," I say. "They seem convinced Amanda's killer was a client. So I was wondering if you . . . I don't know, whether you could make some inquiries? Pull a few strings?"

Hardy shifts on his seat and regards me for a long moment without speaking. "Frankly, I have nothing to do with the police. It's way outside my remit."

"But you could find out who to speak to, couldn't you?"

Hardy sighs. "Stella . . ."

"You knew her," I add. "You met her . . . Don't you think it's the least you can do? She's dead. And Kristen is beside herself. She could lose the flat, everything."

I fix him with an earnest expression.

"Is that all?" He glances at his watch.

I nod.

"I'll look into it," he says, his voice terse. "But I have to go. I've got a departmental meeting in half an hour."

I reach over and grasp his hand in mine. He gazes at it in surprise before withdrawing it. "Thanks," I say, making myself appear suitably grateful. "I really appreciate it."

He stands, straightens his coat. Looks down at me.

"I'll stay on here for a bit," I add. "You go ahead."

Hardy gives me the briefest of smiles and walks away. I see him pull out his phone as he heads back up the street, presumably calling his driver. I glance over at the old man. He's shuffling along toward the cottages, his lopsided gait suggesting a recent stroke.

I've done it, I think, with a sense of finality. I've stepped over the brink. Now it's simply a matter of waiting for whatever will happen next.

Either way, I figure Alex has his answer.

TWENTY-EIGHT

rarely do overnights. It's not the dearth of sleep that bothers me. Or even the endless sex.

It's the pretense that's such hard work. Having to bite my tongue, or force myself to talk when I'd rather be silent. Never revealing the boredom or antipathy lying beneath my smile, behind that little gasp of pleasure. I can keep it up for one hour, even three or four—but the façade wears very thin on a twelve-hour shift.

But when Ben calls, I don't hesitate. I've spent the last two days in a London swathed in fog, jumping at shadows. My flat no longer feels like a sanctuary, and the thought of escaping for the night is beyond tempting. Not to mention I'm surprised and pleased to hear from him again.

Maybe a little too pleased.

We meet at the Japanese restaurant I suggested in Soho. It's one of my favorite haunts—authentic, understated, filled with natives. The kind of place you suspect has a private room for the yakuza hidden away downstairs.

Ben is waiting at a tiny table in the back corner. He stands to kiss me on the cheek. "Amazing restaurant," he says. "Good choice."

"It's great, isn't it? The next best thing to actually being in Tokyo. Not that I've ever been."

"It was pretty tough getting a reservation. I rang twice before they got a cancelation. Otherwise it would have been the Nando's up the road."

I glance round as I sit. The small dining room is crammed and it looks like we're the only non-Japanese in here. "That's the problem with this place. It's always busy."

"I'm assuming you've been here before?"

I smile. "Do you really want to know?"

He takes the hint. "No."

A diminutive waitress with skin like bone china hands us each a menu.

"So, how are you?" Ben asks, examining my features for clues. I make myself hold his gaze. I'd nearly forgotten how attractive he is. The way his hair curls around his forehead. That wry smile. I'm oddly disarmed by his presence.

"Wonderful. Thank you." I wonder how he'd react if I told him the truth. Probably run a mile. Clients can bear only so much reality. "How about you?"

He shrugs. "What can I say? Work . . . you know."

"Wife?"

The word pops out of my mouth before I can stop it. I want to slap myself around the head. Why do I do this with him? *Act the fucking part, Grace.*

Ben raises an eyebrow. "Well, yes, as it happens. But let's at least order some drinks if we're going to discuss that."

"No need. To talk about it, I mean." I examine my menu, feeling my face flush.

Neither of us speaks for a minute or two. I'm just thinking the whole appointment has gone south again when he looks up. "I've got a confession to make."

"Yes?"

He holds up the menu. "I'm not very familiar with Japanese food. Or Japanese, come to that."

I glance down at mine. It's written first in kanji characters, the ensuing English offering few clues as to what's on offer.

"Are you're saying you'd like me to order?"

"Please."

I stick to Japanese-lite. Edamame and maki sushi. Six pieces of tuna sashimi—the beginner's raw fish. Vegetable and prawn tempura and some agedashi tofu. A jug of good sake.

"So why do you ask?" he says, once the waitress has retreated. He's sitting back in his seat, regarding me with something close to amusement.

"Ask what?"

"About my domestic situation."

"I don't know," I say, flustered. "I didn't. I was just being flippant. Sorry, it's none of my business."

Ben laughs. "That's what I like about you, Stella. The real you just can't help breaking through."

I smile awkwardly, remembering that Alex said something similar. The waitress returns with the sake. Pours us both a glass, then sets the rest on the table.

Ben takes a sip, nods approvingly. "Anyway, since you did ask, I am married. Nominally."

"Ah," I say, savoring the dry flavor of the rice wine. "The nominal marriage. Sounds like the title to a literary novel."

"'Nominal' as in we're just going through the motions."

"Isn't everyone?"

He grins. "There you go again."

This time my smile is genuine. Suddenly I'm not making an

effort. Given the alternative of another night alone chewing over Amanda's death and my bust-up with Rachel, I'm genuinely glad to be here.

Two waitresses appear, serving all our food at once. There's barely space left on the table. "I never could get the hang of these," says Ben, gripping his chopsticks. I show him how to pincer them between thumb and fingers. He imitates my scissoring action—badly—dropping a piece of the tuna into the soy sauce and struggling to retrieve it.

I look over and mouth "fork" to the waitress. She dips her head and retrieves one from the kitchen.

"So," says Ben, finally able to eat. "How about you?"

"How about me what?"

"Married?"

"Not anymore."

Ben looks like he wants to pursue this further but decides against it. He spears an edamame pod with his fork and pops the whole thing into his mouth. I let him chew it for a full minute before I start to smirk. I pick up another with my fingers and squeeze out the succulent soy beans.

Ben groans and swallows with visible effort, chasing it down with a gulp of sake. "Christ, I wondered why they were so . . . gristly."

We steer the conversation into safer waters. He talks about his job. His megalomaniac boss, and the time he persuaded Ben to apply for a position with a rival firm.

"What on earth for?"

"He wanted me to report back. You know, on how they pitched to clients."

"What, you mean he wanted you to actually join the company? While you were still employed by him? How the hell could you do that?"

"They let a lot of their employees work from home, at least

for part of the week. He reckoned I could come and work for him on the days I was supposed to be homeworking."

"You're kidding. That's ridiculous."

He lifts his hands in a gesture of surrender. "True story."

"So what on earth did you do?"

"I applied for the job and I got it. And never went back to my old boss. Left the bastard completely in the lurch."

I put my hand over my mouth as I chew and laugh at the same time. "Priceless."

He spears a lump of the tofu. Downs it in one. "Your turn."

I give him a questioning look.

"Come on. Don't tell me you haven't had some laughs in this job."

"It's confidential," I say. "How would you feel if I gossiped to my other clients about your astonishingly small dick?"

His face falls for an instant, then he grins.

But I do tell him Anna's burqa story, suitably disguised—in case he's ever seen her. Though I find that's something I don't even want to consider.

"Anything else?" The waitress materializes and relieves us of our embarrassment of dishes.

I look at Ben. He looks back.

"Let's skip dessert," I say, watching his mouth widen into a smile.

It's different this time.

We undress each other slowly, intently, letting every movement, every action count. Leeching each moment of sensation, like sucking the juice out of the flesh of an orange.

He goes down on me, his tongue exploring, teasing me into orgasm. I drop my head to return the favor but Ben pulls me up into a kiss. Long and sensuous and I taste myself on his breath, the rich musk of my excitement.

"Stella," he breathes, pulling back to fix his gaze on mine. It's all he says and I don't reply. This isn't the time for words.

When we fuck, it's urgent, but slow and measured, if such a thing is possible. Like a surgeon performing lifesaving surgery, every movement executed with fierce concentration, an absolute focus of attention. And weighted with something I'd almost forgotten existed.

Tenderness, I realize as I come with a yowl of pleasure, biting back tears that rise, unbidden, like floodwater from an underground aquifer.

Something feels as if it's come loose inside me.

"So, tell me," Ben says afterward, arm curled around and head nestled against mine. "What's your secret fantasy? The thing you most long to do."

"If I told you that, it wouldn't be a secret." My standard response.

He grins. Waits.

Out of nowhere, I get the urge to answer seriously. I turn on my side. Run a hand through the mess we've made of my hair.

"Live on an island. It's a mile from the mainland, so I can go back in a boat to get food and stuff. I have a small white cottage with a few rooms. Cozy, but sparsely furnished, because I wouldn't need much, but lots of books. And pictures on the walls. Line prints, landscapes. That sort of thing."

He props his head up on his elbow and looks at me. "Interesting. But that wasn't quite the sort of fantasy I had in mind."

"I know."

"Okay. What kind of island?"

"Somewhere wild. And uninhabited," I say. "Apart from me." I pull the duvet closer. The room still feels cold. I wonder if something's gone wrong with the heating.

"So what's yours?"

He sniffs. "This pretty much covers it, I reckon."

"Honestly?"

He nods.

"Blimey. You do lack imagination."

"Well, thankfully you don't." He grins. A filthy, lascivious grin. Then exhales, slowly, not quite a sigh. "All right, tell me what you really think about sex—you being the expert and all."

"What I really think about sex in general? Or what I think about during sex? Haven't we come full circle?"

"In general."

I stare into space, mulling it over. "I guess I believe sex is primal, however much we might pretend otherwise. No one is immune to its power."

Ben laughs. "Except perhaps my wife. We haven't had sex in over a year."

I confine my curiosity to a raised eyebrow. "Well, it's different for women."

"How so? You just said no one was immune."

"I know. I mean, with men, sex is something hardwired, automatic; show most guys a picture of an attractive girl with nice tits, and they'll get a hard-on. They can't help it." I pause, choosing the right words. "With women, it's much more subtle. It's all about context. To arouse a woman you have to engage her mind, her imagination."

"Her heart?"

"Not necessarily."

His lips twitch. He lets his head flop back onto the pillow. "Well, it seems I've failed to engage Helen on any level."

"Helen?"

"My wife."

"Your nominal wife," I remind him.

He turns to look at me. "So you're saying you don't enjoy any of this, then? You fuck men but you're not engaged. You could have fooled me just now."

I feel a flicker of embarrassment. Followed by irritation. "Don't make assumptions, Ben. You know nothing about my imagination or how it works. For all you know, this is exactly the sort of thing I fantasize about."

"Being paid for sex? You find that erotic?"

"Why not?"

He lets his gaze linger on my face. "You're quite an enigma."

An image of Alex at the party, using the same word. Jesus, why do men always talk in clichés?

"Enigmatic," I muse. "I must add that to my website."

Something slumps in Ben's face. His mouth twitches before he speaks. "Well . . . okay. How long are you planning to carry on with this?"

"This?" I glance at the clock. Nearly midnight. "Approximately eight more hours. If you're up to it."

He scowls. "You know what I mean."

"I do. I'm just choosing to misunderstand." I quell another wave of frustration. Why does everyone keep asking me this?

"Eight hours." Ben withdraws a little. Tucks both arms under his head. "What shall we talk about, then? Life, death. The universe?"

"As you please."

He thinks for a moment, frowning slightly. "Do you believe in God? An afterlife?"

"I don't think so."

"All right, so what do you imagine there'll be? After we're gone?"

"Nothing, I hope. Silence. Peace."

He looks thoughtful. I let my eyes drift across the line of his jaw. Study the steep curve of his chin, the hollow under his bottom lip. Have to suppress the urge to reach out and touch it. "So, what do you think there will be?"

He lifts his hand and scratches his cheek. It's a while before he answers. "I think it will be like waking from a dream, and realizing that what you were dreaming wasn't real. And feeling it slip away, the life you led while you were asleep, just fall away, like a mistake."

"Wow," I say, feeling oddly moved. "Very profound."

His mouth widens as he turns to face me. "I am profound."

"So, you believe this is all a dream?" I indicate the room around us.

"I reckon all we're doing right now is forgetting the true nature of things."

"But it seems so real." I stroke his thigh, enjoying the delicious tickle of the hairs beneath my fingertips. "And so appealing."

"So do dreams—feel real—when you're in them." He lets his eyes drop to my breasts, and I shift forward to offer him a better view. "'Life is but a dream within a dream.' Shakespeare?"

"'*All* that we see or seem / Is but a dream within a dream.' Edgar Allan Poe."

"Ah," he says, taking my hand and placing it on his erection. "I stand corrected."

TWENTY-NINE

I sleep fitfully, unused to another body in my bed. We make love again in the early hours, fast and furtive, and I drift back off and awake again when it's light. Ben is lying on the duvet, dressed only in his jeans, watching me.

"Morning, gorgeous." I muster a smile as he leans over and kisses my nose. "Coffee?"

"God, please."

I lie there, listening to him move around my kitchen. Cupboards opening. The clink of spoons. The sound of the kettle coming to a boil.

I look at the clock. Half past seven. Nearly time for him to leave.

Ben appears with two mugs of coffee on a tray I'd forgotten I had. Puts one on the bedside table beside me. I prop myself up against the pillows, registering the ominous draggy feeling in my head that presages a hangover. I shouldn't have had that third glass of sake.

He sits on the side of the bed, looking at me. After a minute it comes perilously close to getting on my nerves. "What?" I ask. "Have I got mascara down my cheeks or something?"

Ben's smile is wide. Optimistic. "I like you, Stella . . . or whoever you really are. I like you. I want to get to know you better, that's all."

I retrieve my work voice. "So let's do this again," I say, too brightly.

Ben's happy expression fades. He looks down at his bare feet. "I can't . . . I mean I can't afford this. Not so often. I'm not loaded, like your other clients. Before I met you it was only something I did now and then—an escape from the eternal winter *chez moi*."

"Are you asking for a discount?"

He whips his head back round to face me. "No, Stella, I'm not. That's not what I'm asking for at all."

I take a sip of the coffee and close my eyes. When I open them again he seems to be waging some kind of internal battle with himself, squeezing the knot of skin between his brows hard enough to turn it pale.

"Look, I just want to get to know you. The *real* you."

I stare at him. A pain starts to pulse in my forehead.

"The *real* me?" The vehemence in my tone startles both of us. His eyes widen slightly and his back stiffens.

"Christ, Ben, this isn't fucking *Pretty Woman*," I snap. "I'm not going to pull off my wig and shake my hair loose and become everything you ever dreamed of. That's what you want, isn't it? The fantasy. If you got to know 'the real me,' as you put it, you'd find out I wasn't so very different from your wife."

"I doubt it," Ben fires back. "As far as I'm aware, she doesn't charge her lover twelve hundred quid a night."

I feel my cheeks flame with indignation. "And there we have it. You want to know me better, but you're never going to let me forget that I'm a whore."

Ben looks away, his jaw tight, the tendons in his neck distinct. I hear him exhale, see him force himself to calm down before he turns back to me.

"Stella, I'm sorry. I didn't mean . . . I shouldn't have said that." He rubs his forehead with the heel of his hand. "Look, what's going on with you? I can tell there's something wrong. You're tense, on edge . . ."

"I'll give you a refund."

"What?"

"If the service hasn't been up to scratch, I'll give you a refund."

"That wasn't what I meant and you know it." He's struggling now to keep the anger out of his voice.

"Don't you see?" I say, trying not to raise mine. "This is what I *do*. Provide a screen for men like you to project their fantasies on. It's not about the sex—if it were just about the sex you'd be happy with a quick wank. It's all about the fantasy, Ben, and you're paying me not to let the reality of myself intrude on that."

"I don't agree. I—"

"You don't know anything *real* about me. Not even my name."

"So tell me."

"Stop talking like a fucking cliché, Ben. Listen, there's nothing going on here, okay? It's just business. I don't know where you got the idea that—"

"So why are you crying?"

A question like a slap in the face. I lift my hand to my cheek and it comes away wet. *What the . . .*

Christ, I really have to pull myself together. "I'm sorry," I say, chastened. "This isn't what you're paying for."

"So how about I stop?"

"Stop what?"

"Paying you. What if we do this again? But on equal ground. What if I were to join you on that island?"

I snort.

"I mean it."

"I bet you do. It'd certainly be a bargain for you."

I see the hurt on his face, followed by resentment. "It's not about the fucking money, Stella. I'm not trying to save myself a few hundred quid. It's about us. *You and me.* Or are you telling me this is all fake? Were you just acting last night? This morning? Are you telling me I imagined all that?"

I shut my mouth, biting back my words. We stare at each other as I try to stop my lip from quivering. I should ask him to leave, I think, but can't bring myself to say it. We sit like this for nearly a minute, then he sighs and runs his hand through his hair. "Shit. I've got this completely wrong, haven't I? I expect you get this crap off punters all the time."

I gaze at him, but can't think of any response—even though it's not true. I just watch the agitation in his face.

"You're good, Stella." He gets to his feet and grasps his shirt. "I give you that. I don't mean the sex, although it's first-class. I mean the rest of it. You really have a way of drawing people in, making them believe—"

"None of this is deliberate."

He searches my face as he pulls on his trousers. "I know. I'm sorry. It's my fault. I let myself get carried away, thinking . . ."

"Ben."

"What?"

"Let's not go through this right now. *Please?*"

He falls silent. I listen to a faint ringing in my ears, like a warning bell. When he speaks again it's so quiet it's as if I imagined it.

"I can't do this again." He doesn't look at me as he puts on his socks and reaches for his jacket. "I'm sorry. I've been really stupid. You're right, I've fallen into that age-old trap, haven't I? Mistaking fantasy for something real."

A feeling in my stomach, cold as dread. For a second I have the urge to grab his arm and ask him to stay. I force myself to remain silent.

He retrieves the envelope and tosses it onto the bed. "Good-bye, Stella."

I close my eyes as he walks out of the bedroom, holding my breath until I hear the clunk of the door closing behind him.

This time I don't count the money.

THIRTY

At least business is booming, I think bitterly, even if the rest of my life feels like it's entered some sort of terminal phase. I skim through half a dozen e-mails from men with itches to scratch. The usual lineup. Men whose wives won't screw them. Men whose girlfriends won't go down on them. Men who are too fucked up to maintain any kind of relationship at all.

Not that I'm one to talk.

The bell rings at 4 P.M. exactly. I open the door to a man of medium build, black hair. Not attractive, but not unpleasant either. A nondescript face, bar a slight indent in his left cheek, a little too big for an acne scar.

I smile and usher him in. He's wearing one of those ubiquitous dark gray suits, topped with an overcoat. No bag or briefcase. He stands in the lounge, sizing me up with an expression that's neither a smile nor a scowl, but somehow has elements of both. It's a cool stare, clinical almost.

I feel a jolt of uneasiness. Maybe he's going to bolt.

"Stella." His voice an even monotone. "How nice to meet you at last."

I smile again. "Indeed."

He remains there, unmoving. But not at rest. It's more like a pause, a lull that only emphasizes his latent momentum. For a second or two I wonder if I've ever met him before. Not as a client, perhaps, but somewhere else. He seems familiar in some way—or maybe it's his air of somehow knowing me.

"Can I get you a drink?" I offer, breaking the silence.

"Not for me. But you go ahead."

I walk into the kitchen and pour myself a glass of wine from the open bottle in the fridge. Notice my hand is trembling. Low blood sugar, I tell myself. Shouldn't have skipped lunch. I swallow a couple of mouthfuls before returning to the lounge.

My client has removed his overcoat. He hands me the white envelope straightaway.

"Thanks." I drop it on the coffee table and nod toward the bedroom, keen to dispense with small talk. Not that he seems inclined to make any.

He follows me without a word, walking to the end of the bed, then coming to a standstill again. There's something curiously detached in his manner. No trace of desire in the way he regards me. No attempt to put me—or himself—at ease. It's as if he . . . I struggle to formulate the thought . . . as if he's *trying* to make me uncomfortable.

I walk toward him. Lift my hand to loosen his tie. He grabs my wrist and shakes his head.

"Strip."

It's not an unusual request, or even an unreasonable one, but something in the way he says it chills the air. I feel a pulse of emotion. Indignation? Humiliation?

No, I realize. *Fear.*

I unzip my skirt, trying to keep my expression relaxed and

sensuous as my mind spirals in alarm. Should I just stop, ask him to go? Or walk right out of the flat, get myself outside, somewhere safe?

I dismiss both options. If this man intends to hurt me, he won't leave—asking will only provoke him. Ditto running away. I wouldn't stand a chance; he'd stop me before I even reached the door.

Play it cool, Grace, I say to myself. *Pretend you're perfectly at ease.*

But my mind leaps inevitably to Amanda, to her last moments in that dingy hotel room. Have I got it all wrong? Was it a client after all? A man much like this one, perhaps, watching her with those same impassive eyes.

I step out of my skirt. Fiddle with my blouse, undoing the buttons as slowly as I dare. All the while weighing up my options.

Show no emotion, Grace, says the psychologist in my head. *Don't let him know you're afraid.*

I'm down to my lingerie. I pause, as if allowing him to soak in the sight of it. After all, most women look sexier with their underwear on than off. But his head flicks toward me, telling me to get on with it. Like he has no time to waste with seduction.

I reach behind my back and release the clasp of my bra, letting it fall away from my breasts. Bend over and slip off my briefs. Then stand there, wondering what the fuck to do next.

The man stares back, his face entirely devoid of expression. And I realize that's what is making me so edgy. There are no tells. Those tiny physical signs people give off when they're nervous. Because clients always are, on a first time with someone new. Even the experienced punters.

But this guy, nothing. It's almost as if he's been trained to repress them. Or perhaps has none to repress.

"Get on the bed," he says, simply.

I lie on my back, legs slightly apart, hands half covering my breasts, feeling more exposed than ever before in my life. The room feels impossibly cold, though I checked the heating earlier and I know it's on.

He removes his clothes. To my surprise he already has an erection, its stiff bulk in unexpected contrast to the lack of enthusiasm in his demeanor. He takes a couple of strides toward the bed, picks up a condom from my bedside table, and deftly slides it on. Then lowers his body over me, nudging my legs apart with his knees, keeping his arms outstretched so his face and chest tower above me.

His eyes bore into mine. His expression still unreadable.

"So, *Grace*," he says. "Here we are."

The temperature in the room drops several more degrees. The breath catches in my throat and I swallow hard.

He knows my name.

He knows my fucking name.

My mind blanks in panic. Then suddenly I remember where I've seen him before. Something in the tilt of his jaw, the shadows forming in the angles of his face.

The funeral. The man outside the crematorium.

"Why are you here?" I ask, trying desperately to keep any trace of fear from my voice. "What do you want?"

He smiles, finally, but there's no warmth in it. "I came to deliver something, Grace. Two things." His tongue sliding over my name, caressing it.

"What?"

He lowers his torso and pushes himself inside me. I draw back instinctively, but he lunges forward and pinions me to the bed.

"First, a warning," he says, thrusting hard.

Breathe, I tell myself, my mind almost calm now, with the dread focus of knowing I'm in real danger. *Don't move or show you're intimidated in any way. Don't challenge his sense of control.*

Because this is clearly his game. He wants me to lose it, to be afraid.

"Your beautiful friend, Grace. The lovely Elisa—or should I say Amanda. You should learn from her mistakes."

At the sound of her name my whole body stiffens.

It's him. This is the man who killed her.

The certainty nearly makes me whimper in terror. My heart rate escalates into panic. I wonder if he can sense it through my skin.

He drives himself into me again with a force that makes me wince. I shift my hips to adjust his angle of penetration, to make it harder for him to get in deep. But I don't move a muscle in my face. He lowers himself so his chest lies heavy on mine, his face pressed against my cheek.

A couple more jabs, then his whole body shudders and stills. We lie there for a minute, and I wonder at what point he will kill me.

And I wonder too if I'll resist, or simply let him do it. All at once I feel too tired to fight the inevitable.

As if reading my mind the man lifts himself onto one elbow, putting his left hand round my neck. He stares deep into my eyes, something like a smile forming around his lips. His grip tightens. His fingers dig into my skin while his thumb traces the line of my throat. At the base, in the hollow where it joins my chest, he presses down. Not hard enough to stop my breathing. Just hard enough to make me very afraid indeed.

This is it, part of my mind declares, and I wonder what it will be like. How long it will take. I feel curiously detached from it all now. Resigned. As if this were always going to happen.

The pressure from his thumb increases. My breath stops somewhere in the base of my throat and I sense my body beginning to fight back, to lose control. *Fuck*, I think, tears springing to my eyes as the pain builds and my vision blurs.

Oh God . . . it really hurts.

Suddenly he releases his grip. Sits up, swinging his legs over the side of the bed, turning his back on me. I look around for anything I could hit him with. But there's nothing, just an alarm clock, several paperbacks. And the certain knowledge that the instant I tried to hurt him it would all be over.

He removes the condom, tying a knot in the end and wrapping it in a tissue. Puts the whole thing on the bedside table and pulls on his trousers. He dresses quickly, not even glancing in my direction. I lie still, watching, willing myself not to look at that little parcel.

The man shrugs on his jacket. Then walks back to the bedside table, picks up the tissue, and drops it into his coat pocket, his mouth jerking briefly into a smile.

I pull on my dressing gown and follow him to the door, my hand twitching with the need to lock it fast and hard behind him. But as he opens it, he turns, and my heart rate goes wild again.

"Oh yes, the second thing." His lips lift in a way that makes me shiver. "A message."

He raises his hand and strokes my cheek. The blood drains from my face and my pulse starts to sing in my head, and I feel his breath on my skin as he leans in and whispers three words in my ear. Three words like punches, like a kick to the guts.

"Michael says hello."

THIRTY-ONE

Tony examines me as I stand dripping on his porch. I forgot my umbrella and the five-minute walk from Clapham Common tube to his house on Navy Street has left me drenched.

"Okay, Stella, what's up? Why didn't you want to talk on the phone?"

I use my hand to wipe the rain from my face. "Are you going to let me in?"

Tony retreats a couple of steps and holds the door open. I go on through to the living room.

"Any chance of a drink?"

He gauges me for a second or two. "The thing is, Stella, I'm rather seeing someone at the moment, so if you're . . ."

"Give me a break, Tony," I snap. "Do I look like I'm here to drum up business?"

He runs his eyes over my wet hair. "I've got to admit, you're not looking your best. Unless you've really let your standards slip since I last saw you."

I glance down at the jeans and old sweater I pulled on as I left the flat. Hardly what you'd call seductive. I haven't checked in a mirror, but somehow I doubt my makeup is flawless.

"Right. I'm out of wine." Tony nods toward the kitchen. "But I've a few bottles of beer in the fridge. Or there's always gin and tonic."

"I'll have a G and T. Thanks."

I scan the living room while he pours the drinks. Piles of books and magazines still ranged along the walls. Clippings and torn-off pages of newspapers stacked in untidy bundles on the vast desk at the far end. Nothing seems to have changed since I was here last, though back then he'd have my clothes off by now, leaving me scant opportunity to inspect my surroundings.

I walk over to the large mantelpiece above the ancient gas fire, study Tony's collection of Japanese netsuke. A coiled hissing snake. A bald man with a fat belly and a sneering expression. A heap of tortoises, crawling over one another. Several rats. Assorted demons. I pick up the nearest. A dragon or some other kind of monster emerging from a cracked egg, one malevolent eye peeking out from beneath a folded wing. The detail in the carving is astonishing, the ivory smooth and warm in my hand. I have to force myself to put it down.

Next to the netsuke is a little glass snow scene, the kind you saw a lot when I was a kid. I lift the dome and give it a good shake. A miniature blizzard swirls around the tiny house among the trees.

A lump forms in my throat. My eyes begin to sting. All at once I feel lost. Utterly, hopelessly, irretrievably lost.

"There you go."

I spin round to find Tony offering me a tumbler of clear liquid. He's even added ice and a large slice of lemon.

"Cheers." He clinks his glass against mine. "Good to see you again."

Sinking onto the rather worn sofa, I stretch my legs out in front of me and try not to shiver. Tony sits in the armchair opposite, still watching me intently. He hasn't changed much since we last met a year ago. Same mess of wavy brown hair, always a tad too long. Broad, pleasant face, well lived in.

"So, what's up, Stella? Are you in some kind of trouble?"

I take a sip of the gin. It burns down my throat, making me shudder. But seconds later I feel warmer, and somewhat calmer.

"I suspect I am."

"Is it money? Because I'm sorry, but I haven't got—"

"No, it's not money."

"What, then?"

I gaze at him, wondering if my next words will save or damn me. Because the visit from that man an hour ago left me in no doubt that if I ever see him again, it will be the last time.

I swallow another mouthful of my drink. "I think there's something going on, something big. And I think it's to do with Elisa— Amanda Mansfield."

Tony's eyes narrow. "I saw it on the news. Fucking shame. She was a smashing girl."

He looks genuinely upset. I wasn't sure if he'd known her or not, though Tony's one of those dedicated punters who's worked his way through most of the women on the London scene. That said, I'd have thought Amanda was a bit outside his price range— her hourly rate was double mine.

"Are you saying you know something about her death?" Tony takes a large swig of his gin.

"I'm not sure. Maybe. I don't know what I know, if that makes any sense." I clench my jaw. I'm trembling, I realize, my teeth chattering. "But it seems I know enough to have hit a few nerves."

He leans forward. "You look terrible, Stella. What happened?"

I cough to clear my throat. "I don't suppose you've got any cigarettes?"

Tony frowns. "I don't smoke. I didn't think you did either."

I nod. Take a deep breath and exhale slowly. And tell him. More or less from the beginning. The party. The men. The deal on the TV. Tony's eyes widen at the mention of Edward Hardy. I don't need to explain who he is.

I relate everything I know about Amanda's death. The man at the funeral. The visit to the police station.

And the one that man just paid me.

Tony listens carefully, interrupting only to ask the odd question. When I finish he whistles, leans back in his armchair. Stares up at the ceiling, sucking his teeth.

"Jesus, Stella. This sounds like some major shit."

"Yeah," I say, grateful that he even believes me.

He drops his gaze to my face. "This man—the one who just came round—did he actually hurt you? You seem pretty shaken up."

"Not really. Just tried to freak me out."

"It appears he succeeded."

I don't reply, but it's true. *Michael says hello.* All the way over here I've been thinking what that means. Could he be some friend of Michael's? Has he got another con to track me down, rough me up a bit?

Or maybe he has nothing to do with Michael. But somebody who knew that even the mention of his name would be enough to intimidate me?

"So you want me to, what . . . look into this for you?" asks Tony, finishing his drink.

"I was hoping you could dig something up. You being a journalist."

"An ex-journalist. I got kicked off the paper, remember?"

I do remember, though he never explained why. Something to do with that whole phone-hacking scandal, I heard.

"Yes, but you must still have contacts—know people you can ask. I just want to find out who he is, this man who came to see me. And the others, at the party."

"Are you sure?" he says. "Sounds to me, whoever he was, that man was warning you off."

I swallow. Take another sip of my gin. "Wouldn't you?" I ask. "I mean, if it were you. Could you drop it? Walk away?"

He shakes his head and laughs. "Maybe not. But then I always was a stupid bastard who never knew what was good for me."

I let that rest as my answer.

He wrinkles his nose, thinking. "Why not go back to the police?"

I hesitate before I reply. "Because I'm not convinced that will get me anywhere except deeper into the shit." I focus on the timing of Alex's request to meet me at Westfield—only a few days after I spoke to DI Shaw. Was that what prompted his proposal?

I want you out of London.

Though I'm fairly sure that offer has now well and truly expired.

I drain the rest of my drink. Study the bottom of the glass, the half-melted ice cubes and the rather clumsy chunk of lemon. "Besides, what new evidence have I got for the police? I'm not exactly what you'd call a credible witness."

Tony doesn't respond, but I can see he takes my point.

We sit there in silence for a minute or so. I hear a key in the front door. Two voices and footsteps on the stairs.

I glance up at Tony.

"Lodgers," he says. "Students. Got to pay the bills somehow." He thinks for a while. Gets to his feet. "All right. I'll make some calls."

"Thanks," I say as Tony accompanies me to the door. His expression is kinder than when I arrived, edged now with concern. "Listen, Stella, I've no idea what's going on or even if you're simply paranoid . . ."

I stiffen at his words. He raises a hand.

"Hear me out. I'm suggesting you get out of town for a while. I'll be as discreet as possible, but I can't guarantee that my asking questions won't cause a few ripples. You need to understand that."

I nod.

"So perhaps it would be wise to make yourself scarce. Until we've got a better idea what we're dealing with."

"Okay."

He puts a hand on my shoulder, then pulls me into a hug. "Take good care of yourself, all right? I'll get back to you as quickly as I can."

I tighten my coat around me. Glance toward the road, the rain illuminated by the streetlight.

"Thanks," I say, "and good for you."

"What for?"

"Finding someone you're serious about. I must admit I had you down as a serial polygamist."

"You mean one of those sad bastards on PunterWeb who screws all the girls and gets reductions for good reviews."

"You deserved the discount." I manage a grin. "You always had a way with words."

THIRTY-TWO

G race!"

I spot Kristen standing in front of the huge cross section of an ancient sequoia at the top of the stairs. It towers behind her, like a giant wooden sun, as she scans the gallery below.

Her smile is fleeting as I climb to meet her. "How are you?" I ask, though one glance tells me that's a stupid question.

"Thanks for coming at such short notice."

Kristen's text, sent late last night, was brief and urgent. The kind you can't ignore. "Is there somewhere quieter we can go?" she asks, glancing around.

I think quickly. "There's a café round the back of the stairs. I saw the signs as I came in."

We descend toward the huge diplodocus skeleton dominating the ground floor of the Natural History Museum. I'd forgotten how beautiful this place is, inside and out. Maybe one day I'll come back.

"I wanted to see it one last time," says Kristen, as if reading my mind.

"One last time?"

She looks directly at me. "I'm moving back to Scotland."

So this is why she wanted to meet. I refrain from asking more until we're seated in the café, with hot drinks and a slab of fruitcake. The museum has been open only half an hour and the place is nearly deserted; only a couple of women at the far end, deep in conversation.

Kristen cradles her mug of tea in her hands, looking tired and fragile. She's removed her coat but is still wearing her thick scarf, despite the heat indoors.

"So why are you leaving?"

Kristen's gaze again slides away from mine. I'm beginning to wonder whether I've done something to upset her. "I can't meet the mortgage payments on my own. And Amanda's family want her half of the equity."

"Jesus. Can they do that?"

"She didn't make a will. We're not married. They're her next of kin."

I flash back to the funeral, to the tall blond woman who so resembled Amanda. The man with the manicured beard. Wonder if they have any idea how much pain they're causing the person their daughter loved. Grief makes you selfish, I muse, studying the hollows beneath Kristen's eyes. Blinds you to other people's suffering.

Her expression is so wretched I lean forward and pat her hand. "Come on, Kristen, you can fight that. You have rights. It's the last thing Amanda would have wanted."

She presses her lips together. Blinks a few times, then looks away again. I sense there's something she's holding back.

"Have the police come up with anything yet?" I ask.

Her gaze swings back to meet mine. "I've no idea. They don't tell me a thing." She clears her throat. "I take it you didn't get any- where either."

I stare at her, surprised. How does she know about my interview? Would they have told her?

I shake my head. "I'm sorry. I should have said something to you."

"Why did you go to them?" Her tone is taut, panicked.

I shrug. "I don't know. I thought maybe I could help. All that stuff that doesn't add up over Amanda's death. I wanted them to take it seriously."

Kristen stares at me. Sizing me up. "I think you should drop it, Grace. The whole thing. Forget about Amanda, about what happened, all of it."

I frown. "Why? Don't you want to know?"

She looks down at the table. "You're making everything worse. I know you don't mean to, but . . ."

"How do you mean, *worse*?"

She swallows. Her eyes dart around the café, then come back to rest on mine.

"I had a visit."

"A visit? Who from?"

"This . . . this man." She takes a deep breath.

Everything around me seems to recede. The building, the noise, the people—all suddenly nothing more than a distant background.

"What man, Kristen?"

"I don't know who he was," she says in a near whisper. "He didn't give a name." She looks up into my eyes, her face pale. "But he was scary, Grace. Really fucking scary."

My throat feels too dry to swallow.

"What did he look like?"

She shrugs. "Medium height. Dark hair. A funny indent on his cheek. Like a pockmark, only bigger."

Him. Who else?

"What did he say?"

She sighs. Rubs her left eye. I notice her hands are trembling.

"Nothing specific. It was all sort of suggested. But the gist seemed to be that stirring things up wouldn't be in anyone's interests. That it was best just to let Amanda go."

"Stirring things up?"

Her eyes fix on mine. She clears her throat. "He said he knew you'd been to see them—the police, I mean—and that it really wasn't a good idea. He said he—" She stops. Bites her lip.

"Tell me."

"He said he'd hate there to be any more casualties."

I feel the color bleach from my face. I clench my hand, trying to breathe evenly.

"And he asked me to give you a message."

"What?"

She keeps her gaze fixed on mine as she pulls the scarf away from her neck. I see a line of deep purple bruises circling her throat. Some small and round, like fingertips.

I gasp. "Jesus . . . oh fuck, Kristen . . ."

Kristen adjusts her scarf back up over the bruises.

"When?" I stammer.

"Yesterday."

Fuck. He must have gone from her to me. Or vice versa. "We should go back to the police," I say. "Now. Both of us."

She shakes her head.

"Yes!" I hiss. "Listen to me, Kristen. We must show them. They can't ignore this."

"The burglary," she says almost inaudibly. "I'm not sure it was druggies."

"Who told you that? The detective?"

"I'm not stupid, Grace. I can work things out for myself. I reckon they were looking for something."

"But you said they stole money. Amanda's jewelry."

Kristen shrugs. "I reckon that was just to make it look like a burglary."

A hitch in my throat as I swallow. "So what do you think they were after?"

She peers right into my eyes. Hesitating. Affirming something in me.

"Kristen, listen, you don't have to tell me. Not if you don't want to."

She runs her tongue over her lips, then appears to come to a decision. Pulls her purse out of her bag. At first I assume she's going to offer me money for the tea. Instead she reaches inside and removes something I can't quite see.

"Hold out your hand."

I look at her, perplexed, but do as she says. She places it into my palm. I stare at the small rectangle of black plastic. "What is it?"

"An SD card. The kind you use in cameras and computers."

I lift my eyes to hers. "This was Amanda's?"

She nods.

"Where did you find it?"

"Between one of the bed slats and the bed frame. It fell out when I was taking the thing apart yesterday."

I inhale slowly. Feel a buzz of curiosity. Underneath, deeper, an insistent hum of dread.

"What's on it? Have you looked?"

"It's a list," she says, pausing to gulp down the rest of her tea. "Of all the clients Elisa ever saw—or at least, a lot of them." Her eyes lift to survey the café, but it's empty now, the two women gone. "And details about them, things they told her, other things she must have found out. And . . ."

She falters. I glance at the little piece of plastic, lift my eyes back up to her face.

"Pictures." She says the word quietly, holding my gaze. Again, that sense she's gauging my reaction.

"Photos?"

"Taken with her phone, I'm guessing."

"Showing what?"

She ignores my question while continuing to study my expression. "You mean you don't know?"

"No." I shake my head. "Kristen, honestly, I've *no* idea what you're talking about."

A few more seconds of silence. Then her lips twitch in anticipation of her next words. "Not only pictures, Grace. Videos too."

She shifts in her seat, eyes suddenly unable to meet mine. "Of Amanda doing stuff with these men."

"Stuff . . . you mean sex?"

She nods, clearly embarrassed. "But not just Amanda . . ." Her cheeks flush. She looks away.

I stare at her. Then finally I get it. "You mean *me*?" My mouth drops open. "You're saying I'm on this too?"

"You. And Janine. At that last party you did together."

"Shit."

An image of Amanda holding her phone when I was with Harry and Rob. Not texting, I realize, with a drop in my stomach like vertigo. Not fucking texting at all.

That crap about a family crisis. I feel a stab of anger, of betrayal. Then fear. *Amanda, Jesus. Why?*

"That's one reason I'm giving it to you." Kristen's voice slices through my thoughts. "It's not the sort of thing you'd want getting into anybody else's hands. Especially not the police."

I take a deep breath. Try to focus on what she's saying.

She closes her eyes briefly. Presses the tips of her fingers into her forehead. "She was blackmailing them, Grace. And not just for a few quid."

My jaw drops, my gazed fixed on her face. I can't speak for ages. Maybe a minute.

"Jesus . . . are you sure?" For a moment I wonder if the stress of Amanda's death, the burglary, her encounter with that man, has somehow sent Kristen over the edge.

"Take a look." She nods at the card. "You'll see."

I close my fingers around it. Find myself scanning the empty café. Checking.

"Fuck, Kristen," I breathe. Realize my hand is trembling.

"There were bank details on it too. Not the account she used normally. I managed to work out her password, checked it out online."

"How much?" My mouth can barely form the words.

"Half a million. Slightly more."

"Fuck." Surprise stiffens my features. If anyone were watching, the shock on my face would be easy to read.

"She's been stashing money away for years, making deposits nearly every month. Usually a good few thousand pounds or more."

Her eyes glistening with tears. And something else. Shame? Anger?

"I mean . . . hell . . . how else could Amanda get that kind of money?" She balls her fists and presses them against the table. "She always said she was going to get out soon, but that she wanted to earn enough for us to be secure. I never imagined she meant like this."

I look at her. "Are you going to keep it? The money, that is."

Kristen glares at me. "I don't want it," she says indignantly. "I don't want a fucking thing to do with it."

"So what are you going to do with it?"

She sighs. "I considered handing it over to the police. I did. I know I should, but I can't bear the idea of anybody . . ." She stops. Presses her fist to her mouth. "I don't want anyone knowing that about Amanda. Or seeing those . . . those things."

Her voice trails off. Her eyes fill with tears again. She lowers her clenched hands, her knuckles white.

My mind flashes back to the party. What Kristen must have seen in those pictures. I can hardly meet her gaze when she raises her head.

"So, no police, okay? I know it's wrong, but it's what I want."

I open my hand. Pass the SD card back to her.

"No." She waves it away. "You have it. I never want to set eyes on it again."

"But the bank details . . ."

"I've deleted them."

"So why give this to me?"

She swallows, her lips beginning to tremble. "God, I miss her so much, Grace, and at the same time I'm so, so angry with her for leaving me in this mess. These last few days I've been thinking that, if she were still here, I'd probably kill her myself."

I look at her, surprised by the vehemence in her voice.

"I can't stop going through it all. Who he was, the man that murdered her. Why she met up with him. The ridiculous risk she was taking."

A tear rolls over her left cheek, pursued by another. She wipes them away with the tips of her fingers. I try to imagine what Kristen was like before all this. How happiness or contentment would have lifted her features. I've only known her unhappy, I think; only seen this broken side of her.

And all I've done is make her impossible situation worse.

"Grace . . ." Her voice so quiet I can hardly hear what she's saying. "Do you reckon this is what got Amanda killed?"

I gaze at the black rectangle in my hand. Amanda must have gone after someone. Only this time she picked the wrong man.

Or men.

You should learn from her mistakes.

I take her hand. "Kristen, I'm sure she was careful. You know she—" I stop dead. The expression on her face tells me to go no further. Fierce and furious. Desperate.

"I don't know," I continue. "Maybe," I say more honestly.

I clutch the chip in my fingers. Consider what it cost Kristen to bring it to me—she had no idea, after all, if I was in on the blackmail. And the risk she's running today, simply by being here.

The risk both of us are running.

I glance around again, but we're still alone. "I don't understand though why you're giving it to me. Why not just throw it away?"

"I was going to destroy it," she says. "Pretend it never existed, because I'm fairly sure he . . . that man isn't aware of it. If he were, I'm certain you wouldn't have it now."

I meet her eyes. I suspect she's right.

"So I figured you might need it. That maybe you could use it in some way to make them leave you alone."

I blink. "And you, Kristen? What about you?"

"I'm taking his advice." She puts her purse back into her bag. "I'm getting as far away from here, and all this, as possible."

"When are you going?"

"Tomorrow."

"Where . . ." I pause. Hold up my hand. On second thought, perhaps it's better not to know.

She leans over and writes a number on the napkin. "I've got a new mobile phone, a pay-as-you-go. Untraceable." She laughs. "At least Amanda taught me that much." She pushes it over to me. "In case you ever need to get in touch."

I pick up the napkin and stuff it in my pocket. We both stand. Kristen pulls on her coat with such a dazed expression that I can hardly bear it. I step forward and wrap my arms around her, suddenly reluctant to let her go.

"You don't think this kind of thing could be real, do you?" she says when I release her. "Part of me can't believe it's actually happening, that I must be imagining it."

She adjusts the scarf around her neck. Looks me right in the eyes. "But the rest of me has never been so scared in my entire life."

THIRTY-THREE

I go straight back to my flat. Double-lock the door behind me and cancel my afternoon appointment, pleading a cold. The client sounds disgruntled, like not getting his rocks off is a major inconvenience.

Tough.

I boot up my laptop, hardly able to bear the minute or so it takes for all the icons to settle on the screen. Consider running back out and buying that pack of cigarettes.

"Focus, Grace," I mutter to myself as the egg timer over my cursor finally disappears. I insert the SD card into the little slot below the mouse pad. "Import pictures and documents?" my computer asks. I click "No," then bring up the file directory and open the Removable Disk icon.

About thirty files fill the screen, each headed with initials. I click on the first—"DRH." It reveals a Word document and half a dozen photographs. I glance through them. They're slightly blurred and obviously taken in a hurry, but you can plainly see a man in various poses, all of them nude. All of them incriminating.

The last few images have a Movie icon next to them. I hover over the first and press Play. A man lies on the bed, looking straight at me.

"What the hell are you doing, Elisa?" His tone commanding. A little plummy.

A woman answers in the background. "Hang on a sec. Just switching it off."

Seconds later Amanda comes into view. She's wearing her hair piled loosely on top of her head, a style that makes her look particularly glamorous. She climbs astride the man and slowly lowers herself onto him.

"Richard," she says teasingly. "You really have missed me, haven't you?"

The man laughs. "You know damn well I'd see you every day if I could afford it."

The angle of the film is slightly skewed, their heads bobbing in and out of shot. I'm guessing Amanda propped the phone up somewhere inconspicuous. On a chair, maybe, piled with clothes, or on the desk.

I imagine her routine. Photos would be simple enough. Pretend you've got a text come in or you've forgotten to turn off your mobile. Take a sneaky snap or two while fiddling with your phone, or set the delay to get a shot of the action. Videos would be even easier—simply press record and prop the phone somewhere with a view of the bed.

Amanda's voice pulls my attention back to the video. I can't quite hear what she's saying, but I can tell it's dirty. Nothing much from him. Murmuring. The odd incoherent grunt. The clip goes on for nearly five minutes, then abruptly ends. Maybe the phone ran out of battery, or perhaps she put it on a timer. After all, how much do you need to blackmail somebody?

Not much.

Amanda, I think as I click open the Word file accompanying the pictures, *definitely not just a beautiful face*.

The document is only one page long. "Richard David Harris," it says at the top. Below, a list of details:

Chairman of the Harris Clothing Group.
Age 57.
Married to Louisa.
Two kids—John and Geoffrey.
The Beeches, Guildford Road, Godalming, Surrey.

Below that another column of figures:

15/4/13—£1,500
13/7/13—£1,000
1/3/14—£1,000

Right at the end is a mobile number, along with an e-mail address. An anonymous Gmail account—presumably the one she used to contact him.

I click back to the first picture. Check the Properties tab to see when it was taken. Ice in my stomach as I read the date.

Three weeks before the initial payment.

The next file has only two photos. A man in his forties, lean and muscular. And another video. This one more distinct, though less dialogue. Amanda getting fucked from behind, his body obscuring hers so I can't tell exactly what he's doing, but I guess for Amanda's purposes it hardly mattered.

The Word document tells me this is John Leesham, manager of a well-known football team. He has a wife named Audrey, one daughter, and a house in Cheltenham with what I suspect is a good address.

He paid her over five thousand—one lump sum in April last year.

I work my way through the rest of the files, which appear to be in date order. The lineup includes a TV presenter, the editor of a tabloid newspaper, and the head of a large private school, as well as a motley collection of MDs and CEOs—at least half in banking. And four men in government—two Conservative MPs, a top-ranking civil servant, and a Labour backbencher.

Some of them have given Amanda several smaller amounts; others what look like larger, one-off payments.

I pause halfway through. Calculate that she had amassed nearly three hundred thousand by last summer alone. I sit back in my seat. I'm sweating, my fingers sticky on the keys.

So easy, when you think about it. So easy, if you're prepared to cross that line. I find I'm feeling almost sorry for these men who got so much more than the mind-blowing sex they bargained for.

Taking a deep breath, I carry on. The videos become noticeably sharper, the sound less tinny. Obviously Amanda upgraded her phone, got one with a better camera. God knows, she could afford it.

I force myself to check every file, every single photo and video, in case there's more to discover. After a while it's like viewing a series of tedious amateur porn movies. I notice Amanda talks a lot, describing what she's going to do in graphic detail. Less for titillation, I realize, than to implicate these men even further.

"You cunning little minx," I mutter, pondering the psychology behind all this. Surely it wasn't just about the money. There's something playful in Amanda's manner; not quite coquettish, more like she's toying with them.

Which, of course, she was.

What happened to her? I wonder as I watch Amanda fellating an MP. What lay beneath the contempt she clearly harbored for these men? Because they're not all bad, those who visit women like us. They're bored, they're lonely, they're curious—they're simply human.

They surely don't deserve this.

I open the second-to-last file. And freeze. My stomach flips as I recognize the face staring back at me.

"Harry Arthur Elliott," says the Word file. "Fifty years old. Senior partner at Trellum, Bailey and Company."

I switch into Google. Trellum, Bailey and Company turns out to be a sizable private equity firm, specialists in emerging markets. Harry is one of its top dogs, by the look of it. I go back to the photos. His ruddy face beams out at me. I check the stats. Two sons, both at a top private school.

Then I see it. At the bottom of the document is a single figure: £15,000. The largest sum Amanda ever demanded.

And no payment date.

There's only one video. I click the Start arrow. A flinch inside tells me what's coming. Harry, kneeling behind a girl with mid-length dark hair. His hands clamped around her hips as he eases his way into her anus. Beneath her, another man, his face obscured by the angle of the shot.

Me. Sandwiched between Harry and Rob.

"You enjoy fucking girls up the arse, don't you, Harry?" Amanda's voice. Mocking, almost derisive. "Does it make you feel big and powerful?"

Did she really say that? I don't remember. I guess I was too busy to notice.

The girl in the image looks up into the lens. Her eyes widen, her face contracting into a frown as she spots Amanda fiddling with her phone.

I can't bear to watch any more. I get up and make myself a cup of tea and stand by the kitchen window, waiting for it to cool. It's getting dark outside, and there's no one much around. A couple struggling to get a buggy into the boot of a car. At the end of the road, on the other side of the street, a man leaning against the wall of the pub on the corner, smoking. His face is turned in my direction, though it's too far away to see clearly.

Am I under surveillance? Is that possible? Or just paranoid?

I stare as he drops the cigarette on the ground, grinds it under his shoe, and disappears back into the pub.

A draft pushed its way through the gap in the sash window, making me shiver. Would this be enough to go to the police? I wonder. I know I promised Kristen I wouldn't, but surely it's the most sensible thing to do? I have proof now. They'll have to take all this seriously.

But what if they don't? I think, remembering those marks on Kristen's neck, dark and livid. And even if they did take it all on board, would they be able to protect Kristen? Or me?

I go back to my laptop and force myself to open the last file on the list. Inside are some pictures from the party. Several of me with Edward Hardy. Christ, how did Amanda get those? She must have sneaked into the bedroom when we were screwing. Unless she'd already set up a camera in the room.

I examine the remaining photos. Study their faces. Hardy. Harry's friend Rob.

And Alex. He stares back at me, his expression blank yet somehow challenging. I feel a lurch inside. A kind of ache.

I open the accompanying Word document. Hardy's listed there, with his full ministerial title—Amanda had obviously caught the news reports. I wonder if she was planning to blackmail him too, or decided that was too risky. Robert Mulligan, it says next to the picture of Rob, along with his job title and the name of Harry's bank.

My eyes drop down to see what Amanda had dug up on Alex. But there's nothing. Clearly she hadn't yet worked out who he was.

I switch to the Internet, bring up Hotmail, and create a new e-mail address. I know strictly I should do it from a different computer, to mask my ISP, but there isn't time. From this new account I paste in Tony's address and type "The Others" into the subject line. Below I paste pictures of Harry, Rob, and Alex, along with those details I have. I add a note that I'm leaving town for a while, and tell him to contact me via this address.

The second I've sent it I delete the message from the e-mail site and shut down my computer, removing the SD card. I hold it between my fingers and stare at it for a few moments. So small, so insignificant.

"Amanda," I mutter out loud, picturing her beguiling smile, that gorgeous mask she wore to the party. Hiding so much more than any of us could ever have guessed.

"Jesus Christ, Amanda. What the fuck were you thinking?"

THIRTY-FOUR

WEDNESDAY, 1 APRIL

There's nothing here. I drive along the seafront searching for Ryall Close. Double back at the roundabout where the high street meets the promenade, craning in the darkness to read the road signs.

Stacy said it was just off the main road. Told me I couldn't bloody miss it.

I glide past a desultory-looking block of flats and several ugly beach chalets masquerading as guest houses, vacancy signs swaying in the wind. Several pebble-dashed bungalows. Even in the dark I can see it's a far cry from the cheerful little resort I went to with Rachel and Tim. Of all the coastal towns of the South West, I seem to have landed up in the most desolate.

Pulling up next to the seawall, I lean my head against the side window and watch the rain slashing across the windscreen. I've been driving for five hours solid and have the kind of headache that makes you want to throw up. Why didn't I hire the car with the GPS? It was only an extra fifty quid for the week. But I was paying in cash and hadn't reckoned on needing quite so much of it—as it is, I got the smallest model on the forecourt.

I lift my head and scan the horizon. In the distance, on the outskirts of the town, glows a giant luminous Tesco sign. I set off toward it, pulling in at the adjacent garage.

"Could you point me toward Ryall Close?"

The man behind the counter thinks for a second, then draws me a map on the back of a discarded till receipt.

"Can't miss it, love. Just off the main road."

I detour into the car park and dash into the store to pick up some provisions. Only the basics. Plus an umbrella and a new phone. I choose the cheapest, and pay for everything in cash.

Five minutes later I find the squat little bungalow at the end of a cul-de-sac. Cliffview Cottage. Finally.

I'm there again.

In that room, in that flat, on a stained mattress on the floor. It's chilly. My skin prickles, the film of sweat where my belly had touched his is cooling now that he's peeled himself away.

He's standing by the window, bare chested, jeans slouching low on his hips, looking over the estate and the city beyond. Just standing there, looking out that window, and then he turns and fixes me with those blank blue eyes and he says, "You shouldn't have done that, Grace."

And I wake. I wake with a cry and a gasp and the sensation that I'm falling, plunging downward through the bed, through the floor, through the earth beneath. Sweat soaks the T-shirt and knickers I fell asleep in. I'm sticky and clammy and cold all at once.

Things fall apart.

I sit up, straining to take in my surroundings, the half-light of approaching dawn barely visible behind the thin curtains. No

sound, except for the ringing in my ears, a high-pitched whine
I've been spared in London's ceaseless clamor.

The bed is a double, and I'm tucked between a sheet and the thick
cream cotton bedspread. Opposite looms a large wooden wardrobe,
a thin strip of mirror down the central panel. On either side of me
are two matching bedside tables, their varnish orange with age.

I peer into the mirror. A dark shadow for a reflection. I lie back,
struggling to remember where I am.

My friend Stacy from the crisis center. Her holiday home in
Devon.

Yesterday's relief at leaving the city seems to have curdled during
the night. My mind hums with anxiety. I feel almost paralyzed with
dread, dregs of that headache still lingering like an echo in my skull.

Deep in my stomach something churns. I stumble into the bathroom and throw up into the toilet bowl. Nothing much to show
for it, but the retching sensation is so violent, so shocking, I'm left
weak and shaky even after it subsides. I lean on the basin, trying
to ignore the acrid smell of vomit and damp, then run the cold
water, scooping several handfuls into my mouth, forcing myself to
breathe slowly until the panic recedes.

Michael says hello.

One sentence and here he is, resurrected from my five-year
attempt to bury him in the deepest recesses of my mind. My own
special purgatory, the penance for my sins.

Michael. He may be locked up, but that man let him loose in
my head. Knowing, I'm sure now, the damage he would do.

I dress quickly, shivering, my breath visible in the frosty air of
the bedroom, and find the thermostat in the hallway. I twist the
dial, listening for a responding click in the central heating. Nothing.
Maybe there's a switch somewhere. I search in the nearby cupboard,
around the lagging surrounding the hot-water tank, but find only
dust balls and an old pair of swimming trunks. Child-size.

Outside, the streetlights are still visible against the watery sunrise. I pick up my new phone and text Stacy to let her know I
arrived. In the kitchen I find the supermarket bag I dumped on the
table before collapsing into bed, and confirm I forgot to buy coffee
or anything for breakfast. A cursory scan inside the cupboards
reveals nothing besides a pack of aging peppermint tea bags and
a jar of instant that looks like it's been here since Stacy's aunt died
and left the place to her.

I pull on my coat and boots and set off into town. Halfway
there I realize that nowhere will be open yet, this not being the
city. So I turn left toward the seafront. The rain has stopped, but
the streets are still lagooned with puddles. It's nearly light, the sky
above the sea watery and pale, and I can see properly now just
what a dreary little place this is. I can't imagine spending a week
here, let alone a summer. Or a life.

But the sea is the sea wherever you are, so I trudge down to
where the water laps and teases the shingle. I watch the restless
gray waves for a minute or two, then pick my way along the beach,
listening to the soothing suck and swish of the tide. It's hard going,
the stones constantly subsiding under my feet, and it takes nearly
fifteen minutes to reach the distant point where the headland nar-
rows to a few rocks covered in greeny black seaweed.

I stop underneath the cliffs, sheer crags of red mud. Not very
stable, judging by the landslips slumping toward the tide line, the
absence of any vegetation suggesting recent collapse. Some thirty
feet up several stunted pine trees are growing precariously close
to the edge. I stare at them for a few minutes, wondering if they
have any sense of their predicament.

Christ, it's cold. The wind nips my face and sidles between my
neck and my coat and I make a mental note to buy myself a scarf
when the shops open. I take my phone out of my pocket and check
the time.

Six fifty-nine.

I turn and climb the steps to the concrete promenade separating the town from the sea and head back toward civilization. Walk past the little rotunda café, closed up for the winter, boards over the windows and a padlock on the door. Farther along, a stretch of empty ground. This must be where they put the beach huts in summer. Stacy mentioned you could rent one in high season, though quite why you'd want to sit in a glorified shed and stare at this desultory little patch of coastline is beyond me.

I pass a block of toilets, a small gravel garden surrounding a large rusty anchor, and, at intervals, huge metal gates guarding the various entrances to the promenade.

Sea defenses, I realize—the last resort against storms and high tides. God only knows what this place is like in winter.

Up on the high street most of the shop windows are dark. I'm on the verge of giving up and going back to the house when I notice a light on in a small café farther up the hill.

The man behind the counter looks up from his newspaper.

"Are you open?"

"Just about." He smiles, folding his paper. "Given you're so keen. What would you like?"

I scan the menu board above the counter. "A cup of tea. And a couple of slices of toast, if it's possible."

"That I can manage."

He disappears into the little kitchen out the back. I sit at one of the tables by the window, watching a few cars climb the hill toward me and disappear inland. Other than that, the town appears deserted.

Somehow putting this distance between myself and London has brought everything into sharper focus. My mind churns over all that's happened. Amanda's death. The blackmail. That man's hands around my throat, those bruises on Kristen's neck.

Feeling, in some vital way, that it's all my fault. That everything I've done—or tried to do—has only made the whole situation worse.

What the fuck can I do to put it right?

As I struggle for an answer, I sense my anxiety settle into something darker, bleaker. I've known this, I think, exploring the feeling, its depth and texture. Remember emerging from the hospital nearly five years ago, brain numbed by antidepressants, to face a wasteland no medication could restore. Different situation now, granted, but the tone is familiar. The sense of disintegration, of options narrowing.

What did I do then? The only thing you can do when you've tried and failed to end the life you have—construct a new one. And make it so very different that nothing can ever touch you again. Or so I wanted to believe.

So what to do this time?

I have absolutely no idea.

"Here you go, love." The café owner places a large mug of tea and two slices of buttered toast in front of me.

I thank him and take a tentative sip of tea. It's hot, strong, and bracing, and instantly I feel a little better. The toast helps too, and by the time I pay and walk out the door, I've found the strength to face the rest of the day.

THIRTY-FIVE

Time passes more slowly this far from the capital, like a spaceship light years from Earth. With so little to fill them, the hours stretch out before me as a wilderness, nothing on the horizon except my next meal, and the more distant prospect of bed and sleep.

I shun the Tesco megastore and explore the high street. The usual suspects—Boots and WHSmith and a sizable collection of charity shops. I stock up in the independent grocery near the library, cooking myself the kind of comfort food I haven't eaten in years. Bangers and mash and shepherd's pie, a rich creamy curry and a stodgy cauliflower cheese. Even an apple crumble. I become addicted to those cheap little cheesecakes you get in plastic tubs, their cloying sweetness an antidote to the general cheerlessness of the landscape—within and without.

My days quickly assume their own rhythm. Every morning I go to the café for toast and strong tea. An affable greeting from the owner, but beyond asking how I am, he leaves me to eat my breakfast in peace.

Afterward I lug my laptop up to the Costa in what passes for the town's shopping precinct and check my e-mails using the free Wi-Fi. Same routine every day. Delete all the junk mail, dumping client inquiries into a separate folder. Then open what's left.

There's never much. No word from Rachel, and so far none from Tony. One—after a few days—from Stacy explaining how to turn on the heating, though by this time I've bought thermals and a thicker sweater and have grown used to the chill.

Nothing from Alex. Or Ben.

A couple of afternoons, when spring gets the better of winter, I venture out in the car. I don't plan where I'm going—I have no map—just drive and see where I end up. I discover a resort a little way up the coast. It's famously appealing, but its studied air of quaintness, its arty gift shops, and boutique cafés seem contrived. Too obvious, somehow.

Another trip lands me up in a well-to-do market town with a handsome stone church and an impossibly chintzy tea shop on the central square where I'm served a cream tea by a large man in an apron, his bulk in painful contrast to all the flowery delicacy. He looks as if he should be off grappling with bullocks in some sodden field rather than serving scones and jam on rose-motif china.

Most of all I enjoy pottering around the country lanes, irritating more time-pressed locals with my sedateness behind the wheel. This is how I'll drive when I am old, I imagine. Assuming I ever make it. This is how you descend into old age, I realize—first ironically, then unavoidably.

Sometimes as I'm driving I find myself thinking about my ex. Wondering how he's getting on. Part of me would like to call, to find out; another tells me to leave well alone.

Other times I catch myself rerunning that video in my head, the one Amanda took at the party. I see that girl, pinioned between

Rob and Harry, staring into her phone camera. The look of shock and mild outrage on her face as she frowns into the lens.

Stella.

Leaving me wondering who the fuck she really is.

Evenings are the best. Toward dusk, I walk along the beach. It's more pleasant at night, the soft orange glow of the lamps on the seafront lending the place a coziness it lacks in daylight. It's quieter too, once the gulls have hit the sack. By day the seagulls own this town, perching on rooftops, screeching and catcalling like pissed-up youths.

Usually at this time there's no one around except a few people walking dogs and the odd fisherman casting off from the shoreline. Now and then a bunch of bored-looking teenagers, hanging out in the concrete shelters under the cliff, the tantalizing smell of cigarette smoke and the occasional spliff mingling with the air of palpable boredom.

I remember how I felt at their age, on the cusp of adulthood, waiting to find out what numbers you'd drawn in life's genetic lottery. A good brain or a pretty face the winning ticket to a less tedious existence; neither, and likely as not you were destined for dull anonymity, a life stalled in the mundane.

Or like me, I think, hovering somewhere in between, with maybe four numbers out of a possible six. Making the best of things.

Or possibly the worst.

Back at the cottage I hole up in the lounge, huddling on the sofa, draped in the wool blanket found in the bedroom wardrobe. I watch telly on the bulky old set in the alcove—the picture isn't great, but at least it works. I stick to sitcoms, soap operas, and anodyne chat shows. TV analgesia. Nothing that might upset the delicate mental equilibrium I've established in this unlikely bolt-hole.

Time out, I tell myself whenever anxiety surfaces about my self-enforced exile. I'm just taking time out. Like a satellite orbiting Earth, continuously falling at a speed and angle that keeps it suspended in space, safe from the turbulence below.

And it seems to agree with me, this hiatus. In a week I've rounded out, my jeans beginning to pinch around my waist and thighs, my pubic hair reclaiming whole areas razed by wax and razors. I haven't bothered with makeup since I got here. I'm comfortably numb, I realize, as London recedes in my mind. I feel safe here, anonymous. Finally off everyone's radar.

This morning, as I drag myself out of bed, it occurs to me that I could stay. I could rent somewhere, one of those shabby little flats off the seafront. Get a job when my savings run out. Work in a tea shop or behind the tills at Tesco.

Over breakfast in the café I ponder how easy it would be to set up a new life under a different name. I could change it by deed poll, apply for a new passport—should I ever need one. I'd live alone, confining myself to brief chats with neighbors or customers. I'd get hairy and fat and no one would care—least of all me.

Not an island, exactly, but close enough. A sanctuary of sorts.

It's a sustaining thought. A comforting one.

At least until I open my e-mails.

THIRTY-SIX

Back down to earth with a sickening bump, before I even read them.

My eyes gravitate to the first, sent from an address I haven't seen for several years. I stare at it for a while, my finger hovering over the Delete button. Eventually I click it open.

It's not from my father, but his wife. His second wife.

She informs me, curtly, that my father's heart condition has taken a turn for the worse. And suggests pointedly that I might like to ring him.

Thank you, Julia. I can think of nothing I want to do less.

I read the e-mail several times over. Let its import sink in. So my father wants to talk to me. He really must be sick. We've not spoken since the trial, since he told me I disgusted him and that he didn't want anything more to do with me.

Don't imagine for a minute that this absolves you, Grace. Nothing absolves you of what you did.

His exact words. A life sentence—in contrast to the one they gave Michael.

I close the e-mail and open the next. It's from Tony. Finally.

"I've got news. Let's meet tomorrow."

I haven't the heart to cook on my last evening in the bungalow, so order a takeaway from the garishly decorated Indian on the corner of the shopping plaza. I watch a show about computer dating while shoveling doughy naan bread and biryani into my mouth, barely tasting any of it.

None of the carefully matched blind dates lead to anything. So much for science. I switch off the TV, bored. I try reading the paperback I picked up in a charity shop, but the words flatline on the page.

Fuck. I've been jolted out of orbit. I've lost my equilibrium and all those nerve endings that have been happily anesthetized are reviving, leaving me tense and edgy. Restless as hell.

Don't do it, Grace. You know you'll be wasting your time.

I can't stand it any longer. I pick up the phone and dial his number. It rings over and over, and I fight the urge to end the call before he answers. A little worm of worry when I think he won't.

"Hello?"

In that one word I hear the toll that illness and advancing age have taken on my father.

"It's me. Grace."

Silence at the end of the line. Perhaps a full ten seconds before he speaks.

"Grace."

It's a statement. A fact. Nothing else.

"Julia e-mailed me. She said you've been ill."

"Yes."

I swallow. "How are you, then?"

Another long pause. "Better than I was. Thank you for asking."

There's just the faintest edge of complaint in his voice. The perpetually injured tone of the lifelong narcissist. I suppress a sigh, noting the absence of any inquiry into my well-being.

"I was wondering if I was ever going to hear from you again." My father's resentment now undisguised.

"It was you who said you didn't want any more contact, Dad," I remind him.

He makes no response to this. I hear him cough, then clear his throat. A distant voice murmurs in the background. Julia, maybe? Or perhaps the TV.

I have a pain in my chest like heartburn. *I can't do this again*, I think, remembering how he always manages to reduce me to this.

Hopeless. Flawed. Wanting.

A psychology degree, three years training in clinical therapy, five years in practice, and my father can still make me feel like crap with just a few words.

"Is there anything you need, Dad?"

I'm desperate now for the conversation to end. I want to get off the phone and go up to the supermarket and buy enough wine to help me forget this ever happened.

"I don't believe so," he says finally.

"Well, ring me if you do."

I give him my new number and end the call with a simple good-bye. Then sit there, dazed, my head in my hands and my breath stilted, bitter memories flooding my defenses like waves breaching the seawall.

THIRTY-SEVEN

WEDNESDAY, 8 APRIL

The campus is a vast sprawl of lawns and low-rise buildings wedged between two dormitory towns on the outskirts of London. I find the car park, using up most of my remaining cash to feed the meter.

The café, a giant Starbucks up by the student union, seems to form the beating heart of the whole university. The place is heaving, full of undergrads nursing huge lattes and raspberry muffins that must eat through their loans like a cancer. Girls, boys—hopelessly young—peering into the screens of their smartphones and laptops, affecting that slightly bored, seen-it-all expression universal to those who've not lived enough to know they've seen nothing.

Everyone dressed in a uniform of T-shirts and skinny jeans, the girls wearing those flat little ballet shoes that are impossible to keep on your feet. Only one, a tall blonde in her early twenties, bucks the trend, teetering in a pair of the highest stiletto heels I've encountered in a long while. If she took them off, I reckon she'd be a head shorter.

You have to wonder how she might be supplementing her student loan.

I join the end of the queue, feeling disoriented, having lost the knack of tuning out so much noise and bustle. Christ, how will I cope again in London?

The idea of my empty Pimlico flat prompts a surprising surge of nostalgia for the little house in Devon. *You could go back*, says a voice in my head. *You could walk out of here, hit the motorway; you'd be there in four hours. You could forget all this and start again.*

I reach the front of the queue. There's still no sign of Tony. He's had a change of heart, I think, before another thought steals up behind it and shallows my breathing.

Perhaps something or someone has stopped him coming.

Don't be ridiculous, I tell myself, ordering a mug of tea and sitting in the far corner with a view of the entrance. Stop being so bloody dramatic.

A second later two uniformed police walk through the door. My heart leaps. Christ. For one insane moment I'm convinced they've come for me, though I can't for the life of me imagine why.

Or maybe they're here about Tony, I think irrationally as they approach. Fuck . . . something really has happened to him.

The officers stride past me, round to the back of the counter. Over the rush of blood in my ears I hear them asking the way to one of the student blocks. I feel a surge of relief. Most likely a break-in, something like that.

I take a sip of tea, trying to calm down. At the next table three boys watch the policemen leave, bantering in voices pitched just loud enough to be overheard. The conversation seems to revolve entirely around how drunk they're going to get tonight, everything uttered with the kind of studied insouciance you can muster only if you're very young. Or very rich and good-looking.

Freshers, probably. Irritated, I eye their Gap hoodies and

smooth chins. Then recall my own first nervous, blundering weeks on campus.

Another lifetime, I realize, suddenly feeling old. And very weary.

The nearest boy turns round and catches my eye, his gaze appreciative. I look away. Check the time on the clock above the counter. Quarter past eleven. Tony should have been here half an hour ago. He must have got cold feet. Decided this is way more trouble than I'm worth.

An instant later I see him hurry through the door, phone pressed to his ear. He glances around, spots me, holds up five fingers.

I feel stupidly relieved, as if somehow Tony being here at all is going to make everything okay.

Five minutes later he's removing his rucksack, dumping it next to the chair opposite. He looks hassled, disheveled. A little paunchy round the midriff.

Tony checks me out too. Doubtless comes to the same conclusion. "Apologies, Stella. Bloody traffic. Unbelievable. I should have got the train."

"It's not the easiest of places to get to," I admit.

He sits down. "I know. I'm sorry, but that was half the point. I thought we might be better off out of town. And I've arranged a meeting in the media faculty later to give me an excuse."

I nod, trying not to dwell on the reasons for his caution. Glance at his large glass of Frappuccino and supersize chocolate muffin. "That stuff'll kill you."

He eyes it thoughtfully, then looks up. "Right now, I'd say my odds are better than yours."

Something shrinks inside me. The remaining sedative effect from the last week evaporates as the reality of my situation hits me anew.

I fix my gaze on his. "Explain."

He shifts his chair round so it aligns with mine, reaches into his rucksack, and pulls out a laptop, one of those superslim Ultrabooks. He presses a button and icons fill the screen. Sliding his finger across the mouse pad, he brings up the browser, scrolling through a folder full of bookmarks. He clicks on one and a picture appears.

"I've been doing a bit of research," Tony says. "In fact, a lot of research. And it's not pretty."

I hardly hear him. I'm too busy staring at the photograph.

Alex.

"Do you know who he is?" I ask, trying to keep my voice steady.

"His name is Alex Lennart. I didn't get anything on that Paul Franklin name you gave me—obviously an alias."

I nod.

"I had a devil of a job pinning him down, actually, but then I stumbled across this."

Tony pulls up another website. The *Berkshire Daily Herald*. There's a picture of Edward Hardy standing outside a modern office complex. The sign to the right of him tells me it's a company called Palmer Wentworth. Hardy's shaking the hand of someone I'm guessing is the managing director, while several other men cluster around them, all beaming at the camera.

"Hardy seals the deal for a new future for UK defense industries," reads the caption underneath.

I peer again at the men in the background. Only one isn't smiling. Alex Lennart. My stomach contracts as I study his face. I can feel his gravitational pull, even from here.

"What does he do?" I force myself to look back up at Tony.

He swallows his mouthful of muffin. "It's rather hard to define, and it's even harder to dig up real information on him. But basically he's an arms broker."

"An arms broker?" My breath stalls on the inhale. "You mean he *sells guns*?" My mind leaps immediately to the one I saw in his hotel room drawer.

Tony laughs. A hollow laugh hardly designed to put me at ease. "Essentially, yes, but not the type you're thinking of. More bulk weaponry, the kind of stuff you'd see on the front line in Afghanistan or out in Gaza. Tanks, rocket launchers, antiaircraft, that sort of thing."

I make myself breathe out. "Christ."

"You ever heard of Stephan Kock? He was involved in that arms scandal during Thatcher's reign back in the eighties."

I nod. "Vaguely. I read something about it once."

"Essentially Lennart is Kock upgraded to the twenty-first century. A kind of intermediary, smoothing the way between big arms firms and the government contracts they're hoping to attract. Some of it legal, in the sense that the deals aren't breaching any international arms embargoes. But he also helps arms manufacturers find a way round international law."

"How do you mean?"

Tony slurps at his coffee through a straw and leans back in his seat. "Say there's a ban on exporting arms to Iraq or Afghanistan. People like Lennart get the weapons there by diverting them through countries we don't have such an issue with."

I close my eyes briefly, trying to get a handle on all this. "So you reckon he's got an arrangement with Hardy?"

Tony nods. "I suspect Hardy's been helping steer contracts toward the companies Lennart represents, and in return he's been laying the groundwork for British firms wanting to export arms to places they shouldn't. I expect Hardy's been getting some nice little kickbacks along the way—and a few of his ministry chums, no doubt."

"So you're saying this Abstar contract was illegal?"

Tony shakes his head. "Not in this case. We've been selling stuff to the Middle East for years, especially to the Saudis—over four hundred million pounds worth per year, on average. The issue is more why Abstar got the contract over other bidders who looked better on paper. There's been a lot of grumbling and rumors. Hence the select committee."

I digest this for a moment.

"So where does Harry the banker come in? He was the one who was so cock-a-hoop over the deal."

"Think about it. These contracts are huge. Multiple millions of pounds, enough to significantly boost a company's share price when it's announced. All Hardy or Lennart need do is give Harry a little advanced notice, and he can buy up shares ahead of the announcement. Then make a killing when their price goes through the roof."

I close my eyes again. Inhale slowly.

"It's basically a win-win-win situation," says Tony, breaking off another piece of muffin and stuffing it into his mouth.

I open my eyes. "And Rob?"

"Robert Mulligan. Harry Elliott's sidekick at Trellum, Bailey. He's bound to be in on it, but I doubt he's pulling any strings."

I chew the side of my cheek for a few seconds. Then force myself to make eye contact with Tony.

"So what happened with Elisa, do you think?"

He sighs and wipes crumbs from his lips with a napkin. "I reckon our lovely friend stumbled into a minefield. I'm guessing she discovered something about one of these guys, or had something on them. Somehow or other made a nuisance of herself. Lennart in particular is not somebody you would want to piss off."

I drop my gaze. Run my palms across the legs of my jeans. Should I tell him about Amanda's files? The figures without dates?

It's all beginning to make sense. She must have sent the usual blackmail package to Harry, expecting him to cough up like the rest. After all, she'd heard him bragging at the party about the money he'd made. No doubt had him down as an easy mark.

An image of Amanda wiping Harry's spunk from her eye. *That fucking pig. I'll make him pay for that.*

But she hadn't counted on his friends. What effect her little party trick might have on them. "I think possibly she upset Harry," I say guardedly. "I suspect it was something to do with money."

Tony's look is appraising. He knows I'm holding out on him. I can see him wondering whether to pursue it. "Well, I'm guessing he didn't like that." He takes another slug of his coffee. "So he called in his friends. Difficult to say who might have set special ops on her. Could have been Lennart or Hardy—or both."

"Special ops?"

Tony shuts the lid of his laptop. Shifts his seat back round to face me. "That bloke, the one that came round and tried to freak you out. I made some inquiries. Sounds like special ops, one of the elite covert units working under the Foreign Office."

I stare at him. "Since when is screwing escorts part of their remit?"

Tony grimaces. "Everything's part of their remit, Grace. Whatever gets the job done."

I swallow, reliving the pressure of his thumb on my throat. Those bruises on Kristen's neck. "So you reckon this . . . this elite unit . . . they were the ones who killed Elisa?"

"Quite possibly."

I think it through. Amanda probably contacted Harry via e-mail. It would have been easy for them to set up a meeting with her, under the guise of handing over the money. Only it wasn't Harry waiting when she arrived, but them . . . that man.

Christ, what did he do to her? I don't even want to ask myself the question, but answers manhandle their way into my consciousness. Questioned her. No, *interrogated* her until they were sure she'd given them everything. Then took her to the hotel and killed her, making it look like a client.

Which would explain why there was no DNA found anywhere on Amanda's body. After all, these people know how to clean up after themselves.

I examine my tea. I've barely drunk any of it, but suddenly the idea of swallowing anything feels impossible. She held out, I realize, filled with a surge of admiration. Amanda. She didn't tell them about the SD card.

Though they must have suspected there was something—hence ransacking her flat.

I raise my head. Tony is studying me as he chews his way through the rest of his muffin. I screw up my courage to ask him what I can no longer avoid. "This special ops force. Why would they turn their attention on me?"

Tony sucks the chocolate from his teeth. "You were at the party. They may suspect you were involved with whatever she did that so got under Hardy's skin. That, or they know somehow you're onto them."

I mull this over for a minute. "I went to the police," I tell Tony. "And Hardy, when details from Elisa's death didn't add up."

"Let me guess. The police didn't take it any further."

I nod. He's right. I never did hear back from that detective.

"Most likely they've got someone in on the investigation, keeping an eye on it for Edward Hardy."

"Then why not just get rid of me, like Elisa? Wouldn't it be safer for them?"

Tony leans toward me, resting his hands on the table. "I'm not saying they won't, if pushed, Stella. But I'm guessing they'd rather not. One strangled call girl can be brushed under the carpet; two starts to attract more attention. They'd have to pass it off as a serial killer or something, and that would mean the police cranking up their investigation. And there's the chance somebody might uncover the connection between you and Elisa, and that would stir things up for them."

"I met him," I say. "Alex Lennart. He offered to set me up with an exclusive contract—conditional on me leaving London."

Tony gives me a measuring look. "I take it you turned him down."

"It didn't make any sense. I mean, I hardly know him."

"Sounds as if he was trying to protect you, Stella. Offering you a Get Out of Jail Free card."

That was before I went off to meet his ministerial chum. Poked my stick further into the hornet's nest.

I briefly squeeze my eyes shut, watching the stars spark and dance in the darkness behind my lids, then stare at all the guileless faces around me. "Christ, I remember being in their place, everything ahead of me. How did I fuck up my life like this?"

"You came here?" Tony asks.

"No. But close enough." I clamp my hands between my knees. "So what do I do?" I ask Tony. "How do I deal with this?"

He glances at me, then his empty plate. "Fucked if I know, Stella."

I sense he's backing off, trying to put distance between himself and this whole sorry mess I've got myself in. Or maybe he's simply afraid. Scared of straying into the firing line.

"Do you think if I went to the police, told them everything, showed them all this"—I nod at his laptop—"they'd act on it? Surely they'd have to do something. I'd get protection, wouldn't I, as a witness?" Though that wouldn't help Kristen, I realize.

Tony raises an eyebrow. "Not my best advice, to be honest. I don't imagine you'd get very far. And then you'd really be in the shit."

He leans forward again, lowers his voice. "Think about it, Stella. You still need proof. Everything I've told you, it's all conjecture—we don't have any hard evidence. And for the police to act on it would mean opening the biggest can of worms this government has ever faced. You're talking a major investigation into corruption, not only at Westminster, but in the arms industry and the banking sector. And right on the heels of the select committee inquiry."

"What came of that? Do you know?"

"Not much. Clearly people have their suspicions—it's near impossible to prevent things leaking out. But Hardy and his cronies seem to have convinced everyone there's nothing untoward going on."

I consider the SD card, tucked deep in my purse. "So even if I had firm evidence connecting Hardy and the others with Elisa, you don't reckon it would be enough?"

Tony blows air into his cheeks. Releases it. "You'd be taking a huge risk, Stella. And even if by some miracle the police and the Crown Prosecution Service did manage to drag Lennart or Hardy into the dock in a murder trial, you'd be a key witness. You'd have to testify."

He pauses. "And then everyone, I mean *everyone*, in the country . . . in the whole world . . . would know about you and what you do."

And what I *did*, I think, heat rising to my face.

"Consider your credibility issues in the witness stand," Tony adds. "They'd crucify you."

He knows. He knows I'm Grace Thomas and he knows about Michael and the trial. He knows no one will believe a word I say.

I clear my throat. "Thanks, Tony, I owe you one."

He smiles and drains the last of his drink. "I might have to take you up on it one day. Especially if the girlfriend ever finds out what I've been up to on your behalf."

"My lips are sealed." I stand and pull on my jacket.

"As are mine." He puts his laptop away in his rucksack, then pauses and looks me over.

"My advice, Stella, if you don't mind me offering it, is to get the fuck out of here. Preferably abroad. And not for a week, not even for a month. As long as you can manage. Get as far away as possible for as long as possible and keep a low profile. You need to send these people a clear signal."

"Saying what?"

"That you're no threat. That you have no intention of pursuing this any further."

Follow Kristen's example. I chew this over for a second. Imagine running away. Finding that island.

Then feel something well up inside. "But they'd get away with it," I blurt, more loudly than I intend. Knowing how silly I sound. "Pulling off corrupt deals. Insider trading. Abusing government office. Breaking international arms agreements—you name it. *Ordering Elisa's execution, for fuck's sake.*"

Tony nods, slipping on his jacket and heaving the rucksack onto his back.

"Yeah, you're right. They'd get away with it, Stella. I don't want to sound harsh, but boo hoo, it's an ugly old world."

He eyes me one last time before heading for the door.

"But look on the bright side, kiddo—at least you'd still be alive."

THIRTY-EIGHT

This time, when I hand him the cash, the clerk doesn't turn a hair. Just takes the form I've filled out and puts the keys on the counter. Points to a beige Volvo out in the car park.

It's not the same car I had before. I've splashed out on something more substantial. Something with a bit more clout. And GPS.

I drop my bag on the backseat, turn on the ignition, and program in the address. The satnav talks me through central London and out onto the M25. Another thirty minutes and I'm cruising up the M1, passing signs to Milton Keynes and Northampton, Rugby, and Leicester.

Clouds loom, growing denser and darker as I head farther north, eyes focused on the endless gray tarmac of the motorway. I stay in the slow lane with the trucks, driving at a steady sixty miles an hour, overtaking only when they slow to a crawl on the hills.

Another hour passes. I fiddle with the radio, searching for something to distract me. Find nothing but music or news. I'm in the mood for neither.

It's not too late to turn back.

The thought rises unbidden. I could go home. Pack my bags. Take the tube to Heathrow and buy a ticket to somewhere. Anywhere.

I keep on driving, watching the speedometer chalk up the miles between me and my escape route. I count off the junctions, stopping for half an hour at Donington Park services for a pee, a cup of tea, and a soggy tuna sandwich.

Ten minutes past Nottingham it begins to rain, a sudden deluge that slashes visibility to a few yards and forces all but the most reckless to cut their speed. I put the windscreen wipers on full, keeping my eyes trained on the taillights of the red truck just ahead. The sun is setting, the sky fading toward dusk.

It's not too late to go back.

The thought mirrors the rhythmic sweep of the wipers. Back and forth, back and forth. The truck in front grinds to a walking pace, and I see a string of red lights curving up the road in front of me. Possibly an accident up ahead.

Half a mile later, the traffic speeds up again. I switch into the middle lane to overtake. Just as I draw level with the red truck, it indicates and starts to pull out. I check my mirror and try to move into the fast lane, but a black Range Rover appears alongside me, blocking my path.

I smack my hand on the horn for it to let me in, but the car doesn't alter its speed. Inside the front passenger's window I glimpse a man looking right at me, his face impassive.

Shit.

I hit the brakes at the exact moment a light goes off in my eyes, like an internal firework. I can't see a thing. I pump the brake, already feeling the car going into a skid, the scream of car horns as I careen across the highway.

I'm dead, I think as I lose control of the steering, still half blind. No fucking way I'll survive this.

No way at all.

The car hits the verge on the other side of the hard shoulder and goes into a spin. The blare of more horns, and my vision clears just in time to glimpse a juggernaut thundering toward me.

I close my eyes and wait for everything to end.

"You okay, miss?"

I open my eyes slowly. A police officer is tapping on the car window.

"Miss? Can you open the door?"

I can't breathe. My chest feels crushed, stamped flat. I can't inhale.

"Miss?" I look at the officer. He's pointing at the button that releases the central locking. "Open the door."

I stretch forward, just reaching it with my hand. A click as the locks release and he opens the driver's door.

"Handbag," I manage to stammer, nodding toward the backseat. He leans over and hands it to me. I find my inhaler. Squirt albuterol into my rasping lungs.

"You okay?" he asks again. I nod, closing my eyes as I wait for the drug to work. A minute later I can speak.

"Jesus." It's all I can think to say.

"What happened?" asks the officer. I peer out the windscreen. A squad car is parked on the hard shoulder in front of me, a mini-van a few yards behind it. I realize I'm facing the wrong way, toward the oncoming traffic.

"Miss?"

"I'm not sure." My voice comes out hoarse and shaky.

"Sounds as if you had a narrow escape. This gentleman says you lost control and spun right across the highway." I look up to see a young bloke in a hoodie standing by the officer. The van must be his.

"Do you remember what happened?" the officer asks again.

I think hard. "I was overtaking a truck, but it pulled out in front of me. Then I was dazzled by something, I couldn't see."

"A light?"

"Blinding."

"Did you notice anything?" the police officer asks the other man.

He shakes his head. "Only the car going into a skid. Nearly got hit by a semi."

"It was like a torch," I say, remembering. "Like when somebody shines one in your eyes. But stronger. Brighter."

"A laser light?" suggests the man. "Maybe it was someone on the bridge." He nods at the overpass in the distance.

"Possibly kids," says the officer. "Wouldn't be the first time."

"There was a black Range Rover," I add. "I tried to pull into the fast lane but it wouldn't get out of the way."

The officer looks over at the traffic belting along the motorway. I can see him weighing up what to do next.

"There's some services a few miles up the road. You can come in the car with me, and my colleague will turn yours round and follow on behind. We'll check it over when we get there."

By the time the police have filled in the paperwork and given me and the car the all clear, it's getting late. I drive slowly, cautiously. Shouldn't be driving at all, as the officer said, not till I'm over the shock. Although he had no idea how shaken I am. As Tony pointed out, strangled call girls attract attention—but not if they're flattened on a motorway.

I've no choice though. I have to get there tonight. Whether what happened was an accident or deliberate, I still need to get a move on.

Even so, it's gone ten by the time I find the right road on the Leeds estate, and only streetlights illuminate the long row of houses. It's a cheap seventies row house, the kind that appears to have been slung together with giant slabs of concrete, PVC windows stuck in like an afterthought. All the front doors set into a glorified lean-to; the scraggy grass outside barely meriting the word "lawn," let alone "front garden."

I slow the car and peer at the number on the nearest property. Count forward in twos until I spot the one I'm after.

Number 71. A bucket by the door and a red moped parked in front of the window.

I look around, study the road behind me in my rearview mirror. Toward the end, up near the junction, I make out the back of a couple walking a Staffie. The dog stops, sniffs, cocks a stocky leg, moves on a few yards, and goes through the whole rigmarole again. The man tugs at the lead and they disappear round the corner.

I check around again. No one. Grabbing my handbag, I get out of the car, locking it behind me. My legs still feel trembly and I almost hobble to the front door, relieved to see the light glowing behind the curtains, the sound of a TV.

The bell doesn't seem to work, so I tap on the window with my knuckles. A hand pulls a curtain aside and I glimpse the silhouette of a man's face. A few seconds later the door opens and the hand gestures me inside.

Raffey's standing at the foot of the stairs, eyeing me curiously. As he reaches past to shut the door, I'm assailed by a powerful smell of cooking fat and stale tobacco. And something underneath, something more pungent.

I pull my attention back to Raffey. Though it's only been five, maybe six years, he looks older, the lines on his face deeper. He's dressed in jeans and an old black sweatshirt—not much different from the prison-issue clothes I last saw him in.

"So, Grace Thomas," he drawls in a voice craggy with age and cigarettes. "Never thought I'd see you again."

I don't bother with a greeting. It would be wasted on Raffey. "Do we have to stand out here?"

He studies me for a few seconds longer, then nods toward the living room.

The heat hits me first. Then the smell, the undertone in the hallway now transformed into the distinct reek of skunk and something earthier. I glance around. In the corner of the room I catch sight of the cages—wire mesh, three stacked one on top of the other.

Christ. What on earth does he keep inside them? Rats? Reptiles? I decide not to ask.

"You look rough," Raffey sniffs.

I don't bother to reply. Raffey walks over to the TV and turns off the sound. "How'd you get my number then?"

"I called in a favor. Someone at the probation office."

"Right," he says, sucking his teeth loudly.

"So do you have it?"

He shakes his head. "Not yet. Tomorrow."

"Okay."

I keep my face expressionless, but he laughs huskily. "This isn't Argos, sweetheart. These things take a bit of time. And money."

I take the hint. Dig into my handbag and hand him the bundle of notes. I haven't bothered with an envelope—Raffey's not one for niceties like that.

"It's all there," I say, but he insists on counting out the used twenties one by one. He may have an IQ in the low eighties, but there's clearly nothing wrong with Raffey's ability to add up.

"Not out the cashpoint?" he confirms, evidently assuming such a large amount of cash would be a problem for me.

Little does he know.

"So, what time tomorrow?" I ask, when he's finally reassured himself that I haven't pulled a fast one.

He doesn't reply. Goes over to the corner, opening a little door in the top cage and retrieving a metal tin from under a pile of hay. Stashes the money inside and replaces the tin in its hiding place.

Then he turns to me, letting his gaze travel from my breasts down to my crotch before swiveling back up to my face.

"Should be here by five."

THIRTY-NINE

Where am I?

My eyes focus. Bed, desk, TV. Cheap plastic chair. The kind of bathroom that comes in one easy-to-install unit. The dismal internal vista furnished by budget motels across the world. I turn my head on the pillow to see if there's anyone beside me, but I'm alone.

More alone, perhaps, than I've ever been.

I eat the buffet breakfast—watery orange juice, dry croissants, and the nastiest coffee I've tasted in a long time, bitter and burned. I feel groggy, blurred at the edges, after half a night lingering between sleep and wakefulness, my nervous system still on full alert.

I check out, chuck my bag into the boot of the car, and climb in behind the steering wheel. I rest my forehead against it, wondering if I've lost my nerve.

It's not too late to go back.

I've no idea where I'm going. It's only when I sit up and turn the key in the ignition that the inevitability of it hits me.

The one destination I simply can't avoid.

Forty minutes later and I'm swinging into Sweetland Road. Another half a mile brings me face-to-face with the stark brick building. I drive past and pull up opposite the car dealership. Check I can still see the entrance in my rearview mirror.

There it is. The crest above the doorway. Spirals of razor wire just visible above the high perimeter walls.

I take a deep breath, gripping the steering wheel with both hands. There's a gritty pain in my chest, and my breathing feels strained. I lean over and grasp my handbag, find my inhaler. Aim it at the back of my mouth.

Nothing comes out. I shake the canister and try again. A brief hiss. The chemical taste on my tongue, not as strong as it should be. Obviously running low. I breathe slowly, deeply, until the urge to cough fades into a faint tickle deep in my throat.

Another glance in my mirror. Where is he? I wonder. I check the time—half past ten. Not in his cell, then. In the gym, perhaps. Michael was always careful to keep himself in shape; not easy, given the prison diet. Or maybe he's in one of the education classes. Though God knows I can't think what anybody could teach him that he doesn't already know.

I stare at the stone walls of the prison, estimating the distance between us. A hundred yards, maybe two? Even being this close makes me feel nauseous. I sit back in the seat and shut my eyes. Fill my lungs with air, inhaling through my nose, out through my mouth, all to a count of five. The same breathing exercise I taught to dozens of inmates inside that very building.

How many are still in there? I wonder. How many outside, picking up the shards of their lives?

I adjust my mirror, pointing it toward the main block. Remember the narrow corridors, the claustrophobic little cells with their metal beds and stainless steel sinks and toilets. The ubiquitous scent of disinfectant. I can hear the barked commands of the prison guards, the endless chatter of the inmates, their comments and catcalls, echoing around the building like ugly birdsong.

Michael. My mind seeks him out again, his face surfacing like an old photograph. Young still, those carved cheekbones, those soulful blue eyes.

"Michael." Just saying his name again after all these years feels like blasphemy, but it springs to my lips like a mantra. *Michael.*

I imagine the days, weeks, months, stretching out before him. I know how that must make him feel. Know how much he hated being inside.

And I'm glad, I realize. I want him to suffer. It's the only thing that makes my life bearable.

A sharp rap on the glass by my head. I jump. Look up to see a man peering in. A man I recognize. I turn the ignition and press the button to lower the window.

"Is there a problem . . ." He sees my face more clearly and his expression changes, his mouth drooping with surprise. "Grace! What the fuck are you doing here?"

I stare back at Ed. I don't know what to say. I can't think of a single decent excuse to explain my presence.

"I . . ."

He stares at me. "Let me in."

I lean over and release the catch to the passenger's door. He walks round, glancing at the building behind him as he slips inside.

Ed turns to me and frowns. "I can't hang around, Grace. I've just finished my shift and I've got to get up to the surgery. But seriously, what the hell are you doing here?"

"Only passing through, Ed, okay? I just . . ." I search again for a plausible reason. Then decide on the truth. "Actually I've no idea what I'm doing here. I was in the area and I needed to . . . I just needed to not avoid it anymore."

"So you heard?" He nods his head toward the prison.

I gaze back at him. "Heard what?"

Ed studies my face for a moment, then frowns. Raises his right hand and rubs his forehead. "Shit, I assumed you knew."

"Knew what, Ed?" My tone sharper, more urgent.

"He's out. On probation."

"How?" I yelp. "He got an indeterminate sentence. He's classed as a dangerous offender, for God's sake."

"Farrish served his minimum term, Grace. He was up for parole."

"Yes, but surely they wouldn't fall for . . . not again." I groan. Cover my mouth with my hands. I feel hollow. Like my insides have melted and drained away.

Ed sighs. "You know how it goes. New guy heading up the board. Farrish giving him the full butter-wouldn't-melt routine."

"But they know his record . . ."

"Matthews brought it all up. But the board decided he no longer poses a risk to the public."

"That's insane." I swallow, the threat of tears making my eyes sting. "The fucking stupid bastards."

Ed clears his throat. "You can't blame them, Grace. You remember what Michael Farrish is like . . . how convincing . . ."

He doesn't go on. Thank God. Doesn't spell it out for me.

I don't reply.

He studies me, his eyes searching for mine. I can't bring myself to look him full in the face. We sit in silence for a few minutes before Ed speaks.

"Grace, no one really blames you . . . Farrish is a clever bastard. Very"—he searches for the word—"very . . . charismatic. You just got caught up in it all."

I lift my eyes to his, wanting to smile. Note how his hair still curls to the right, a little cowlick that makes him look like the soft touch he isn't. I always liked Ed. He's that rare thing—a prison officer with genuine compassion. Somehow maintaining an optimistic view of human nature in the face of daily examples to the contrary.

"That's a very generous way of looking at it," I say.

He keeps his gaze fixed on my face. "You can't go back, Grace. You've got to let yourself off the hook and put it behind you."

I nod again.

"I mean it. You've paid enough for this already. Let it go."

He puts his hand on the lever to open the car door.

"Wait," I say, grabbing his arm and asking him the one thing I know I ought not to. "Where is he?"

Ed gives me a pitying look. "C'mon, Grace. You know I couldn't tell you that, even if I had any idea."

He gets out of the car quickly, half slamming the door behind him, then walks round to my open window. Reaching in, he pulls my chin up so I have to meet his eyes.

"Good to bump into you, girl. Really. Now fuck off and make sure I never see your face round here again."

FORTY

I get to Raffey's place just after five. Park on the opposite side of the road and suss out the two lads hanging around outside. They're both smoking, laughing, and kicking at a tennis ball, jostling each other as they slam it against the wall of the house.

I decide to chance it. Walk up to the front door, fully aware that they're both hovering a few feet away, sizing me up.

"Fuck off," Raffey says to them as he opens the door and pulls me into the heat. The taller one scowls and drops his cigarette end on the ground, grinding it out. They slink off down the street.

This time he leads me straight into the kitchen. It's surprisingly neat, all the surfaces clean, almost gleaming. No dirty crockery in the sink or clutter on the worktops. A load of laundry quietly revolving in the washing machine. It seems Raffey picked up some good habits while doing time.

I stand there, half hoping he'll offer me a drink. Even a cup of tea. But the swiftness of his movements and the way he avoids my eyes tells me he doesn't want me hanging around any longer than I have to.

Shit, I should never have asked him to do this. To take this kind of risk. What the hell was I thinking?

He leans down and reaches into the cupboard under the sink. Removes a shopping bag with a Primark logo and places it on the kitchen table. Pulls out a shoe box and raises the lid.

I look inside. Nod.

"You ever used one of these before?"

I shake my head.

He lifts out the gun. Then puts his hand back in the bag and takes out a small black plastic sack, the kind people use to pick up dog muck. Removes several bullets and loads them into the barrel, clicking it shut.

"It's that simple, really." He pushes a little switch with his thumb, holding the gun at an angle so I can see what he's doing. "That's the safety catch. Release it like this if you want to fire." He flicks the switch off again and hands the gun to me.

I take it from him carefully. There's a star on the handle and a model number with MADE IN CHINA etched underneath in crude uneven capitals. It's like something you'd buy in Toys "R" Us; only this is heavier, the dark metal cold to the touch. It can't have been here long, I realize, or it would have adjusted to the heat in the house.

I picture the two boys outside. Did they deliver this? Another pang of guilt as I think how many people I've already dragged into the mire with me. Step over the line, and the consequences ripple out all around you.

"Here." Raffey shows me the remaining contents of the Primark bag, holding it open by the handles so I can peer inside. I reach in, feel the cool metal.

Exactly what I asked for. Prison issue, by the look of them.

He stands back, leaning against the sink. Subjects me to his unnerving scrutiny.

"Long way to come to tool up," he says, running his tongue over his teeth.

I shrug. "Easier than trying to make connections in London. Besides, I needed to get out of town."

"Not come looking for him then?" Raffey's look has a kind of leer in it that makes me feel physically sick. I don't even grace it with a reply.

"I hear he's out. Farrish," he persists, nodding approvingly at the gun in my hand. "Shame you didn't have it before, Grace. You could have shot that cunt back then. Saved everyone a load of trouble."

I think of Michael's flat, the one he moved into after his initial release. That sordid high-rise out on the Pallesey estate, with its piss-reeking corridors and broken lifts.

Would I? I wonder. If I'd had this gun in that gloomy little room, would I have used it?

But that's not the right question, I realize, as I examine the places where use has worn the color from the metal. The real question is not whether I'd have shot Michael.

The real question is whether I would simply have turned it on myself.

FORTY-ONE

Anna's late. Twenty minutes so far. I sit on the park bench, shivering in the cold snap that's descended on London, winter's giving spring the finger before departing. I'm wearing jeans, a thick sweatshirt, and a coat, and I still feel underdressed.

Eventually I see her in the distance, hurrying up the hill toward me. She has her hands thrust deep in the pockets of her jacket. She is wearing a giant wool scarf wound loosely round her neck, her chin hidden in its folds. It looks like something your gran would knit you, but probably cost more than my whole outfit.

Anna drops onto the bench beside me, wincing as the chill in the wood penetrates her jeans. "This is a bit rural, isn't it? Why not just meet at the pub?"

"I thought it would make a change," I lie.

Anna's expression is skeptical. "So where have you been? I tried ringing you several times on your new number, but your phone was always off."

"I had to go and sort a few things out."

Another quizzical look. But this time she doesn't comment.

"Why the new mobile anyway?"

"I lost the other one." I feel myself flush. The lies are stacking up like interest on a bad debt, and it's not making me feel any better.

Over in the playground a couple of kids start whooping with excitement, chasing each other around the elaborate rope-climbing frame. Anna glances over and quickly looks away.

Hell. I should have chosen somewhere else.

"Let's go." I get up and head over to the patch of woodland on the crest of the hill, Anna's pace falling into step with mine. We walk side by side between the bare trees, neither of us speaking. Watching our breath disperse into the air like smoke.

"Fuck this," Anna says after a few minutes. She pulls me toward the café on the edge of the park. Orders two hot chocolates and a huge slab of carrot cake. We sit at a table by the window; you can see the lake through the trees. I keep an eye on everyone who passes by, while trying to hide it from Anna.

"Eat," she says, handing me a fork. "You look like you haven't bothered in days."

I take a mouthful of the dense sponge and chew it slowly, letting the sweetness spread across my tongue. A sip of the hot chocolate to chase it down. I hope all this sugar isn't going to make me sick.

"So what's going on?" Anna's expression tells me she's had enough of being fobbed off. "You're as jumpy as a scalded cat."

I study the pattern of the froth on my mug, the heart-shaped dusting of cocoa powder. What can I tell her? I can't bear to keep lying; equally I can't think of anything I can say that won't involve her further.

"Is this something to do with Elisa?"

I look back up at Anna, sharp as ever. I still don't answer.

"Okay, I get it." She gives me a once-over. "Best if I don't know."

"Sorry."

"No need to be. I'm concerned about you, that's all."

I nod.

"So, if you're not here to tell me what's going on, and we're clearly not just meeting for a casual chat, what exactly is it you want me to do?"

"Actually . . ." I hesitate. "Okay . . . I do have a couple of favors to ask you."

"Fire away."

"I need Janine's address. You've been there, haven't you? You did a duo with her, I seem to remember."

She squints at me across the table. "Why not ring her and ask?"

I swallow. "I'd rather go round and see her." Calling would forewarn her. I want the element of surprise.

"Okay, it's in Islington. Belbridge Road. Number 17, I think. You can't miss it 'cause it's the only house with a bay window. Middle flat."

"Thanks." I make a mental note of the address.

"So what's the other one?"

I gaze at her.

"Favor? You said you had a couple of things to ask me."

Reaching into my coat, I pull out a small clear plastic box containing the SD card. Press it into her hand.

"Take care of this for me, will you? Put it somewhere safe, somewhere no one can stumble across it."

She examines it for a moment, then picks up her handbag and zips it into an inside pocket. "I suppose I can't ask what's on there?"

I shake my head. "And please don't look." I reach over and place my hand on hers. "It's a big ask, Anna, I know, but can you do that for me?"

Anna's eyes fix on my face. I see her fighting the urge to know more.

"You have my word."

"Only, if something happens to me . . . if I . . ."

"What the fuck are you talking about, Grace?" Her voice is a suppressed growl, lowered but insistent. "Are you in some kind of trouble? I mean real trouble? Not just money shit."

I stare out the window. Realize I'm on the lookout for them—not only for them, but him too—examining every male that walks past. Though I know he's miles away. No way Michael would risk breaking probation. Not this time.

"Grace?"

I turn back. "Yes, I am. But I'm going to deal with it, all right? But in case something does happen . . . if it all goes wrong, even if it looks like an accident, I want you to do two things for me. I want you to copy the stuff on that card and send it to every national newspaper in the country. And then I want you to take it to the police."

"And say what?" Her expression both astonished and horrified.

"Say it came from Elisa's flat."

"But how do I explain how I got hold of it?"

I chew the inside of my lip. Think for a few seconds. "Tell them I took it when I went round to see Kristen."

Anna leans forward, resting her elbows on the table. "Jesus, Grace, this sounds like some serious crap you've got yourself mixed up in."

I grimace. Don't bother to deny it. There's no point bullshitting Anna. She may lack my clinical training, but she has a natural lie detector honed by years of being screwed around by men.

"Why me?" she asks suddenly.

"Because you're about the only person I can trust not to look."

She frowns. "What is this? Pandora's box? Open the lid and unleash all the evil into the world."

"Or all the good. It's hard to tell at this point."

Her eyes search my face for clues. I can sense her desperation to ask more. "Grace, I'm suddenly more than just worried about you. I'm really *scared* for you."

I swallow and stare back out the window. A sparrow lands on

one of the outside tables, pecking at crumbs. Another dive-bombs
in beside him and they both fly away.

"I'm scared too." I say, facing her.

She leans over and takes my hand in hers. Gives it a squeeze.
"Is there nothing I can do to fix this? Nothing else I can do to help?"

I shake my head again. "I wish you could. Honestly. But I've
got to sort this on my own."

Anna blinks. Downs the rest of her drink and gets to her feet,
slinging her handbag over her shoulder. "I have to go. I'm due at
the Carlton in a couple of hours."

She leans over and kisses the top of my head. "Good luck," she
says, straightening up and winding her scarf back around her neck.

It's only then, as she turns toward the door, that I see she is
crying.

FORTY-TWO

Belbridge Road is a short walk through the backstreets from Islington tube. It's not long before I'm standing in front of Number 17, ringing the bell for the middle flat.

No answer.

I ring again. Wait another minute. *Oh God, please let her be in*, I think as I glance up and down the empty street. Certain now that I don't have much time.

"Who is it?" Janine's voice on the intercom, sounding terse.

"Stella."

There's a pause. I wonder if she's going to leave me standing here on the doorstep.

I never much cared for Janine, being the kind of whore who views every client as fair game, a glut of resources waiting to be tapped. Rumor has it one guy was schmuck enough to buy her a sports car, though I can't see any sign of it out here.

The buzzer sounds. I push on the front door and climb the stairs. Janine is hovering in the hallway of her flat, dressed in a white cotton dressing gown, her hair piled up in a towel. I've never seen her without makeup before. She seems smaller, more vulnerable, and . . . well . . . duller. Where Elisa, barefaced, was even prettier, Janine simply looks plain.

"Why are you here?" Her tone hardly welcoming, though she stands back to let me in. "I was in the shower."

"Sorry," I say insincerely. "I don't mind waiting till you get changed."

"I had a visit from the police a few weeks ago," she says accusingly as she closes the door behind me. "They were asking all sorts. About the party, about Harry. I got the distinct impression you'd pointed them in my direction."

"What did you tell them?"

"What's to tell? It was only a little get-together. I don't see what the fuck it's got to do with Elisa getting herself knocked off in some hotel."

I stare at her. She scowls back.

"You don't care, then," I ask. "What happened to Elisa?"

She snorts, but her eyes won't meet mine. "Of course I fucking care, Stella. Everyone cares." She tightens the belt of her dressing gown around her waist. "It's not nice knowing there's some kind of nutter out there. You have to be careful. Elisa should have known that."

"You think it was her fault? That she was careless?"

She shrugs.

I gesture toward what I assume is the living room. "Aren't you going to invite me in?"

Janine runs her tongue over her immaculate veneers, then jerks her head inside. "Go on through."

I walk into a room entirely furnished in cream. Cream carpet. Cream leather sofas. Cream display shelf and coffee table. Cream cushions and cream curtains. It looks like something from an early Bond film.

"So why are you here?" She drops into one of the sofas, pulling her dressing gown over her exposed knees. Christ, does she imagine I've come round to seduce her?

"He wasn't a nutter," I say, staying on my feet.

"Who?" Her look is sharp. I must remember not to underestimate Janine—she has the kind of feral intelligence of somebody entirely out for themselves.

"The man who killed Elisa. It was a professional job."

Janine stops scowling. Her mouth drops open. For once she has nothing to say.

I give her time for my revelation to sink in, but don't let my gaze leave her face for even a second.

"How can you possibly know that?" she asks finally. Her tone accusatory, like maybe I've come here purely to wind her up.

"I just do."

I remain standing, looking down on her. I figure the only way forward with Janine is to frighten her into cooperating with me.

"How?" she asks.

I ignore the question. Let her stew for another minute. *Play this steady, Grace*, I tell myself. *Don't scare her off too soon.*

"I still don't get it." She stares up at me. "Why you're here. What's any of this got to do with me?"

"A lot," I say simply. "Quite likely, you're next—or me. Probably both of us. And sooner rather than later."

Her mouth falls open again. I watch her breathing turn shallow, the pupils of her pale brown eyes dilating as her heart rate begins to elevate.

"Don't be ridiculous. You can't know that. Why would anyone want to hurt *me*?"

Despite the bravado, I can see in her eyes she's genuinely afraid. This fuck-'em-and-eat-'em thing Janine's got going is only skin-deep; underneath, she's as vulnerable as the rest of us.

"Because, Janine, you were there. You were at the party too. We're loose ends."

She pulls her dressing gown tighter across her chest. A subconscious gesture of self-protection.

This might just work.

"I don't understand." Her voice smaller now.

So I explain. Slowly and clearly, without embellishment.

She stares back at me, her expression a cross between fear and disbelief. "Let me get this right. You're saying they had some sort of dodgy deal going and Elisa found out about it?" She's huddled on the sofa now, her knees drawn up tight to her chest.

"No, Janine. I'm saying they had some sort of dodgy deal going and they *thought* Elisa had found out about it. That's why we're not safe either. We don't have to actually threaten or blackmail them to present a risk—they only have to think we *might*."

"But they can't just *kill* us. I mean, how?"

I shrug. "Anyhow. Simply make it look like an accident."

She swallows. Swipes at the tip of her nose with the heel of her hand. "So what do you reckon we should do?"

Now it's my turn to hesitate. This is the moment where I tell her what I've planned—and put my fate in her hands. If Janine bolts, goes to Harry, trades what I've got up my sleeve in return for her safety, I'm as good as dead.

I study her face. The defiant jut of her bottom lip. The sly expression that seems always to lurk at the edge of her eyes.

Is this really a gamble worth taking?

I take a deep breath and tell her my plan. And her part in it.

She glares back at me, horrified. "You must be fucking joking, Stella! Why would I go along with this? Harry's a good client, a regular. I see him practically every week."

I fix my eyes on hers. Force her to hold my gaze. "Have you seen him recently, Janine?"

No answer.

"It's been, what? Eight, nearly nine weeks since the party? Have you met up with him since?"

She thinks for a second or two. Slowly shakes her head.

I take a couple of steps toward her. Square my shoulders so I tower right over her, trying to make myself look as intimidating as possible.

"He's a lost cause, Janine. And he's also the man who had Elisa murdered. For what she *knew*, Janine, for what she *heard*." I pause, to place greater emphasis on what I'm going to say to her next. "So what do you imagine will stop him doing the same to you?"

Janine goes pale. I can almost see her trembling. "He wouldn't do that. Harry's really into me."

I snort. Make my voice sound a great deal tougher than I feel. "Wouldn't he? How long till he . . . they . . . decide you're a liability too?"

I watch her. I can tell she's wavering.

"Get real, Janine. You honestly believe you're that special to him? That there aren't dozens of girls who could give him what he wants? It'd take him, what, five minutes on the Internet to come up with a replacement?"

Janine's face slackens. She wipes her nose on the sleeve of her dressing gown, trying to stay composed.

"Elisa's dead, Janine. *Dead*. Don't you get it? You're batting way out of your league here."

She swallows. Blinks twice, slowly. "I can't, Stella. I just don't think I can do it."

"You can have my fee too. Double your rates—that's got to appeal."

Her face brightens a little at the mention of money. "But like you said, Harry hasn't been in touch since the party. How am I going to get him to agree to see me now? In the next few days?"

I smile down at her. Moisten my lips before I speak.

"You're an inventive girl, Janine. I'm sure you'll think of something."

FORTY-THREE

He's lying in bed in a private room, head and shoulders sunk into the pillows, looking smaller than I ever remember. His eyes are closed, his face turned away.

I walk in quietly, half hoping he's asleep and I can come back later. But his head moves and his eyelids flicker open as I approach, as if he knew I was there all along.

"Grace." His voice so quiet, uncertain, I can barely make out my name.

"Dad."

"You came."

I lower myself into the chair beside the bed. "So it would seem."

He clears his throat. Speaks a little louder. "I didn't think you would."

I glance at the paraphernalia around his bedside. He's hooked up to a drip, the tube running across to the hand resting on the sheet, gnarled and scrawny, mottled by age spots. Behind the bed, a heart monitor bleeps softly to itself, the screen a muddle of green lines and figures.

"How are you doing?" I force my gaze back to my father's face.

It twists into a scornful expression. "Do you really need to ask?"

Still enough strength to be snide, I note, then feel bad. In his place, I doubt I'd be very cheerful either.

Beyond the room, in another ward, comes a screech. A female voice shouting words I can't quite make out. My father groans. "That bloody woman. All day. Never stops." He tries to heave himself up into a sitting position. Slumps back down. I get up to help, but he waves me away.

I've already seen the doctor. A nice Indian guy, younger than me, with that precise way of speaking that comes with a second language. He told me my father was dying of congestive heart failure. That he could have a heart attack at any moment, and that the next one would almost certainly be fatal. Or his heart might simply lapse into arrhythmia.

Either way, he hasn't much time left. Days, probably. Maybe hours.

I study him now. His skin is pale and sallow, and the bulk he's carried all his life seems to be falling away. His flesh, what I can see of it, appears slack and untethered. His gray hair has thinned, and the rheumy sheen in his eyes makes him look tearful.

His face, however, still retains the expression of concentrated displeasure it's always worn.

"Is there anything I can do to help?" I ask, in the absence of any effort at conversation on his part.

"Bit late for that." I catch him watching me to see the effect of his words. Still measuring the extent of his power over me.

My dad's eternal M.O., I think, suppressing a sigh. Every interaction not so much a chance to relate to those around him as an opportunity to score a few points.

No wonder his heart is giving up on him.

"Have you spoken to Julia?" he asks eventually.

I shake my head.

"I've told her I want to go home, that I'll never get well in this place. But she keeps saying she can't cope." He turns his head toward the window. "Stupid bitch."

"What did you say?"

I stare at him, wondering if I actually heard him right. I'm not sure my father has ever sworn in front of me before, though God knows you could tell he was often tempted.

But I'm more shocked by the venom in his tone. The contempt.

He looks at me with the same disdain I imagine he directs at Julia when she's here. I can't blame her for not wanting him home.

"You always were a disappointment," he says, apropos of nothing, a trace of spittle oozing from the corner of his mouth.

I lock my eyes on his, leaving a pause before I speak. "You know, that's the funny thing, Dad. I've always thought much the same about you."

"What do you mean?" His cheeks flush. The bleep of the monitor picks up speed.

"You've got through two wives and one daughter, and none of us lived up to your expectations. But do you ever wonder how well you've lived up to ours?"

He scowls. Looks away. "I've taken care of all of you. You never went without a thing when you were a girl—or your mother, before she died. You had a good childhood. I can't recall a single thing to explain why you—"

"Explain what, Dad? Why I turned out the way I did? Is that what you mean?"

I wait for him to deny it. Though I know he won't.

He turns his head back to me. "I loved you, Grace. I've always loved you."

I hold his gaze, but his words leave me untouched.

I love you. I picture Michael, waiting outside that first parole hearing. Whispering into my ear when he was sure no one was looking.

But I know now what I didn't even suspect back then. There was nothing in his eyes. He was simply saying what he imagined I wanted to hear.

"I did my best for you, Grace, whatever you might think." My father's voice pulls me back to his bedside. "But you couldn't expect me to stand by you after what happened. You disgraced yourself, all of us. I was ashamed."

I let his words drop through me like pebbles thrown into a lake. Wait for the ripples of emotion to disperse.

"I made a mistake, Dad. A big mistake, sure, but still a mistake." I keep my voice steady. "Everyone screws up, you know— even you. What counts is having the courage to admit it."

His eyes rest on mine for perhaps a second, then slide away. "I'm tired now."

I get to my feet, noticing the background odor of the disinfectant. And the metal hospital bed, so similar to the ones they use in the prison.

Solitary confinement, I think, observing the uncertain rise and fall of my father's chest. A life sentence that's fast coming to an end.

"Good-bye, Dad," I say quietly. "I'm not sure when I'll be able to come back."

I wait for him to speak. To say something. But there's nothing except another shriek from the woman in the other ward.

I walk toward the door.

"Grace?"

I turn around.

"There was someone here looking for you. A man."

My father runs his tongue over his lips. I feel my pulse begin to race, outpacing the blip-blip-blip of the monitor behind the bed.

"He said he was a friend of yours. He wanted to know if I'd seen you."

"A friend of mine? What did he look like?"

I sense my father calling up a mental picture. "Brown hair. Around forty."

"Did he have a funny dent on his cheek?"

My father frowns. "Not that I noticed. Why?"

"No reason." I go to leave.

"He said he was an old friend and he'd been away for a while and just wanted to catch up. Said he'd lost your contact details."

Ice in my heart, sharp and cold. *Been away for a while.* Oh fuck. It couldn't be, could it? My breath turns to short staccato gasps while my father watches me dispassionately. Probably enjoying the effect his words have finally had.

"What did you tell him?" I say, straining to speak. "About seeing me?"

My father makes a noise resembling a snort. "I said I'd be lucky if you bothered to show up at all."

I manage to get outside before I throw up. Run round to the side of the main hospital entrance where there's a thick planting of shrubs and bushes and retch onto the bark-covered soil. Nothing much to show for it though—all I've eaten is the cake Anna foisted on me earlier. I start to shake, trembling uncontrollably, leaning against the wall for support.

Breathe, Grace. Breathe.

I sink onto a nearby bench. Inhale cool clean air while I dig around in the bottom of my handbag for a tissue. I find loose change, a lipstick, a couple of tampons. Nothing I can wipe my face with.

Shit. I close my eyes, trying to steady the flow of my breath.

It's not him, I try to tell my panicking brain. *Get a grip. It's not Michael. It can't possibly be Michael. It must be somebody else.*

A hand on my arm. I let out a small squeal of alarm.

"You all right, love?"

My head whips round and I see a woman standing in front of me, a hanky in her hand. A real one, made of cotton, neatly folded and ironed. I mouth "thank you," then take it and swipe it across my lips. The woman sits beside me and puts a hand on my shoulder. Suddenly I'm crying, really crying. Big gulping sobs, shoulders quaking, snot streaming from my nose. The full works.

People shoot me the odd glance as they pass, but otherwise seem unconcerned. This is a hospital, after all; as with prisons, tragedy is not something in short supply.

The woman sits there, witnessing, not speaking. I smile at her briefly, try to pull myself together, only to be ambushed by more tears.

"Bad news, was it, love?"

I turn to face her. See pale blue peering out from under heavy folds of skin. The flesh around her chin has turned to jowls, but there's still a vibrancy to her complexion, a liveliness that suggests she's had a good life.

"I lost my husband a couple of years back. Knocked me for six. But you do get over it." She's dressed in a hospital uniform, the kind support staff wear. A cleaner, perhaps, or maybe she works in the kitchens. I imagine her struggling on her widow's pension, working part-time for barely the minimum wage.

Christ. I probably earn more in an hour than she makes in a week.

"You'll be all right." She squeezes my shoulder. "It's never as bad as you imagine."

Oh, but it is, I want to tell her, *and sometimes it's worse. Sometimes it's simply more than you can take.*

But I don't say anything. Just smile, grateful for her kindness. "Thanks."

The woman looks at her watch. "I'd best go, love. My bus leaves in five." She leans over and pats my hand again, a thin gold band on her wedding finger. I try to hand her back the ruined handkerchief but she waves it away. "You need it more than I do."

"Thank you," I say again.

She stands, slowly, painfully. Bad hips or knees, I think; perhaps both. I watch her walk toward the main road, each step clearly an effort. And wonder if I'll ever make it as far as she has.

It's only when she disappears around the corner that I remember my phone and switch it back on.

Almost immediately it vibrates. I look at the screen.

Janine.

FORTY-FOUR

have to hand it to her—this place rocks. Right on the river at Greenwich, it's all exposed brickwork and warehouse chic. God knows who Janine managed to borrow it from. A client, obviously—possibly some property developer, since this apartment appears to be the only one in the building that's inhabited. A show home, I'm guessing.

I'm impressed she's pulled this off at such short notice.

"How long have we got?" I ask her, taking in the cavernous lounge and its sparse but stylish furniture. Half a dozen canvases fill the walls. All by the same artist, I'd say; bold abstracts in shimmering peacock shades. More like a high-end gallery than anywhere you'd actually live.

"Three hours. I have to get the keys back by seven."

We size each other up. Janine's sticking with the Bond theme, I note, vamped up in a sleek black catsuit and black Gucci heels. She's wearing heavy dark eyeliner and pale lip gloss, her hair hoisted into a jaunty ponytail.

I have to admit she looks fabulous. Amazing, the power of carefully applied slap to alter a face. Not that I can fault her figure. Janine has the kind of lean, toned physique you'd expect to see on a professional athlete, rather than some self-indulgent escort.

"You look great," I say sincerely. "Fantastic."

She grins back at me. "I was going to say the same to you. In fact, I really wouldn't have known it *was* you."

I check myself out in the mirror above the fireplace. I'm wearing a blond wig I borrowed off a girl I once did a duo with. It's quality, not some cheap synthetic deal. This is real hair, cut in a sharp bob, with a perfect ash tone that completely alters my complexion.

It's a bit creepy, looking at my head, wondering who this used to be attached to. It's one thing to sell your body—after all, you get it back afterward. Quite another to sell your hair.

Instead of my usual minimal makeup, I've laid it on thick. Even purchased a set of the false eyelashes that are Janine's stock-in-trade. Without Elisa to help me, it took me half an hour to attach them, but I have to admit the result is worth it. My eyes are wider, more striking; with eyeliner and silvery shadow, quite mesmerizing.

My pièce de résistance, however, are the colored contact lenses. I went for the most expensive I could find, a subtle blend of blues and grays that looks both authentic and arresting. They transform me in seconds from a dark-eyed Celt to a cool Nordic blue-eyed blonde.

Janine is right. You really wouldn't know it was me. Every time I glance in the mirror the unfamiliar girl reflected there looks surprised, even a little shocked.

I check the time on my phone. Three fifteen. Harry should be here in a few minutes. I go into the kitchen, put the champagne I bought into the fridge. Janine follows me, removing another smaller bottle from her bag.

"Want one?" She holds it up. "It's vodka. He won't smell it on your breath."

I nod. I'm feeling almost sick with nerves. Maybe it will help.

Janine pours an inch into two glasses. She downs hers in one, then roots around again in her handbag. Pulls out a small plastic bag of white powder.

"You sure you'll be okay with that?" I ask as she makes herself a line on the polished work surface.

She ignores me. Bends over and sniffs it up her neat little nostrils. She straightens and offers the bag to me. I shake my head. A stiff drink is more than enough. I'm going to need my wits about me.

"I'll give him some when he gets here." Janine wipes the end of her nose. "It'll blur his edges a bit. Make him less likely to notice anything."

I lift an eyebrow but leave it at that. It's way too late to argue this out. Besides, she's clearly nervous herself, going back into the lounge and pacing up and down its considerable length, avoiding my eyes.

I stand by one of the windows overlooking the Thames. Run through everything again in my head, making sure there's nothing I've forgotten. "You remember what to do?" I grab Janine's arm as she walks past.

She nods. "Don't worry. I've got it."

I pull her round to face me. "If it gets rough, Janine, you go, all right? Leave me to handle him."

She nods again, but her fingers come up to the base of her throat, fluttering nervously. Suddenly, behind all the makeup, I see her for the young girl she still is.

Another person I've dragged into the mud.

I check the time again. Nearly half past. Where the fuck is he?

Janine clocks my expression. "Don't worry about it. He'll show. He's always late."

But what if he doesn't? I wonder. What if he's got wind of what

I'm up to? Or simply changed his mind? I walk to the window and peer down at the river. Feel my pulse beginning to race as the minutes tick by.

I turn to see Janine downing another shot of vodka. Christ, at this rate she'll be legless by the time he turns up.

"Perhaps you should give him a ring?" I ask, trying to keep the anxiety from my voice.

She nods. Retrieves her phone from her bag. I watch as she finds his number, presses the call button, and holds it to her ear.

Half a minute later she snaps the phone cover shut. "No reply."

Christ, it's quarter to. He's not fucking coming. My mind races. What on earth do I do now?

The truth is, I have no idea. There is no plan B.

A loud buzz on the intercom makes us both jump. Janine shoots me a panicky look, then half runs to answer it. I settle myself on one of the sofas, taking a deep breath and adopting a pose I hope looks relaxed and seductive.

Janine buzzes him up. Neither of us speaks as we wait for the lift to bring him to the apartment.

A minute later Harry's moon face swings into view. He scans the room before striding in and kissing Janine on the cheek. She takes his coat and jacket into the adjoining cloakroom, leaving him free for a moment to focus on me.

I give him a lazy smile and get to my feet. "Hello. My name is Lene. You must be Harry."

I pronounce his name "hairy," speaking a little more slowly than usual, as if unsure how to say it. The Norwegian accent sounds convincing, at least to my ears. God knows, I've practiced it enough, spending several hours on the Internet studying every YouTube video I could find, trying to perfect the lilting tone and the different emphasis on words.

Janine returns, standing behind Harry, her eyes fixed on me. I sense her holding her breath as he looks me over.

"Very nice," Harry croons appreciatively, extending his hand. "Pleased to get the opportunity to meet you, Lene. Janine tells me you're only in town for a few days."

"Two," I say as he turns to Janine, giving her an approving nod. She beams. "I knew you'd like her."

The introductions over, Harry slumps onto a sofa, one hand loosening his tie. Janine disappears into the kitchen to get the drinks. Harry eyes me for a moment or so, then glances round the apartment. "This yours?"

I shake my head. "It belongs to a boyfriend."

"Lucky fella." He grins. "On both counts."

I return his smile, stretching out my legs, knowing the low-cut stilettos give the illusion of extra length.

Janine returns with the champagne. I can tell by the slight flush on her face that she's already downed one in the kitchen. I send her a warning look, but she ignores me.

Despite my best efforts to stay calm I feel myself break into a sweat. One foot wrong and we're in more shit than we ever dreamed of.

"Oh, I almost forgot." Janine retrieves her handbag and gets out the coke. Harry nods approvingly and they both help themselves to a line. I calculate just how high she must be by now and my confidence wanes even further.

Perhaps I should call the whole thing off. Walk away. Take Tony's advice and clear the fuck right out of this country.

"Get your gorgeous little arse over here," Harry commands, and Janine perches on the armrest beside him, all but sitting on his lap. His arm snakes up round her waist and he raises his glass in the other hand.

"To good times," he toasts.

"To good times," we echo, and I manage to get Janine's eyes to meet mine. She gazes back at me impassively.

Christ, she's fucking loaded.

"Like the outfit." Harry looks her up and down and runs a hand over her breast. "Very Pussy Galore."

Janine giggles obligingly, and I relax a notch or two. Harry turns and beckons me over, raising his arm so I can slide in on his empty side.

"My cup runneth over," he says, ogling my breasts. I give him a cool Nordic smile. He dips his head, pulling me in for a kiss. I hesitate for a second or so, then soften into surrender; there's nothing like having to overcome a bit of resistance to get a man's attention.

"My turn," purrs Janine, tugging him away. She bends over and covers his mouth with hers, acting a little possessive. Or maybe not acting at all. When she releases him I can see a bulge rising in the crotch of his trousers.

"Well," Harry sighs, downing the rest of his champagne. "I'd love to chat, girls, but how about we get this show on the road? I've a dinner to get to by six."

"Sure." Janine gets to her feet, seizing the end of his tie and leading him toward the bedroom. I follow behind, mentally punching the air. The less conversation, the better, as far as I'm concerned—one slip with the accent could give the whole game away.

The bed is enormous, with one of those wider-than-superking mattresses you see in high-end hotels. Tailor-made for an orgy.

I've already scoped out the headboard. Latticework, in dark walnut or cherry. But strong—at least strong enough.

Harry sheds his clothes, draping his trousers carefully over the back of the chair. I note with amusement he's wearing those stretchy metal bands to hold up his socks. How very old school.

He runs a hand over my tight-fitting dress. "Let's get this off, shall we?" I smile, turning my back so he can unzip me. But he nods at Janine. "Let her do it."

Janine, naked, strolls over. Deftly strips me to my underwear.

"And the rest," orders Harry.

I face her and she kisses me on the mouth. No tongues. Just going through the motions, but there's still something hard, even aggressive in it. She runs both hands down the curve of my back, releasing my bra, then, tucking her fingers into my panties, shoves them downward.

Harry watches as she pushes me back on the bed, spreading my legs and kneeling between them. She kisses me again, hungrily—or at least with a show of hunger. I see Harry's eyes fixed on the pair of us, one hand caressing his growing erection.

Janine abandons my mouth and moves to my breasts, her tongue circling then engulfing each nipple, teasing each between her lips before moving her head down between my legs. In one deft movement she finds my clitoris and I gasp in surprise. Every working girl knows you only simulate oral; anything more is time-consuming and pointless—clients don't have the patience to wait for the recipient to actually get off.

Janine lifts her eyes briefly and looks into mine. Then takes my clit between her perfect teeth and gives it a sharp little nip. I yelp in pain, only just managing to disguise it as a gasp of pleasure.

The bloody bitch. The corners of Janine's mouth lift as she sits up. Revenge, I think. Her own little payback for getting her into all this.

"Actually I have something much more interesting in mind for her." Janine turns to Harry. "Remember what I said she enjoyed?"

She reaches down, locating the bag I tucked under the foot of the bed. Takes out the handcuffs. They're the plastic kind made for sex play, only strong enough to give an illusion of restraint.

She hands one to Harry and grabs my arm, motioning him to take the other. They attach one end of each handcuff around my wrists. Janine goes to clip the other to the headboard, but Harry shakes his head.

"The other way round."

Janine looks at him for a moment, then grasps his meaning. She rolls me over onto my stomach and threads the handcuff through the lattice. Harry follows suit. Now I'm forced to crouch on my knees, arse sticking up into the air.

I hear Janine going back to the bag. She passes the blindfold over my eyes and the world goes dark. As she slips the gag into my mouth, I'm filled with a flood of anxiety. What if I have an asthma attack?

Steady, Grace. Breathe through your nose. I force myself to inhale slowly, calmly. I give the handcuffs a tentative tug, feel them cut into my wrists. Hell. They may be only for show, but now it comes to it, I'm no longer sure I could get out of them.

This is all going exactly as you intended, I try to reassure myself. But suddenly I realize how vulnerable I am. How easy it would be for Janine to abandon the plan and do whatever she thinks will serve her best.

A hot rush of fear. This is crazy. I'm completely trapped.

I turn my head toward Janine, wishing I could say something, hear her response. Does she really understand how much rides on this? Did I explain it all well enough?

Did she even believe me?

The first sting of the whip on my bare flesh makes me flinch. The second prompts a cry of pain, muffled by the wodge of material between my teeth.

The lash cuts into my arse again. I bite down hard on the gag and blink back sudden tears. Is Janine doing this? Or Harry?

Four, five, six. I count the blows: seven, eight, nine, ten.

The skin on my bottom is glowing, throbbing. Jesus, it hurts. How does anybody get off on this shit?

"My turn," I hear Janine's voice. Harry hands over the whip. The sound of a condom packet being ripped open between his teeth.

"Go on," he urges Janine, and I feel another sharp sting. "Out of the way," Harry commands.

The next sensation is his cock pushing inside me. Hard. I'm not wet and have no time to accommodate his considerable size, so it's painful. I draw away instinctively, but Harry grips my shoulders, driving himself into me more forcefully.

Christ, I think, with another jolt of fear. *What if he grabs my hair?* I never thought of that. I keep my head low, submissive. Harry screws me for a minute or so more, then groans, collapsing onto my back.

I exhale with relief. Wait for him to shift his weight from me, desperate now to be released from the handcuffs, to get on with the next part of the plan. But as Harry straightens up, I feel him nudging at me again, semistiff already—or maybe never flaccid. *Fuck*, I think. *He's taken Viagra. This could last forever.*

He forces a couple of fingers back into my vagina and rubs his cock against my thigh, getting himself fully hard again. It doesn't take long. If nothing else, Janine and I have succeeded in seriously turning him on.

With his erection fully reestablished, there's a pause. I'm hoping Harry is putting on another condom. I wonder what Janine is doing. Watching? Waiting?

Or changing her mind, perhaps, formulating some scheme of her own.

I don't get the opportunity to worry any further. Harry is pushing against me, and by the time I realize what's coming, there's no time to prepare.

Relax, Grace, I urge myself. *Relax.*

Pain sears through me as he forces his way into my anus. I nearly throw up as I sense something tear inside me. *Give me a fucking chance*, I want to yell, but I can't even speak.

He starts to pump, and each forward and backward thrust brings its own kind of agony. I'm crying now, biting on the gag so hard I almost choke. My wrists hurt from where I can't help pulling back against the unyielding plastic.

Harry is grunting now with the effort. And pleasure. His breathing labored, animallike. I get a sudden flash of Michael's girlfriend. What she must have endured. Anally raped. I read the reports when he was in prison. Even saw some of the photos.

Not that he made that mistake again.

And now I'm genuinely frightened. Fear descends like fog, engulfing me, reducing my breath to short repeated gasps. I feel dizzy, start to hyperventilate with panic. I try to calm myself, slow my breathing, but I can't—even the attempt makes me feel more out of control.

Jesus, just come, will you? I scream in my head, wondering if I might pass out. Somewhere deep inside my mind, something snaps and I make myself a promise.

I will never, ever let anyone do this to me again.

Then finally, at that point when I know I can't take any more, I hear Janine, her tone both pleading and seductive. "Save some for me, won't you, Harry?"

The thrusting stops. I feel him withdraw, but the cramp in my anus barely recedes, a pulsing ache radiating right through my torso.

Suddenly the gag is gone, the blindfold slid from my eyes. I'm blinking in the dimmed light of the room, still too bright after the darkness of the last ten minutes.

Janine leans over to release the handcuffs and I catch her look of genuine unease as she sees the tears on my cheeks. But she stays in part, turning and giving Harry a lascivious smile.

"Come on, big boy, it's your turn."

He looks at her dubiously.

"Oh, *come on*," she teases. "We won't hurt you. Will we, Stella?"

Stella?

It's the wrong name. *She just called me the wrong fucking NAME.*

I widen my eyes at Janine in alarm. See from the way she stiffens that she too has realized her mistake.

We've blown it, I think. We've completely fucking blown it.

We wait for Harry's reaction. For him to ask what the hell is going on. But he just looks at us, grinning.

I exhale, my breath jagged. Thank Christ. He hasn't noticed.

"Really, Hairree, you'll love every minute," I say quickly, anxious to move things along before Harry can mentally rewind the last ten seconds. "We promise to be gentle. Not beat you with birch twigs, like at home."

I giggle and Harry's grin widens. He eyes the handcuffs, weighing up whether they present any kind of threat.

"Okay." He lies on his back and holds out his hands. "We're only playing, right, girls? No actual pain."

"Of course not," Janine promises, slipping the cuff onto his wrist and clipping him to the headboard. She chucks the other one to me and I attach him to the far side of the bed, moving his arm wider, allowing him less leverage.

Harry pulls against the cuffs, testing, then lies back, reassured. It's obvious one firm yank from him would snap them in an instant.

Janine approaches with the blindfold, but he pulls his head away. "I'd rather watch."

Her eyes flicker toward me in panic. The blindfold is crucial. Without it there's no way this is ever going to work.

"Come on, Mr. Harry," I coax in my best Norwegian accent. "It's good, not to be able to see. Only feel. It focuses your mind on the"—I pause as if searching for the right English word—"on the *sensation*."

He considers this for a second. Nods his assent. "But no funny business, okay?"

Janine slips the blindfold over his eyes, making sure there are no gaps he might see through. I wave a hand in front of his face, just to make sure. He doesn't flinch.

I nod to Janine. She climbs onto the bed, placing herself between his legs. Slips off the used condom and slides her mouth around Harry's cock.

Contain and distract, exactly as we discussed.

While she's keeping him happy, I go to the MP3 player in the lounge and plug in my smartphone. "All I Want" by LCD Sound-system erupts through the speakers.

I go into the kitchen and open the cupboard where I've hidden the other bag, and bring it back into the bedroom.

"What's the music for?" Harry asks.

"Only a *leetle* atmosphere," I say.

"Bit loud, isn't it?" he complains.

I ignore him. Janine picks up the rhythm of her mouth on his cock, moving up his shaft and twirling her tongue around the tip until he groans in pleasure.

I have to admit, that's quite some technique.

Lifting the first set of handcuffs out of the bag as quietly as I can, I attach one end to the headboard and lay the other carefully across the pillow, making sure it doesn't touch Harry's head. Then repeat the same on the other side.

I tap Janine lightly on the shoulder. She lifts her eyes to mine and in that moment I see exactly how scared she is. I give her a quick smile. She removes her mouth from Harry's cock and posi-tions herself opposite me at the head of the bed. Harry wriggles. His erection stands up from his groin at a right angle, glistening, near purple with engorgement, bouncing slightly as he shifts into a more comfortable position.

"So what's next, girls?" he asks, his voice eager with anticipation.

"This," I say in my own voice, and with rapid, synchronized movements, Janine and I grab the prison-issue handcuffs and snap them around his wrists. Janine manages hers perfectly, opening and clicking them shut, just like we practiced.

"What the fuck?" cries Harry, sensing the weight of them, the cold, heavy steel against his skin. He pulls down hard. The plastic handcuffs snap instantly; the real ones kick in, stopping him dead.

"Jesus!" Harry shouts, almost spitting with fury. "What are you fucking bitches playing at?"

I look at Janine, mouth "thank you" and nod toward the door. She grabs her clothes and darts into the lounge.

I give her two minutes to dress and leave.

FORTY-FIVE

Harry's roaring now, trying to make himself heard above the burst of tortured synth blasting from the speakers.

But there's no one to hear him except me.

I bend down, put my hand back into my bag, and lift out the gun. Position myself at the side of the bed and place the end of the barrel on the bridge of Harry's nose. He flinches at the touch of the metal and twists his head away, kicking out toward where he senses I'm standing.

I step out of the way. Lean over, mouth against his ear.

"Keep still or I'll fucking kill you."

Using the tip of the gun, I draw back the blindfold. Harry freezes as his eyes focus on the barrel. "What the fuck are you—"

"Shut up."

I move to the foot of the bed, holding the gun steady in my right hand. His gaze never leaves it for an instant.

"You fucking crazy Norwegian bitch."

He stops, eyes widening as he watches me pull off my wig and shake out my hair. Transferring the gun to my left hand, I remove the contacts from my eyes, dropping them onto the bedside table.

I'm still naked, but I don't care. My transformation leaves Harry speechless. He stares at me, and I see his jaw stiffen as he realizes who I am.

And what kind of situation he's now in.

His face pales as all hope that this is some bizarre sex game deserts him. I savor the moment. I know what I planned, but now I find I want to improvise, to ad lib a little. I walk to the end of the bed and rummage in the bag. I'm pretty sure I put one in here, almost as an afterthought.

My hand seizes the vibrator. It's one of those neon pink numbers, shaped like a real penis, only much larger than most men can boast. It's equipped with sturdy D-size batteries and a menu that includes rotation as well as vibration.

I hold its obscene bulk up so Harry can see it. His expression freezes as his brain starts to process the possibilities.

Of which, when you think about it, there really is only one.

"Listen . . . Stella, isn't it? Just listen to me. I—"

"Shut up."

I dip back into the bag. Pull out the bottle of lube. Squeeze a liberal dose onto the vibrator's oversize head.

"Stella, for fuck's sake."

His voice is louder now, rivaling the noise from the stereo. He's kicking out with his legs, flailing as I approach him, the handcuffs cutting into his wrists as he tries to twist round and kick me away.

I lift the gun and point it at his temple.

"My name is Grace, as I'm sure you know. And don't imagine that I have anything to lose by killing you. So relax, baby," I croon. "You never know, you may even enjoy it."

His whole body goes rigid as I approach him.

"Lift your legs."

He doesn't move.

"Lift your legs, Harry, or I'll blow your fucking head off."

He raises his knees, a whimper escaping his mouth.

"Please . . ." His words elongate to a howl as I shove the vibrator into his arsehole, as far as it will go. And press the button for high-speed vibrate.

"Aaarggghhhh, God, fuck noooo," he cries, tears springing to his eyes. *"Turn it off, turn it off!"*

I reach for the buttons at the end of the machine. Flick the one for rotate. Harry's words disintegrate into screams. He's writhing now, twisting around, trying to get away from the pain.

I lift my phone out of my bag and take a couple of pictures. Then retreat to the kitchen and pour myself a shot of the vodka. Down in one, just like Janine.

The alcohol burns its way down my throat. I listen to the roars of protest from the bedroom and force myself to picture Michael. *Imagine it's him in there,* I tell myself. *Imagine you had this chance to torture him.*

But it's no good—my initial surge of pleasure quickly palls to disgust. Inflicting pain, even on a scumbag like Harry, is not something I relish as much as I imagined.

I go back in. Harry is lying motionless, half twisted on his side, tears running down his cheeks. I reach over and turn off the vibrator, remove it, and drop it back into the bag. It's smeared with blood and something darker I'd rather not consider.

I walk into the lounge and cut the music. Return to the bedroom. There's no sign of Harry's erection now. His cock lies limp, huddling in his pubic hair like a small creature taking refuge.

I give him a minute to recover. "What do you want?" he asks eventually, his voice quavering.

I stare at him coolly. "Half a million."

He laughs. At least I think it's a laugh. It sounds a bit like he's choking. "You must be fucking joking."

I flick the safety catch off the gun. It makes a barely audible click that Harry senses even if he can't quite hear it.

"Do I look like I'm joking?"

He glares at me for a few seconds. Pulls again on the handcuffs. Gives up. "All right. I'll see what I can do. Just let me out of these."

"Not so fast." I bend and remove a folder from the bag. "This isn't some quick shag."

Keeping the gun trained on Harry, I pull out the printouts from Amanda's SD card and fan the pictures on the bed. Hold each one up in turn so he has a good view. "There's videos too," I say. "Taken at the party. But then you know that, don't you?"

He doesn't reply. I put both hands back on the gun and aim it squarely at his crotch. His legs begin to tremble. There's something leaking from his anus onto the bedspread.

"You know because Elisa sent them to you."

He swallows. "No, I . . ." His words die in his throat.

"And instead of coughing up the paltry fifteen grand she asked for, you went to your mates. And our lovely friend winds up dead."

"She was a nasty little whore," he says, finding his voice.

I raise an eyebrow. "That's a bit rich, isn't it? I'd say we make our money a great deal more honestly than you."

"What, by spreading your legs? Blackmailing people?"

"Sex for money is a legal transaction—at least in this country. Which is more than can be said for some of your deals."

I look him up and down, from his eyes to his cock and back again. "Let's face it, Harry, in a straw poll of public opinion, I reckon your profession would be somewhat less popular than mine."

He glowers at me, but doesn't speak.

"For the record, I don't condone blackmail. There's no doubt what Elisa did was wrong, but it's not like you've stayed within the confines of the law, is it? That little thing you have going with Alex Lennart and Edward Hardy, for instance. If that comes to light you'll definitely find yourself out of a job. And behind bars."

Harry's mouth moves into his habitual sneer, its effect some-what diminished by the tears still drying on his cheeks.

"So what do you want?"

I smile at him. "Actually I'd prefer to see your sorry arse rot in a cell, Harry. You and your nasty little chums. But I'll settle for the money."

He clears his throat. "I haven't got that kind of cash just lying around."

"I realize that. Borrow it if you have to. After all, it's only . . . what . . . half a year's bonus for you? And that's not even count-ing what you make on the side."

I shift the gun into my other hand, its weight beginning to make my arm ache.

"So I'm giving you one day. I've left you detailed instructions of what to do. If by this time tomorrow you haven't done *exactly* what I said, I'm sending these pictures to every interested party I can think of." I count them off on my fingers. "Your wife. Your boss. The head of that exclusive private school you send your kids to. The editors of all the national newspapers. I reckon that'll do for starters."

His face contorts with rage. "You wouldn't fucking dare."

"Really?" I glare back at him. "You sure about that? After what just happened?"

"Fucking bitch," he mutters, but it's more of a grumble now than a threat.

"Yes," I say mildly. "I'm sure I am. But don't underestimate me, Harry. I've taken precautions. If anything happens to me—anything at all, even something that might look like an accident—I've made sure that these will be sent out to everyone on that list. *And* the police. So don't imagine for one second that the solution you and your friends chose for Elisa is an option for me. Or Janine."

I walk round to the head of the bed and hold the gun up to his temple. "Believe me, Harry, I'd welcome the chance to blow you right out of the water. Even from the mortuary block."

He stares at me. All the fight gone now from his eyes.

"Understood," he says. "I'll sort it."

I pull on the jeans and sweater I brought with me. Pack up my things. Harry lies on the bed, watching.

"You're not going to leave me here, are you?" he asks in a panicky voice as I put on my coat. I smile. Sling the bag over my shoulder and pick up the gun. Keeping it trained on him, I go round and release each handcuff.

He sits up, rubbing the weals around his wrists.

"Twenty-four hours," I repeat. "Understood?"

He nods.

I walk toward the door and turn. He's crouched on the side of the bed, bent over, head in his hands.

"Oh, and Harry . . ."

He raises his face. His eyes are red and he looks ill, defeated. I lower the gun, certain now he's got the message.

". . . just one last thing. A heads-up for your mate Hardy. Tell him I don't appreciate visits from his unofficial henchmen—even if they do pay my fees."

I close the door of the apartment behind me and pause for a minute, leaning on the wall, my legs suddenly unsteady.

So far, so good, I think, but knowing there's worse to come. And this time there's nothing I can do except wait.

FORTY-SIX

The bell to my flat rings at ten to three, right as I'm sending the last of the e-mails. I run down and sign for the package, then climb back upstairs, clutching it to my chest. I double-lock the door behind me before ripping it open.

A single ticket. Exactly as instructed.

I examine it briefly, then shove it in the pocket of my jeans. Stuff all the things I need into my rucksack and pull on my coat.

Outside the weather has turned windy and overcast, the sky a shade of whitish gray that casts an unflattering light over everything. People's faces look drawn and pale. Resigned.

It's warmer down in the Underground. I crush myself into a crowded tube destined for Waterloo, join the throng exiting to the mainline station. My pulse begins to quicken as I rise up on the escalator into the main concourse, uncertain what I'm going to find when I emerge.

Will they have someone waiting?

Hurrying over to the announcement board, I pretend to search for a train as I survey the entrance to the luggage service. There doesn't seem to be anybody hanging around. But then there wouldn't—not if they're doing their job properly.

Not too late to call it quits, says a voice in my head. *You've had your fun. You've done your bit for Amanda.*

I take a deep breath and walk up to the counter. I hand over the ticket to a middle-aged man who barely acknowledges me. Just glances at it, then disappears through a door behind him.

A minute later he returns with the parcel. Covered in gray plastic, it's much bulkier than I imagined, and for a moment I think I won't get it into my rucksack. I transfer some things into my handbag, try to squeeze it in.

It fits. Just. The zips refuse to quite meet at the top, but it'll hold. I take another deep breath, ignoring the anxious thump of my heart. Resist the urge to check around me.

Look calm, I tell myself, aware of all the security cameras in the station. *Look casual. Unconcerned.*

There's a Smith's near the main exit. I buy a couple of magazines and ask for a large bag. The cashier hands me one without comment and I make my way to the toilets. Picking a loo with a baby-changing tray, I check there are no cameras overhead.

I work fast, mindful of the attendant lurking on the other side of the door. Remove the parcel and place it on the tray. Grab the scissors, the Bubble Wrap, brown paper, and tape from my handbag, alert for the sound of approaching footsteps. I can't hear anything unusual. A mother scolding a child. Two women discussing whether or not to get a taxi up to Oxford Street.

I close my eyes for a few seconds, then cut open the parcel. Stare, mesmerized, at the fat bundles of fifty-pound notes. Even in a cash economy like mine, this much money is a sobering sight. I pick one up and riffle the corners, the way you would a pack of cards.

It certainly feels . . . and smells real. Papery and fresh. Potent.

I do a quick count. Twenty bundles, each containing £25,000. All there.

I gaze at them for a few last seconds before dividing them up. Four for Anna. Four for Kristen. Two for Janine. The remaining quarter of a million I split exactly in half, removing five notes from each. I wrap the separate piles carefully, first in Bubble Wrap, then brown paper and parcel tape, writing out each address in capitals.

A knock on the door. My heart leaps. "You okay in there, miss?"

"Fine," I stammer, turning and flushing the loo. After a moment, whoever it was walks away. I stuff the tape and scissors and remains of the paper into the shopping bag, along with the magazines, dropping it into the rubbish bin on the way out.

Twenty to five. I fidget as I wait in line for a taxi. I'm barely going to make it.

Ahead of me a trio of businessmen are discussing an upcoming meeting. One glances at me briefly, then his eyes slide away. Nothing about me warrants a second look. I've made sure of that. I'm clean faced, not even a dash of mascara. My hair is pulled back into a clip and I'm wearing my drabbest clothes.

The last thing I need today is attention.

The businessmen disappear into the bowels of a black cab. Half a minute later another draws up beside me. The driver leans across to speak to me. "Where to, love?"

I give him the address in Tower Hill and climb in. We inch into the rush-hour traffic. We've scarcely managed two hundred yards before we're forced to a standstill.

"Know any quicker routes?" I ask the cabbie, trying to keep the desperation from my voice.

He thinks for a few seconds. "We could try Southwark Bridge."

He pulls out into the center of the lane and waits for somebody to let him in, then drags the cab round into a U-turn and heads up Stamford Street. I sit with my hands clenched into fists.

We *have* to make it. I'm not going to get another chance.

Fifteen minutes later we pull up outside the depot. I shove a twenty-pound note from my purse at the driver and wave away his offer of change. Run up to the office and let myself in.

It's 4:55 by the clock above the desk. I'm just in time.

A clerk appears from behind a back door. "Too late," he says. "Can't do deliveries after five."

"It's five to," I object, nodding at the clock.

He doesn't even bother to glance at it. "That one's slow."

"Please." I say, wishing now I'd bothered with some slap.

"Sorry."

He starts to retreat into the back room. "Hang on." I pull one of the fifty-pound notes out of my pocket and slide it across the counter. He looks at it, then up at my face, trying to suss out whether I'm joking.

I nod. Push it farther in his direction.

"Okay," he says, making the money disappear. "I'll see what I can do."

It takes him ten minutes to calculate the cost of sending all five parcels by courier. I pay in cash, inventing a bogus name and address for their forms. Write *Personal Effects* in the bit where it asks what's being delivered.

I send Kristen's parcel to her parents' house in Scotland. Anna's and Janine's to their respective flats. The one for the rape crisis center I address to the head office in Charing Cross. The other goes to a charity: *The Alison Tennant Trust*.

No explanations, and no indications as to my real identity. I have no idea how these parcels will be received, of course, but figure an anonymous donation may be more likely to stick.

Back outside, in the open air, the pressure in my chest begins to subside. I find I can breathe more easily. I stroll along Lower Thames Street, feeling lighter. A weight literally lifted.

I head toward London Bridge, thinking I'll walk home. By the steps, a little way under the arches, I spot the man. He's huddled beneath the ironwork, a bed of cardboard and several ratty-looking blankets draped over his overcoat. I go up and give him the rucksack and the rest of the five hundred quid I kept by for expenses.

The homeless man blinks at me in astonishment. "You sure?" His voice rough, unused.

"Completely."

His mouth widens into a grimy-toothed grin as he raises a hand. "You're a fucking angel," he calls as I walk away.

I climb the steps to the footbridge. Halfway across, my phone rings. I pull it from my pocket and check the screen.

"Number withheld." But I know who it is.

I hesitate, looking over at the gray and white vista of London spread out before me. Let it ring, once . . . twice . . . three times.

Then press the button to accept the call.

FORTY-SEVEN

don't bother with the gun. There's no point. This time, there'll be nothing to be gained by surprise.

This time he'll be well prepared.

I arrive early, five minutes before midnight. Wait by the gardens down on the river. The weather has turned wet again, rain gusting against my umbrella, which fails to keep the water off my legs. I can't see anyone around at all. Just cars sliding past, the hiss of tires on wet tarmac.

I huddle under a holly tree, feeling my damp jeans begin to stick uncomfortably against my skin. Check my watch again. Midnight. *Maybe he's had a change of heart*, I think. Maybe he's got something more effective in mind.

A black Range Rover glides toward me, slowing as it passes. A face at the window. I watch the car turn at the lights. A few minutes later two men round the corner, walking in my direction. It's hard to see them clearly in the streetlights. Dark clothing, suits under raincoats. One carrying something in his right hand. A briefcase?

My heart reacts. *Fuck. I must have been insane agreeing to this meeting. I'm a sitting duck out here. An easy target.*

Get a grip, I tell myself. *They won't take a risk like that. Not now. They've way too much to lose.*

The men are just a few yards away now. One looks up at me inquiringly, his mouth a half smile, his hands obscured in the pockets of his jacket.

I tense, wondering whether to run for it. But it's too late. They're too close. All I can do is wait for whatever is going to happen.

They walk right past.

I'm nearly drenched by the time the car draws up alongside me. A sleek black Mercedes. Tinted windows. Obviously.

The one on the passenger's side slides down noiselessly. Alex Lennart leans over.

"Get in."

He opens the door. I hesitate, peer in at the backseats. Nothing except a suit and a briefcase.

"There's no one," he says. "Like I promised."

The window shuts and I climb into the leather seat. It's warm already—must have some kind of internal heating. Sophie Hunger croons "Let Me Go" from the speakers, rich and silky and sensuous.

Lennart regards me steadily. "Good to see you again, Stella. Or can I call you Grace now?"

I don't bother to respond. He looks at me a moment longer, then pulls off the cycle lane and sets off along Millbank.

"Sorry I'm late," he says. "Flight was delayed."

I nod. Shift in my seat, my legs still cold and uncomfortable.

"This song reminds me of you." Lennart flicks a finger toward the sound system.

I don't react. "Where are we going?" I ask as we hug the river eastward.

"Just somewhere we can talk."

He clicks off the music and we drive in silence, no sound except the rhythmic swish of windscreen wipers sweeping across our field of vision. Like a metronome, beating time as we cruise through the deserted streets.

We turn onto the A13. "That was quite a stunt you pulled with old Harry," Lennart says. "I was impressed."

I don't reply, sensing talk will get me nowhere. And truthfully, I'm not sure I even trust myself to speak.

"I assume you saw the news today?" he continues, undaunted, glancing at me briefly before fixing his eyes back on the road.

Hardy's resignation from the Defense Ministry. It wasn't headline news, but had received a fair amount of coverage. Or rather speculation. Several of the papers linked his sudden departure to his testimony at the select committee.

"Backbenches for the rest of his term," Lennart remarks. "Then I expect the party will drop him at the next election, when the media's no longer paying attention. Thanks to those photos you sent the chief whip. Government minister partying with a dead call girl—seems even the Tories draw a line at that."

I stay mute. We're leaving London now, heading toward Barking and Dagenham. High-rises and squat warehousing. Signs for the Dartford Tunnel. I resist the urge to ask again where we're going.

"So I'm guessing Ted and Harry weren't the only clients Amanda was blackmailing?"

"No."

Lennart smiles, acknowledging the fact I've broken my silence. "So where's all the money, then? I'll bet she accumulated quite a bit."

I shrug. "It's sitting in a bank account somewhere. I can't touch it. No one can."

Lennart overtakes an Audi and accelerates up the outside lane. "I wouldn't worry about it," he says. "I imagine they can afford it."

I check the speedometer. We're doing nearly a hundred. In the rain. On a divided highway. Is he driving like this to scare me? I gaze out my window at the blur of lights and buildings. What will he do if we're pulled over by the police?

Nothing, I suspect. Let them book him, knowing the charges will be buried under paperwork.

We peel off the A13, curve right around the roundabout, and head back toward Barking. *What the hell?* I stare out the window, trying to get my bearings. A minute later we take another right. And another.

Christ. Perhaps I should have brought the gun, I think, as Lennart turns into the car park of some kind of nature reserve and kills the ignition. After a minute or so the lights go out and the engine ticks in the darkness, cooling fast in the night air. I peer out the window but can't see any other cars.

A lurch in my stomach as I realize we're completely alone.

Lennart takes his hands off the wheel, leans back in his seat. Exhales heavily.

"So, nice work, Grace. I like your sense of poetic justice. Deprive the politician of his career and the banker his money. But what are you going to do about me? That's what I've been wondering. Execute me with one of my own weapons?"

I look away as he turns to face me, eyes squinting with amusement. "Trouble is I'm not married. No children. Strictly, I'm not employed by anyone, and I've hardly an impeccable reputation to lose." He sighs. "In my line of work, mud doesn't stick; you're up to your neck in it anyway."

I run my tongue around my teeth and swallow. My mouth feels painfully dry. I can feel Lennart's scrutiny like a prickle on the surface of my skin.

"You interest me, Grace. Not many women do that."

"I'll take it as a compliment," I say, forcing myself to speak.

"You should."

I turn my face to meet his. It's still dark outside, but my eyes are growing accustomed to the gloom and I find I can gaze right into those inscrutable iron-gray eyes. He's more attractive than I remember. And compelling, in that understated way. His effect is unnerving, exerting a kind of force field that somehow saps my remaining energy.

"Amanda was beautiful," he says, his voice softer. "But your face is more interesting." He lifts a hand and touches my cheek. I steel myself not to flinch.

"So, Grace, what are we going to do about our little problem? Or rather, what are *you* going to do?"

He's playing with me, I think. Relishing every moment.

I stare out the front window. Maybe I should tell him the truth. Maybe I should tell him that I have no idea. No plan. Nothing up my sleeve.

He's going to suss it soon anyway.

Because everything he's said to me since I got in this car is true. I can't blackmail him. I can't threaten or embarrass him. I have no leverage over him whatsoever.

But that's not the worst of it. Not by a long way. The worst I daren't admit even to myself.

"You can't help yourself, can you?" he says suddenly. "Like a moth to the flame."

I jerk my face back toward his. "What do you mean?"

His gaze is casual, even clinical. "Don't disappoint me, Grace. I think you know exactly what I mean."

An ancient feeling stirs within me, half-forgotten, now resurrected. A creeping lassitude weighing me down as he lifts his hand again and trails it from my chin to my chest. A warmth between my legs, an ache, dull but insistent.

The mind forgets, but the body always remembers.

I take a deep breath, confronted now with what I've so far managed to avoid—the terrible recognition that some part of me is drawn to this man. Desires him. Despite everything he is, and everything I know he has done.

"Grace," he whispers, slipping his hand through my shirt buttons and cupping my breast in his hand.

Oh God, not again. I close my eyes and find myself standing in that terrible little flat, facing Michael.

"Grace."

Lennart releases his seat belt and mine. Leans across the console between our seats and moves his hand to my thighs, pressing it against my jeans. I force myself to look at him, his features blurring as he moves closer.

"Keep your eyes shut," he commands. I obey as he pulls me toward him, covering my mouth with his. I kiss him back, wanting to devour him, to be devoured. Craving the oblivion that only sex can bring.

But Michael's face hovers in my head, that indifferent, almost triumphant expression in his eyes.

Lennart slides his tongue into my mouth. I push him away and sit upright.

"No."

I start to cough. Try to draw breath but my throat has seized up. Tears sting my eyes as I grab my handbag and grope for my inhaler. Grasp it and raise it to my mouth, pressing down hard on the canister.

Nothing.

Oh fuck, I think, as I remember it's run out. I forgot to get a new one. I fucking *forgot*.

I shake it and try again. Not even a hiss. I drop it and attempt to breathe in. I'm gasping, choking. Stars begin to implode in my head.

Oh God. I can't fucking breathe. Panic surges up inside me. My hands grip the seat as I try desperately to rake in some oxygen.

Lennart leans across me and takes something out of the glove compartment. A small tin. As another paroxysm of coughing engulfs me I see him remove a neatly rolled joint and light it, pulling on it deeply before holding it to my lips.

"Inhale," he orders. "As much as you can."

I try, but the coughing becomes more violent.

"Grace!" He grips my arm, his voice insistent. "You're hyperventilating. Calm down and try again." He raises the spliff to my mouth and I suck on it as hard as I can. Manage to pull some of the smoke into my lungs. A few seconds later the pain begins to ease.

"Again," Lennart insists.

I inhale more deeply this time, and the ache in my chest slowly subsides to a memory. I draw away, clearing my throat.

"Thanks," I choke, barely able to form the word.

He grinds the spliff out on the ashtray in the console. Chucks it back into the tin. "You should be more careful. Keep more than one inhaler. And get yourself on a decent preventative."

"I never had you down for a stoner," I say, my voice still croaky.

He laughs. "Purely medicinal. I find it helps with the headaches." He studies me for a minute while my internal chaos subsides. The pot has taken the edge off the fear; not much, but a little.

"Why did you just do that?" I ask. "Why not leave me? It would have been cleaner, wouldn't it?"

Lennart looks at me with the expression of a parent whose child just said something humorous. "What, and miss the best part? You haven't told me what I want to know yet."

"I thought you already knew it all."

"Not this. Not now. I mean what happened before," Lennart says, his eyes never leaving my face. "With Michael Farrish."

I swallow. He knows. Of course he does.

"Convicted for raping his girlfriend, right?"

I avoid his gaze. But don't bother to deny it.

"You worked with him for how long?" he asks, though I'm sure he already knows that too.

I squeeze my eyes shut. Let my head sink back into the headrest. "Two years." My lips are numb and it's an effort to speak.

Lennart thinks for a moment, his right hand rubbing his chin. "So, your job was to rehabilitate him, guide him through the sex offenders program. Get him to acknowledge the pain he caused his victim, and so on."

I nod, eyes still closed, wondering why he needs to do this.

"I'll bet Farrish did a very convincing job of compliance. Talked about his feelings, his difficult childhood, yadda yadda. You were convinced you were really getting somewhere, right?"

I cough. "Do we have to do this?" I lift my hand and wipe my eyes. I'm suddenly exhausted, wondering how this is all going to end. Almost ready for it to be over.

"Yes, Grace, I think we do," Lennart says, turning to me. "You know why? I think I'm the only person you *can* do this with."

I snort. But my heart's not in it.

"Oh, I'm sure there was plenty of talk afterward, in hospital," he continues, undeterred. "All that counseling and psychotherapy— after you tried the easy way out." The derision in his tone is mild, but unmistakable. I'm not sure if it's aimed at the therapists, or my botched attempt at an overdose.

"But your depression, what was at the heart of it, Grace? That's what interests me—and what should interest you." I feel his hand again on my cheek. It barely touches my skin, but the tiny hairs register its presence like an electric charge.

Don't open your eyes, I tell myself, as if I really am a child. Don't look.

Silence for a while. Long minutes with just the rhythmic sigh of our breathing. It's the only sound in the whole vehicle, besides the patter of the rain on the car. Softer now, less insistent.

"What you forgot, Grace, wallowing in all that guilt, that remorse, was the nature of the beast." Lennart inhales, releasing the breath slowly. "By all accounts, Farrish is a very plausible man. Charming, even."

I open my eyes finally. Meet his. "You've certainly been doing your homework."

He shrugs. "Like I said, you intrigue me." He leans back into his seat, stares out of the windscreen at the landscape ahead. No trees, only an expanse of indistinct countryside stretching off toward faint lights in the distance.

"How do you know all this?"

Lennart's top lip curls. "I've read the reports. The stuff you wrote up on him, the original parole hearing."

"When?" I ask indignantly.

"Way back. Before the party. It was my job to check you all out."

I flash back to our first meeting, his look of recognition in the lobby. The teasing in the hotel room.

You've led such a dull life, have you?

This man will always be ten steps ahead of me.

"Tell me about Michael," he insists. "It was going so well, wasn't it? You built up a rapport. Farrish opened up to you, talked about his girlfriend. *He cried.*"

The ridicule in his voice is unmistakable, and I feel the stir of something. Anger. Irritation. "How on earth did you get your hands on—"

He holds a palm up to interrupt me. "Details, Grace. How does anybody get anything done? You call in a few favors, that's all." He leans his head back on the headrest. I see a faint line of stubble around his cheeks. Part of me wonders when he last got to shave.

"So you were pleased with his progress. Argued in favor of his release?"

I nod miserably.

"And two days afterward he called, on the mobile number you gave him—even though that broke every rule in your book."

"I wanted to . . ."

"I know. You wanted to help, to be there for him." He looks at me. I can't tell if his expression is sympathy or scorn. "Was that what you told yourself when he asked you to go round to his flat?"

I stare down at my hands. See they're trembling. I feel suddenly hot, undo my coat, slip my arms free.

"I've seen pictures, Grace. Farrish. He's a disarmingly handsome man."

I swallow again. Wish I had something to drink. "Where exactly are you going with this?"

He moves his face closer to mine, his voice low and quiet. "Do you want me to stop? Do you really?"

I look outside at the drizzle, at the distant shimmering lights. Consider getting out of the car and making a bolt for it, but I'm too tired to even attempt it.

Time to stop running, Grace.

Lennart puts his hand in his pocket. "Some things are simply very hard to resist, aren't they?" He pulls out a packet of cigarettes, flips open the lid, and holds it out to me. I stare at the neat crowns of the filters. The urge to take one surges inside me. I haven't smoked in five years and yet I've never wanted one more.

I shake my head.

"It's a bit late for self-denial, isn't it?" Lennart removes a cigarette and lights it from the car lighter. The tip glows in the gloom as he sucks it into life. He helps himself to a single puff then hands it to me. "Just one, Grace. It won't kill you."

My resistance crumbles. Like the condemned man, I think as I take it from his hand and put it to my lips. Take a long, deep drag. And start choking again.

Lennart grabs the cigarette from me and waits for the coughing to abate. I feel sick and dizzy and slightly high as the nicotine swarms into my bloodstream, stirs up all those dormant receptors in my brain.

"Better?" he asks, and I nod.

"So let's see." Lennart sucks on the cigarette, releasing a plume of smoke into the car. "You go round there, telling yourself you're there to help. Hiding the real reason from yourself for as long as you can. Only once you're in that room the self-delusion evaporates and you're helpless. Unprepared."

"Alex," I say weakly. "What is this for? Please, can we just let it go?"

He looks over. "Why? Have you got something you'd rather be doing?" The hint of a smirk around his mouth.

I blink hard, remembering where all this has to be leading. "No."

Lennart spins round and leans sideways into the leather of his seat, eyeing me directly. "There you were," his voice low, almost mocking. "Educated, married, successful. Fully trained in the inner workings of the mind. And none of it counted for anything when it came to it, did it?"

I lean forward, open the window, and rest my head on the side of the car, letting the fresh air blow into my face. A few drops of rain land on my skin.

"Did you resist, Grace, when he came on to you? Did you show him your wedding ring? Slap his face?"

I shake my head again. Tears run down my cheeks, merging with the rain. I turn and grab the cigarette from his fingers, take another drag, and throw it out the window.

Then I face Lennart. "I fucked him, okay? You know that. Everyone knows that. *The whole fucking world knows it*. I let Michael screw me and I did it knowing I was destroying everything—my marriage, my career, my self-respect, everything."

"Grace."

Just that. My name.

"What?" I sob, running my hand across my cheek. I feel I've been treading water for the last five years. That now I'm sinking, no strength left to resist. "What's this all about? Humiliate me, before you . . ." I can't bring myself to voice it.

"I'm not trying to humiliate you," Lennart touches the base of my throat with the back of his forefinger. "Far from it."

"So what then? Why all this?"

He withdraws his hand but ignores my question. "Did it never occur to you, Grace, that you were always too big for all that—the semidetached house and the semidetached life? That there was too much in you to ever fit into such a small space?" He exhales. "You didn't know it then and you still don't. You're still punishing yourself for not being small enough, ordinary enough."

I stare out the windscreen. Try to stop crying.

"Tell me," whispers Lennart, leaning in again. His voice nearly a hiss. "Tell me what happened in that flat."

A noise in my throat. Like gagging. "You already know."

"Only the facts," he says. "Not the details."

I listen to the rain. It's picking up again, the faint echo of wind speeding across the landscape. I've lost all track of time. How long have we been here? One hour? Two?

It feels like forever.

I give in. Close my eyes and let the memories overwhelm me. "I honestly didn't believe . . ." I stop. That's not true. The real, ugly, painful truth is that I went to Michael's flat, knowing what would happen, yet denying it was even possible. Still denying it as he kissed me, moments after walking through the door. Still denying it as he undressed me and laid me down on that grubby mattress and fucked me entirely senseless.

I never wanted anyone less—or anyone more.

Lifting my hand, I pinch my top lip until it hurts. Blink back the tears and force myself to carry on. "He . . . Michael . . . Afterward, we . . . Afterward, he got up and walked over to the window. He said . . ."

You really shouldn't have done that, Grace.

The terrible weight of those words. The contempt in his eyes.

"What, Grace?" Lennart's voice close to my ear, his breath on my skin. "What did he say?"

"He said: 'You're all the same, you fucking bitches.'"

Michael wasn't even looking at me when he spoke. He was staring out across the town, toward . . . toward where *she* lived.

"And then I knew," I say hoarsely. "That he'd made it up—the remorse, the confessions, the tears, all of it."

Lennart makes a small noise. Something between a tut and sucking his teeth. He doesn't say a word for a minute or two. Nothing but the sound of my sobbing, ragged and tired, in the stillness of the Mercedes.

"Forbidden fruit, Grace—always the sweetest. You accept that in others, yet condemn it in yourself." He sighs again, a deep heavy sound like disappointment. "Farrish knew you better than you knew yourself. All that time you were analyzing him, peering into his mind, you were simply handing him the keys to yours."

He turns to examine me again. "He exploited you, Grace. Manipulated you."

I shake my head miserably. "I misjudged him. If I'd been any good, if I'd done my job properly . . . if I'd had more integrity, I'd have seen through him, I'd have . . ."

"That's a little naïve," Lennart snorts. "You know he'd have been released anyway. He'd completed the program. The risk assessments showed he was unlikely to reoffend. Besides, the world's full of ex-cons who played the rehabilitation game, only to end up back inside."

"Social and financial pressure, criminal culture, there's many different reasons for recidivism . . ."

"Spare me the psychobabble," Lennart cuts in. "I like you better in your new career."

I shut up.

"So what did you do?" he asks, after another minute or two have passed. "When you realized the truth?"

"Don't you know?" I don't bother to conceal the bitterness I feel.

"I'd like to hear it from you."

I breathe in to a count of five. Breathe out to the same. "I went to the prison governor. Told him what had happened, what I feared about Michael. He brought in the police."

"You told them all you'd slept with him?"

"Yes."

I snap my eyes open before I recall the expression on their faces. The frown of surprise, then disgust. "But they said they didn't have enough to go on. To arrest him."

"So you confessed for nothing."

Lennart's words echo round my skull. I raise my hand to my forehead, squeeze the skin between my eyes as if I can pinch out the past. "I was put on immediate suspension. And twelve hours later, when she went to the police, I was sacked."

"Alison Tennant," Lennart says thoughtfully. Even the sound of her name makes my chest contract painfully. "Only twenty-six years old, wasn't she?"

I nod.

"So . . ." He waits for me to go on.

I inhale slowly. "After I left, he went straight round to her parents' house, broke in when she wouldn't open the door. Raped her twice."

Lennart shifts his weight in his seat. "Only this time he covered it up. Used a condom both times, then dragged her in the shower to wash off any trace of his DNA, right?"

I nod again, aware of the pain building in my head.

"So without any hard physical evidence, it was her word against his. Her crying rape, and him claiming he only went round there to talk. So you had to testify, try to convince the jury that he was lying. I can't imagine that was much fun, Grace. Especially when it came out, your part in it."

I stare back out the window. My stomach seems to have contracted into a tiny ball. I feel like I did then, back there in the witness stand, being cross-examined by Michael's defense team.

As if I were the one on trial.

"I can see it all—Farrish so charming and convincing, his girlfriend in pieces, hardly able to string a sentence together, and your testimony undermined by what happened. By what you did."

I dig my fingers into my palms. "They couldn't make the rape charge stick," I say quietly. "In the end all they could get him for was violating his restraining order and breaking into the house."

"So she knew he'd be out in a few years. Would most likely be after her again."

I close my eyes. Remember the call from a colleague, telling me Alison Tennant had committed suicide five days after the trial. Hung herself in her parents' garage with a bungee cord.

I didn't need photos for that image to burn itself into my brain forever. Wherever I go, whatever I'm doing, she's there, lurking at the back of my mind.

Along with Michael.

I drag my attention back to Lennart. See his eyes glint in the growing half-light. Wonder again when this is all going to end. Where.

I rub my hand across my forehead. My head is starting to pound unbearably. "Your problem," says Lennart suddenly. "Your Achilles' heel, Grace, is your own sense of being fundamentally flawed."

"Since when were you a psychologist?" I snort.

Lennart shrugs. "It's obvious. You convict yourself without trial. Now you're living out the life sentence you gave yourself."

I laugh. A brittle sort of laugh. "I could hardly be accused of innocence."

"Maybe not. But you might be a whole lot better than you believe," he says, looking at me. "Perhaps even good, Grace. A good woman who made a big mistake and now believes herself to be bad."

He smiles and I can just about make out the mockery in his features. "Whereas I'm undoubtedly a bad man who believes himself to be much better than he is."

I watch him, thinking how, in a different time, in different circumstances, we might have been made for each other.

Lennart shifts in his seat, toys with the car keys. I can sense this is drawing to a close, that he's preparing himself for something. Fear starts to seep back into every nerve.

"I know what you did with Harry's money, Grace, if you could call it that. Most of it was actually mine."

"How do you know?"

"Had you followed, of course." He smiles again. "For the record, I approve. And don't worry, dear old Harry will pay me back. I'll make sure of that."

I clear my throat. I can't bear this any longer. "So what happens now?" I force myself to meet his gaze. "What are you going to do?"

Derision lurks at the corners of his mouth. "I could ask the same of you."

We stare at each other. Another minute ticks by.

"It seems we're at something of an impasse," Lennart says finally. "So let me suggest a way out." He bends forward and puts a hand under his seat. A slight click and he sits up.

In his hand is a gun. Not the one he had before. This one is more streamlined, clearly a lot more sophisticated. And no doubt has a built-in silencer, I realize with a primal lurch of fear.

He studies it for a second or two, then looks out the window. It's virtually light now. Sunrise, a thin strip of orange line visible on the horizon.

"Let's take a walk," he says.

FORTY-EIGHT

Lennart opens the car door and steps out. I sit there for a second or two, knowing I have no choice but to follow. The back of my neck prickling, I swing out my legs and stand. One buckles underneath me, pins and needles shooting through my calf.

Lennart strides over and grips me under the arm. Steadies me against the side of the car.

"Wait here."

He walks round and opens the boot. I can't see what he's doing from this angle, but I hear a grunt of effort as he heaves something out. There's a heavy sound as whatever it is drops to the ground.

"Up!" orders Lennart sharply. For a moment I think he's speaking to me. Then in the half-light I make out the shape of someone struggling to their feet. A man, I realize, as he stands, though his face is obscured by a kind of tight black mask.

What the fuck . . . ?

Lennart prods him in the back with the gun and grabs his arm.

He waves the gun at me, using it to point at a path through the undergrowth.

I can't move. I feel sick, my legs quivery. Who is this? What the hell is Alex doing? The reality of my situation finally hits me and I start crying again.

"Come on!" hisses Lennart, pulling the figure toward the open countryside. I stumble after them, slipping in the mud, still not able to see the path clearly. My head throbbing with the effort of movement.

After five minutes or so we emerge into what looks like marshland. I can hear reeds swishing in the wind, a smell in the air of grass and damp earth. Lennart takes my arm again, steers me across to another track. Water oozes up around my feet, seeping into my boots and soaking the bottom of my jeans.

Now it's happening, now all this is finally drawing to a close, part of my mind is alert, racing, calculating my chances of escape. But only a small part. Most of me knows it's futile, and with this admission something settles over me.

A kind of peace.

Somehow I always knew this was coming. Knew my life would bring me here, walking in the dim dawning light with this shadowy man. My Nemesis. Suddenly it feels like it doesn't really matter anymore; with no choices left, I may as well accept the inevitable.

"This'll do," he says as we arrive at a small clearing in the grassland. It's windier here, more exposed. Gusts whip up my hair, tug at my clothes. I shiver in the damp dawn air.

Lennart releases the figure and for the first time, in the gathering light, I notice he isn't wearing shoes. His socks are dark with wet and mud, and I can see he is shaking, either with cold or fear.

Oh God . . . Panic rises up again, closing my throat. I feel my chest contract, my lungs threatening to shut down. I try to breathe more slowly, then force myself to turn and look at Lennart. It's drizzling again, a fine mist of rain settling on his features. I hover there, trembling, as it soaks into my hair, my clothes.

I left my coat in the car, I remember, along with my handbag. I wonder what he will do with them. I guess I've no more need for them now than this man has for his shoes.

I wonder, too, what he's done. How he's managed to get himself on the wrong side of Alex Lennart.

"Ever have the feeling we're simply going through the motions?" Lennart asks, raising his eyes to the fat crescent of the moon, still visible toward the horizon. He stares at it briefly, then withdraws the gun from his pocket. Holds it in his right hand, appraising the fit, the weight of it. "I don't know. You always hope there can be some other outcome. Other than the obvious, I mean."

He turns to me. "A Taurus," he says, showing me the gun. "Very discreet. You ever handled one?"

I shake my head. A double execution, I think. More efficient, I guess, than offing us individually.

Alex studies my face for a second, his expression almost regretful. Then raises the gun level with my chest.

I close my eyes. Stand there, legs trembling so much I can barely stay upright, breath stalled in my lungs. My body trying desperately to prepare itself for its own dissolution.

Just do it, hisses a voice inside my head. *Just fucking do it.*

The seconds fall away from me, one by one. But the impact doesn't come.

"Grace."

Tentatively I open my eyes and look at Lennart. See now what I missed before—he's holding the gun by the barrel, offering it to me.

"Here." Lennart flicks the handle toward me. "Take it."

I step forward and do as he says. "Is it loaded?"

He smiles. "Of course."

Hand shaking, I check the safety catch. I aim at the ground a few yards to the side of me and pull the trigger. There's a loud snap and a chunk of earth flies up into the air and lands somewhere in the reeds.

Jesus. I let the implications of this sink in. Spin round before Lennart can grab me, but he's just watching. Smiling.

Then, swiftly, he pulls the mask off the man staggering beside him. I feel a slam to my guts, a punch of raw emotion.

Fuck, no . . .

No, no, no, no, *no*.

He blinks, eyes adjusting to the light. His face looks slack. Drugged, I realize, though he seems to be coming round. Gaffer tape covering his mouth. But still unmistakably Michael. Though his hair is longer and even in this light I can tell he's aged, two deep lines running from nose to cheek, like scars.

Michael's eyes focus on me, widening as they take in the gun in my hand.

"So, Grace," says Alex, nodding toward it. "What's it to be? Are you ready to cross that line?"

I gaze at him for a second, then down at the pistol in my hands. And remember my first trick. Standing by the door waiting for a man to arrive. Telling myself I could back out at any time, yet no part resisting when the knock came. Letting myself get swept along until it was too late, until there was no way back.

Just like with Michael, I think. Walking right into the trap he laid for me, blindfolded by my own desire.

"Grace?"

I raise my eyes to Lennart. "You killed Amanda," I say. Not asking, stating.

He sighs. "Actually, for what it's worth, that was more Hardy's doing than mine. I may trade in violence, but in my opinion it's rarely a solution for anything. And I was right, because the problem didn't end with her, did it?"

He spreads his hands in a gesture taking in our situation as well as our surroundings. "Here we all are."

I look back at Michael, relishing the weight of the weapon in my hand. The rightness of it. A mounting sense of anticipation that's almost sexual. Lennart doesn't move, simply studies my face, that half smile playing across his lips.

And I understand, as if for the first time, just how very dangerous he is. For someone like me, this man is crack cocaine. My drug of choice. My body feels the pull of him like an addiction. Like the constant craving for nicotine that never quite leaves my consciousness.

As I turn back to Michael and raise the gun, I sense Alison Tennant watching me from the shadows of my mind. I touch the trigger, feeling my arm begin to tremble, remembering that client, the one who was a soldier in the Falklands. That moment he described.

Kill or be killed. What kind of choice is that?

Michael's eyes fix on mine. I force myself to stare right into them. Search for a sign of pleading, of fear, of begging for forgiveness.

Find only contempt.

My finger caresses the smooth curve of metal beneath it. So cool, so . . . seductive. I see Alison's body, hanging in her parents' garage. Michael staring out the window of that flat, turning to me.

You're all the same, you fucking bitches.

I lift the gun a bit higher. Aim for his head. Close my eyes and will myself to squeeze. An instant later I feel the weapon wrenched from my hand and before I can do anything, say anything, there's a sharp whiplash crack and Michael's body folds in on itself, crumpling forward, landing a few feet away.

"Oh God . . ." My legs collapse beneath me and I sink to my hands and knees. I stare at Michael through the half-light, waiting for movement. His body twitches for a moment, then stills.

"Oh God . . ." Something like a scream builds in my throat. A howl. I can't believe what I've just seen. The terrible, unassailable *reality* of it.

Dead. Michael is *dead*.

"Grace. Let it go."

I look up at Lennart, still holding the gun, arm by his side. He's looking at the body with a wistful expression. "I know I said violence is rarely a solution," he says, pulling a plastic bag from his pocket. "Well, this is one of the exceptions."

"But I was going to . . ."

Lennart looks at me. His smile has a touch of indulgence. "Were you? Well, we'll never know, will we, Grace? Maybe you would, maybe you wouldn't, but either way, I wasn't going to leave you with that on your conscience."

I stare back at him, numb with shock. Then watch, bewildered, as Lennart removes the gloves from his hands and stuffs them into the plastic bag.

Gloves? He wasn't wearing those before.

He holds the bag up in front of my face. "Our little insurance policy, Grace; I had to appease the boys with something." It takes me a moment to register what he means. Of course. My prints are all over the gun. All he'd need to frame me for Michael's murder.

After all, it's not like I haven't got a motive.

Lennart steps toward me and pulls me to my feet, gripping my arm. I stagger, try to stay upright. I'm shaking so hard it's nearly impossible, my mind still trying to process everything that just happened.

"If it makes you feel any better, if it wasn't him it would've been you," he says.

"How do you mean?" I stammer.

"I've had somebody watching him, since his release. He was gunning for you, Grace, if you'll excuse the pun. Waiting for an opportunity. Without poor Alison to torment, you were his next best option—especially after you testified against him in court."

I swallow. Think of the visit to my father's bedside. Jesus.

Lennart releases me. I resist the urge to back away.

"Just so we understand each other, Grace. We both walk away from this. We forget it ever happened, okay?"

My eyes dart back toward the body crumpled on the ground. "But what about . . ."

"What about him?" shrugs Alex. "It could have been anybody. A man like that racks up enemies like a dog gets fleas. Nobody will suspect either of us. Besides, I can easily furnish you with an alibi, should you need one."

I stare at him. Of course he can. I'm beginning to think there's nothing this man can't do.

I look back at the body on the ground. Was I going to kill him? I wonder, my stomach sinking, conscience kicking back in like a reflex. Could I really have done it?

I may as well have pulled the trigger, I think. After all, I had the gun. I could have stopped Lennart, stopped all of this.

And yet I didn't.

I glance up at Lennart. He's grinning, as if reading my mind. Taking a step toward me, he runs his hand through my damp hair. "Stop punishing yourself, Grace. He got what he deserved. You know that, so let it go."

He tugs my face up to meet his. Presses his thumb against the end of my nose and draws it down over my lips. "But what about me? Can you leave me unpunished? Are you willing to let me get away with so much?"

I stare back at him, right into those cloud-gray eyes. "There's nothing I can do to you that would make any difference," I say, finally acknowledging the truth of it. Seeing more clearly now. Lennart values his own life no more than he valued Michael's.

"Clever girl," he laughs. "You're right. I made that Faustian pact some time ago, and the devil has my soul in hock. I'm just marking time till he gets his hands on me."

He inhales, looks up again into the sky, then scoops his hand round the back of my head and pulls me toward him. "But equally

I could say the same of you, Grace. Part of you would have liked it to have ended here, wouldn't you? An end to all that torment. Peace, at last."

I don't reply.

Lennart lowers his head and kisses me on the mouth. I don't resist. Simply wait until he draws away.

"But that would be a shame, Grace. To paraphrase Hannibal Lecter, the world is a far more interesting place with you in it."

He releases me and takes a step backward. Stares out across the marshes, seeming to ruminate on something as he surveys the featureless grassland, the pylons and wind turbines in the distance.

"Come on," he says. "I'll take you home."

"So this is it?" I ask. "The end of all of it?"

Lennart smiles. A heavy, sad sort of smile. "Haven't you got what you wanted?"

I gaze out across the rain-soaked landscape, then back at him. And realize I probably have.

FORTY-NINE

Two e-mails again, after I've deleted the backlog from clients. The first from an unknown mailbox. Nothing in the message except a link to an article in the *London Evening News*. I click on it, my heart beginning to race the instant I see the headline.

MAN FOUND SHOT ON MARSHES

The body of convicted rapist Michael James Farrish was found yesterday by a dog walker on Rainham Marshes in Essex. Sources have confirmed that the cause of death was a gunshot wound to the chest. Farrish was released from Brakeford Prison in Leeds two months ago, after serving five years for breaking and entering and violating a restraining order. Police are appealing for witnesses to the crime, which they believe occurred in the early hours of Wednesday morning.

I go back to the e-mail, examine the address. Mephistopheles @outlook.com.

Mephistopheles? Then I remember Faust's demon, the devil's representative, the collector of the souls of the damned.

I click on reply. Write just two words.

"Point taken."

Seconds later a text bleep on my phone: "My offer still stands. Whatever it takes, Grace."

The second e-mail is from Julia, informing me that my father died early this morning. "Peacefully," she says, though it's hard to imagine him doing anything without protest.

I stare at the screen for a minute or two, absorbing the fact of his passing, listening to the ringing in my ears. Tinnitus—one of the few things we ever had in common.

What do I feel? I ask myself after a few more minutes pass. And the answer comes, like a benediction.

Nothing. Nothing very much at all.

FIFTY

The knock on the door makes me jump. I put down my roll of packing tape and peer through the spyhole.

Oh God. I stand there for a moment or two, wondering whether to pretend I'm out. But he probably heard me coming.

I open the door. Ben stands in the passageway, holding a large Easter egg. One of those over-the-top affairs swaddled in layers of cellophane and tied at the neck with a huge gold bow.

"Peace offering," he says, holding it toward me, but shuffling slightly, like someone waiting for bad news. "Good stuff. I figured you prefer your chocolate dark, high cocoa content and all that."

"Thanks," I say, taking it from him.

"Stella, I . . ." He stops and peers past me into the hallway, catching sight of the boxes I've already loaded and sealed. "You're leaving?" he says, unable to hide a flash of disappointment.

I nod. "Come in."

He walks into the living room. I turn off my iPod, remove the headphones.

"You should get an e-reader," Ben says, surveying more boxes crammed with books. "It would save an awful lot of effort." He's trying to sound lighthearted but it doesn't quite come off.

I offer him a smile. "I prefer something with more substance."

He turns and raises an eyebrow.

"Don't," I warn.

He scans the flat. Looks everywhere, it seems, but at me. "Where are you going?" he asks eventually. "Another apartment?"

I shake my head. "I'm leaving."

"Okay," he swallows. "Where?"

"I'm not sure yet."

"How long?"

I shrug. "I don't know. A while."

His features struggle for composure. I can see this isn't what he was expecting at all. "I came to say I'm sorry. About the last time. You know, how things ended."

I shrug again. "It's all right."

"It isn't. It wasn't." He pauses, scratches his nose. "I miss you." His eyes scour the remaining piles of paperbacks. "Actually, I was wondering if you might be able to fit me in . . ." His words trail off. He looks embarrassed.

"For old times' sake, you mean?"

"I know I should have rung and made an appointment."

I look at him and come to a decision. "Okay. When?"

"Now?" His expression sheepish.

I laugh. "The itch that bad, eh?"

He doesn't answer.

"I'll go and get ready," I say, but he steps across the pile of books between us and kisses me.

"No. I'll settle for you exactly as you are."

We go into the bedroom and undress. Or rather I undress. Ben stands there, staring as I peel off my T-shirt and yoga pants. "I want to watch you," he says as I raise my eyebrows.

"Masturbate?"

"No." His voice cross. "Just you, Stella."

I slip off my bra and step toward him. "You're making me self-conscious."

He lifts one eyebrow. "You? Seriously?"

I realize it's true. I've stripped for hundreds of clients, without a thought. But now, in front of Ben, I feel naked.

"Come on." I tug at the button above his fly. He relents and sheds his clothes, all but his boxers. His erection pokes at the fabric like an obscene tent pole. We fall onto the bed. He grabs the condom I hand him, dispenses with his underwear and unfurls it onto his cock. Then pushes himself inside me without preliminaries, fast and urgent.

I feel myself get instantly wet. I squeeze myself around him, letting my hips rock and his tongue roam deep in my mouth, marveling at the perfect fit between us.

"Stella," he whispers into my ear as he fucks me. I close my eyes. Find a merciful blankness there.

"Oh God," Ben gasps, and at the same time I feel the world fall away, leaving me at once both heavy-limbed and light-headed, a deep spreading lethargy radiating out from my crotch like an anesthetic.

"Jesus, Stella." Ben rolls off, one arm still draped across me. "I've been thinking about you . . . about this, for weeks. It got so I thought I must be imagining how good it was."

I don't say anything. Just enjoy the afterglow while it lasts.

At some point afterward I must doze off, because all at once Ben is standing over me, holding a cup of tea.

"I'm sorry," I say. "I keep doing that."

He hands me the mug. "A drop of milk, right?"

I nod, suppressing a smile. He's wearing my dressing gown, looking ludicrous in rose-pink silk. He climbs back into bed beside me. Props himself up on one elbow and strokes my hair.

"I left her," he says, out of the blue. "Helen, my wife. I moved out a couple of weeks ago." He watches my reaction, trying to read my expression.

"I'm sorry," I repeat.

He shrugs. "No need to be. I should have done it years ago. Both of us knew it wasn't working."

I picture my ex, living in that two-up, two-down in Sheffield with the girl he met after we broke up. I hope he's happy, I realize. I hope he marries her and never thinks of me at all.

"So where are you going?" Ben asks again.

I sigh. "Like I said, I'm not sure."

"You're staying in London though, right?"

I shake my head. Something in him seems to deflate.

"Don't worry," I say. "There's plenty more where I came from. I can recommend someone, if you like."

"Stella, don't." He looks away. "Don't do this."

I look up at the ceiling. Chew my bottom lip. "Where will you live?" I ask. "Have you bought somewhere else?"

He shakes his head. "I'm staying with a friend—until I decide what to do."

I don't speak, feeling suddenly weary. All the resolutions of the past twenty-four hours start to slip away.

"Stella?"

"Yes?"

Ben is watching me, gauging. I see him hesitate, then bite back whatever he was going to ask. "It doesn't matter."

I drag myself into a sitting position, take a sip of my tea, and wince. Still too hot to drink. "I'd better get on," I say. "I've got somebody coming round with a van first thing tomorrow to collect all this."

Ben swallows, visibly. Emotion slides across his face. All the things left unsaid hang in the air like smoke.

I get up, pull on my clothes, and walk into the living room. Survey the debris on the floor. Sitting on one pile of books is my mobile. I pick it up. Turn it around in my hand for a minute or two, then click on my messages. Find Lennart's text.

I inhale. Close my eyes. *Whatever it takes.*

Thumbing through my contacts, I locate his number. Let my finger hover for a couple of seconds. Then press delete.

Turning off the phone, I go over to the window. I gaze out across the neighboring gardens, across the roofs of Pimlico, the sky turning golden as the light begins to dim. A few yards away a cherry tree has burst into flower, a riot of white blossom against the backdrop of brick and grass. Spring is here, I realize, with a small lift in my heart. Finally.

At the end of the road I can just hear the distant hum of traffic, the endless London percussion of engines and car horns. I swallow, feeling the tug of leaving before I've even left.

No regrets, I tell myself. No going back. You've made your decision.

Ben emerges from the bedroom, dressed now. He grabs the jacket he slung on the sofa and pulls out his wallet. Extracts some notes. His eye contact fleeting as he holds them out to me.

I wave it away.

Ben raises his eyes to mine, his expression inquiring. "You've changed your rates?"

"I gave it up," I say simply. "I quit."

He stares at me for a moment or two, taking this in. Then drops his gaze, scratching his head. "So what about . . ." He gestures toward the bedroom.

"What about it?"

He takes a step toward me. "Stella, I . . ."

I look at him. Right up into his deep brown eyes.

"Grace."

Ben looks perplexed. Like I've uttered some kind of riddle. "Grace?"

"That's me," I say, closing the distance between us, smiling at the confusion on his face as I lift my hand and place it on his cheek. Detect the beginnings of stubble below my fingertips, the soft skin beneath.

"You?" He looks more confused and reaches up to place his hand on mine. And there it is, only for a second, the temptation to withdraw. Dissemble. Turn back.

But no. Not this time.

This time I'm not running away.

"That's my name, Ben." I let my fingers linger on his face, making myself wait just a few more seconds before I lean in to kiss him.

"My real name," I whisper. "It's not Stella, it's Grace."